A KATE MALONE

TOO SOON A SPY

JACK MACONAGHY

AETHON THRILLS

aethonbooks.com

TOO SOON A SPY
©2025 Jack Maconaghy

This book is protected under the copyright laws of the United States of America. No part of this publication may be reproduced, stored in a retrieval system, or transmitted, in any form or by any means, without the prior permission in writing of the publisher, nor be otherwise circulated in any form of binding or cover other than that in which it is published and without a similar condition including this condition being imposed on the subsequent purchaser. Any reproduction or unauthorized use of the material or artwork contained herein is prohibited without the express written permission of the authors.

Aethon Books supports the right to free expression and the value of copyright. The purpose of copyright is to encourage writers and artists to produce the creative works that enrich our culture.

The scanning, uploading, and distribution of this book without permission is a theft of the author's intellectual property. If you would like to use material from the book (other than for review purposes), please contact editor@aethonbooks.com. Thank you for your support of the author's rights.

Aethon Books
www.aethonbooks.com

Print and eBook formatting and design by Kevin G. Summers. Artwork provided by Steve Beaulieu.

Published by Aethon Books LLC.

Aethon Books is not responsible for websites (or their content) that are not owned by the publisher.

This book is a work of fiction. Names, characters, places, and incidents are the product of the author's imagination or are used fictitiously. Any resemblance to actual events, locales, or persons, living or dead is coincidental.

All rights reserved.

ACKNOWLEDGMENTS

This book would never have seen the light of day without Melissa Gardner's encouragement. She read a beta version of a Kate novel I had written previously and insisted it needed a prequel that told the story of how Kate became to be a spy. I resisted the idea at the time because there were other projects I was eager to get to. But the idea kept gnawing at me, and I finally threw in the towel. Melissa hit the nail squarely on the head and I will always be grateful for her insight.

I want to thank the members of the Dekalb Are Fiction Writers, particularly Connie, Kathrin, Greg, and Bill. Their collective input as I worked my way through the first draft was invaluable, and our after-meeting sessions at PJ's Tavern forged a bond that goes beyond our shared love of writing.

And finally, I need to express my love and gratitude to my wife, Sylvia. Her patience and support as I spent countless hours pounding away at a keyboard was invaluable and very much appreciated.

ALSO IN THE SERIES

KATE MALONE THRILLERS

Too Soon A Spy

∽

Calling all thriller fans: be the first to discover groundbreaking new releases, access incredible deals, and participate in thrilling giveaways by subscribing to our exclusive Thriller Newsletter. https://aethonbooks.com/thriller-newsletter/

Want to discuss our books with other readers and even the authors?

JOIN THE AETHON DISCORD!

CHAPTER ONE

Kate Malone stood by her hotel window admiring the view as the Riyadh skyline shimmered in the oppressive heat. The modern glass and steel buildings towered over the stone and mortar structures of the city's ancient past. The architectural contrast represented a clash of eras, but the underlying culture remained always the same. Today, that culture presented her with a dilemma. With a resigned sigh she stood and went to the dresser. "You're all in or you're not, girl."

She tied her shoulder length blonde hair into a bun and pulled a beautifully patterned scarf from the top drawer. Draping it over her head and wrapping it under her chin and around her neck, she examined the effect in the mirror. Her blue eyes and fair skin still marked her as a foreigner, but the hijab provided the appearance of modesty required of women in Saudi Arabia. She snatched her leather computer bag from the desk before she could change her mind and headed for the door.

As she stepped into the hallway, she bumped into a slender redhead walking rapidly toward the elevators. Monica Lindsey held her phone cradled between her chin and shoulder while her eyes remained glued to the tablet held in her left hand. Multitasking was Monica's normal mode of operation and today was no exception.

"Email it to me and I'll make sure he reviews it on the flight back. I'll call with an ETA once we're in the air." She dropped the phone into her pocket and glanced up at Kate. "The meeting's in ten minutes and …" She stopped dead in her tracks. "You're not really going to wear that thing, are you?"

Kate couldn't hide her grin. Her friend was a feminist to the core and local customs be damned. "You're wearing a high neck top and long sleeves even though it feels like a furnace outside," she replied. "Don't tell me it's because you like the look."

"Yeah, but I'll give in only so far. There are some lines I won't cross."

Kate started toward the elevators. "I have a job to do, and I don't want anything I say to be dismissed. If wearing this can gain me a little acceptance, then it's worth it."

"You think you're going to get to speak at this briefing? This isn't Ankara or Tel Aviv, Kate. Being female made no difference there. The Saudi contingent will be entirely male, and they won't care that you're a top intelligence analyst. All that will matter is that you're a woman. I doubt Phil will call on you."

"Maybe not, but it never hurts to be prepared."

Monica shook her head in bewilderment. "I can't believe you're willing to accept being pigeonholed by a sexist culture."

"Their customs aren't my concern. I'm looking for any advantage I can get and if this helps, then so be it. Did Phil read the updated analysis report I sent him last night?"

"I'm not sure. He's been on the phone all morning."

"There's new information he needs to see before the meeting."

"I'm his executive assistant, Kate, not his babysitter. I can put it in front of him, but I can't make him read it."

They exited the elevator at the conference level. As they reached the door to the meeting room, Monica put her hand on Kate's arm. "I know it's not really my business, but have you told Phil about the job offer?"

Kate shook her head. "I still haven't decided what to do about it."

"What does Dan think?"

Kate looked away and Monica's eyebrows went up. "You didn't tell him either? Trouble in paradise?"

Kate pulled the door open. "Paradise can be overrated. We better get inside before Phil sends out a search party."

The conference room was large and paneled in dark wood. Leather upholstered chairs surrounded a long mahogany table, with additional seating for less senior attendees arranged along the walls. A podium stood at one end flanked by both the U.S. and Saudi flags. A large video screen, currently blank, hung suspended from the ceiling. At the prior stops on their trip, Kate had been seated at the table, but here she'd be relegated to the cheap seats.

The people filtering into the room were mostly Saudi, but there was a great deal of diversity in their manner of dress. About half wore military uniforms. Most of the others were dressed in western style business suits, but a few were attired in traditional Arab robes. The Saudis greeted the male members of the American contingent cordially while ignoring Kate and Monica.

Kate scanned the room, hoping for a chance to speak privately with her boss. The new intel was vital, and she had no idea if he'd taken the time to read the report. She spotted him standing by the podium, engaged in conversation with a Saudi general. The serious expressions on their faces discouraged interruption, so she reluctantly followed Monica toward two empty seats in the far corner of the room. She nodded in Phil's direction. "I assume that's General Haddad he's talking to?"

Monica glanced up from her tablet. "That's him."

Kate studied the Saudi general. He was tall with black hair just beginning to recede and showing the first touches of gray. His confident demeanor spoke of someone accustomed to leadership, and as the head of Saudi military intelligence, he was the main reason they were here.

At precisely 1:00, Phil and the Saudi officer took their places at the podium, and everyone found their seats. Haddad opened the proceedings. "Greetings to you all. This briefing will be conducted in English. Should you require it, a streaming translation in Arabic will be displayed on the video monitor." He glanced down at his notes. "You're all aware of the increased level of cooperation between the intelligence services of Russia and Iran. This development is of grave concern not only to the Kingdom, but to the region as a whole."

Kate noted how he managed to include Israel without mentioning the Jewish state by name.

"We have Phillip DeCosta of the U.S. Intelligence and Security Agency here with us today to brief us on how far that cooperation extends and what the implications are for the rest of the Middle East."

Kate was unsurprised to find that she had been omitted from the introductions. As the lead analyst for ISA's Russia section, she had a prominent role at the briefings in Turkey and Israel. Today, her involvement would be seen as irrelevant.

Phil stepped up to the microphone. "Thank you, General Haddad. ISA has been monitoring these developments closely, and we thought it vital to share what we know with our allies in the region."

An officer seated at the far end of the table looked up from the presentation packet in front of him. "Before you begin, Mr. DeCosta, can you tell us how reliable this information is, and the manner in which it was obtained?"

"I can't discuss the methods used in accumulating the intelligence, but our assessment of its reliability is high. Everything was verified through at least two separate sources."

Phil proceeded through the presentation with occasional interruptions for questions or clarifications. At one point, the same officer raised his hand. "Does Iran have real time access to Russian satellite surveillance, or do they only see what's passed along to them?"

"To our knowledge, Russian intelligence is providing recordings of selected surveillance feeds after they've been reviewed and vetted internally."

Kate swore under her breath. Phil clearly never looked at that report, and now she had a decision to make. She could keep quiet and hope her boss wouldn't get called on it later, or she could try to remedy the situation. She let her briefcase slide off her lap onto the floor. The disturbance distracted Phil, and he looked over at her with a frown on his face. She held his gaze and shook her head imperceptibly. His look of annoyance turned to one of surprise, and he nodded in acknowledgment.

Looking down at the papers in front of him, he cleared his throat. "Let me back up for a moment. What I said about Iranian access to Russian satellites was true twenty-four hours ago, but we have new information I did not have time to include in this presentation. I'm going to ask one of my staff to brief you on the latest developments. Kaitlyn Malone is ISA's lead analyst on Russian security operations."

He looked over at Kate and nodded. She frantically tried to organize her thoughts as she retrieved her case. At the previous stops she had been confident and spoke from a position of authority. That wouldn't fly here. She felt Monica's reassuring pat on the knee and gathered her courage. She rose to her feet, her mind racing. There was one way to start that couldn't hurt.

"As-salaam 'alaykum."

Most of the men at the table seemed surprised to hear her greet them in Arabic. She even noticed a few smiles of acknowledgment at her use of proper protocol. She took a deep breath and took the plunge.

"Before I get into this, I want to apologize. This information only came to our attention in the past day or so. I put it in a report, but Mr. DeCosta is a busy man, and I should have followed up personally. He was not properly informed, and that's my fault."

To her relief, she saw nods of acceptance around the table. That she was willing to take the fall for her boss was what these men would expect. The hijab probably didn't hurt either.

Gen. Haddad was the first to speak. "I appreciate your honesty, Miss Malone. What can you tell us about this?"

"As you know, the region where Iran, Iraq, and Turkey share common borders is heavily populated by ethnic Kurds who have long yearned for a Kurdish homeland. A militant movement hopes to turn the eastern province of Turkey into an independent Kurdish state that would be the foundation of the nation of Kurdistan. Two days ago,

Turkey began moving troops toward the region in what is probably a buildup toward a military operation against the insurgents. Iran played it safe and moved troops toward the border as well in the event the hostilities spilled across into their territory."

"That would be expected."

"Yes, sir, it would. But the Iranian response began within six hours of the initial Turkish troop movement. That's way too fast unless the Iranians saw it in real time. The implications of that are still being evaluated, but it's clear that this would be a major escalation of Iran's intelligence capabilities."

"They had direct access to the satellite feeds?" inquired someone from the table. "Can they monitor military activities in our country as well?"

"Possibly," Kate replied. "I doubt Russia has given Iran total access to the network. They're most likely providing a limited capability to allow them to monitor activities in areas where they have security concerns. At the moment, there's nothing to tell us how far that extends, but it might be possible to find out."

"What do you suggest?" asked Haddad.

"You could conduct an unannounced military exercise along your Persian Gulf coastline, and we could use our satellites to look for an Iranian reaction. If they're watching you in real time, something should happen rather quickly. Then we'd know."

The general nodded. "Thank you, Miss Malone. You have been most helpful."

Kate sat down and took a deep breath. She'd pulled it off. Monica leaned over and whispered in her ear, "You didn't have to fall on your sword for Phil. He's a big boy."

"I did if I wanted them to listen. And I meant what I said. I should have brought this to his attention in person, and you should have made sure he read that report. We dodged a bullet here."

Phil gave her a nod of appreciation from his place at the podium before resuming his presentation. Despite Monica's reservations, she'd been able to contribute in a significant way. She gave a contented sigh and settled back to observe the rest of the proceedings.

At the conclusion of the briefing, she closed her briefcase and followed Monica toward the exit. Their luggage sat by the front entrance of the hotel and three SUVs were waiting to take them to the airbase.

"You and I will be riding in the last car," said Monica. "The first two will be for the men, just like the whole damn country."

"I'm sorry you see our culture in such poor light, Miss Lindsey."

They turned to find Phil and Gen. Haddad standing behind them. Monica took a step backward, flustered at being called out in front of her boss. "My apologies, General. I guess I'm not accustomed to the role women must play in your society. From where I stand, it seems …"

He held up his hand. "I know what you're going to say. You think it unfair? Unequal? Customs differ, Miss Lindsey, but don't for a minute think we fail to recognize the intelligence, insight, and creativity that a woman can possess. But when in another country, one must accept that the social order and customs which apply there may differ from your own. Miss Malone seems to understand that concept very well, and it made all the difference today. She was taken seriously by the men in that room because she showed respect for our ways. Well done, Miss Malone."

"Thank you, sir."

"May my staff reach out to you as we consider how to approach this problem?"

This was a delicate subject. Her job didn't include deciding what intel should be shared with outside entities. "Well, sir…"

"She'll be happy to be of help, General," interrupted Phil. "The source of this intelligence is coming from Russia and she's our expert on their capabilities. Our own security concerns may prevent her from being able to pass along everything, but she'll do all she can to make sure your people stay up to date."

She gave her boss a grateful smile. "I'd be honored, Gen. Haddad. Tell your staff they can contact me at their convenience."

"Excellent. Thank you again, Miss Malone. Now I suggest we all return to the base. Your plane is waiting."

True to Monica's prediction, the male contingent got into the first two SUVs while the two women were waved into the last one. Since this vehicle transported women who were unrelated to the men accompanying them, a soundproof Plexiglass partition separated the rear of the car from the driver and security guard.

As the motorcade pulled away from the curb, Monica sagged back in her seat. "I really stepped in it back there. Phil's not going to be happy."

"It turned out alright," replied Kate. "But you need to rein in that feminist streak once in a while."

"So I've been told. Just don't expect miracles. Okay, now that we're alone, sort of at least," she added with a glance at the men sitting up front, "what's going on with you and Dan?"

"Nothing anymore. I'm going to break it off when we get home."

Monica looked stunned. "But why? I thought you two would end up together. I mean, like permanently."

"He's been talking for a while now about moving in together. The night before we left on this trip, he told me he found the perfect apartment for the two of us. I didn't even know he was looking for one. He just assumed I'd go along with it."

"You've been staying at his place quite a bit lately."

"It's not the same. As things stand, I can spend a night or a weekend with him and then go back to my apartment and my own life. He's looking for domestic bliss, and I'm not even close to being ready for that. I value my independence and I'm focused on my career. If he's thinking long term, then I'm not the right woman for him. I told him so and we ended up in a big argument."

"We've been gone almost a week, and he's had some time to think. Maybe what you said sank in. I've messed up more than one relationship by being bullheaded and selfish. I'd hate to see you do the same."

Kate smiled. "For such a staunch feminist, you're quite a romantic. I'll give it some thought. Are we still on for a girls' night out

Friday? I've heard good things about that new place just off Dupont Circle."

"Oh yeah. After this trip, some downtime is definitely required."

Kate spent the rest of the trip going through accumulated emails on her laptop. She occasionally glanced out the window, never failing to marvel at how much Riyadh differed from the world she was used to. The streets shimmered in the desert heat, but everyone went about their business with no outward signs of discomfort. They passed modern office buildings but also open-air markets where women shrouded in burkas and always accompanied by a male guardian dickered with the merchants over the price of their produce. She understood Monica's distaste for the way this culture viewed women, but Haddad was right. This was their home, and their customs had evolved over centuries. A little respect for that could go a long way.

As the motorcade approached the main gate to the airbase, the cars slowed to a stop to be cleared by base security. She was putting the computer back into her briefcase when an explosion ripped through the square.

Monica screamed as the force of the blast almost tipped their SUV over. Kate looked around in confusion. Flames engulfed the lead vehicle in the motorcade. The driver of the second car backed away from the burning wreck in front of him and the doors flew open as the passengers tried to run for shelter. They were only steps from the car when a deafening blast destroyed that SUV as well. Bodies flew in all directions as fire consumed the vehicle.

The security man sitting beside their driver slid open the partition. "Get out! Now!"

Kate opened the door and ran for the cover of the juniper trees lining the road. She threw herself to the ground and looked frantically around her. A cargo van pulled up behind the motorcade and three men holding automatic weapons leaped from the back and began shooting at anyone who was still moving. Kate lay flat on her stomach and held still, her heart pounding as she watched the scene unfold in front of her.

Monica tried to scramble out of the SUV, but with no way to take cover she made an easy target. Kate screamed in denial as two bullets found their mark and her friend toppled over backward onto the street. The Saudi security guard tried to use the car door for cover, but he too went down in a pool of blood.

Smoke stung her eyes, and the screams of the wounded resonated through the square. Kate fought down her panic and looked around for anything that might provide better cover or a chance to escape the carnage. A movement to her right caught her attention, and she realized she wasn't the only one to make it to the tree line. General Haddad was lying on his back, still conscious but bleeding heavily. She crawled toward the injured officer.

One of the attackers began strafing the area bordering the road with automatic rifle fire. Kate felt a blow to her side and collapsed onto the ground. Gritting her teeth against the pain, she dragged herself the rest of the way and pulled the general's sidearm from its holster. Her assailant walked toward them with his rifle dangling from his right hand. He paused and looked surprised at the sight of a woman in a hijab.

Kate rolled onto her back. The pain almost caused her to black out, but she fought for control and squeezed the trigger three times. Her first shot struck him in the chest. The rifle fell from his grasp, and he toppled onto his back.

Kate stared at the crumpled body. Was he the one who shot Monica? Sirens were going off everywhere and she could hear the gunmen shouting at each other. Her shirt was becoming soaked in blood, but she kept the gun trained on the bushes. Another round of gunfire erupted, and this time she could tell there were a lot more weapons involved in the fight.

Her vision blurred, and she felt herself on the verge of passing out. Someone tried to pull the pistol from her hand, but she fought to hold on to it with what little strength she had left. If she was going to die here, it wouldn't be without a struggle.

"Relax, ma'am. You're safe now."

She tried to focus, but it was like peering through a gauze curtain. "Who are you?" she whispered.

"I'm an Army medic, ma'am. Why don't you give me the gun and let me look at that wound?"

Kate surrendered the weapon and closed her eyes. "How bad?"

"I've seen worse. You were lucky."

Lucky? It didn't feel like that. "My friend's been shot."

"We're doing everything we can. Now lay still and let me do my job."

She stared up at him for a moment and then closed her eyes as the darkness enfolded her.

CHAPTER TWO

Peter Schilling strode through the entrance to the American wing of the Riyadh base hospital. He paused for a moment to take in his surroundings before turning to the man behind him. "Find out where they are and locate the doctor in charge." He went over to the security desk. "Has anyone been here to see Kaitlyn Malone?"

The staff sergeant looked up from his computer. Attired in a tweed sport coat with brown hair just graying at the temples, Peter looked more like a university professor than an intelligence officer. His refined Boston accent only enhanced the image, but he exuded an air of authority seldom challenged by those he encountered.

"Can I see some identification, sir?"

Peter pulled out a leather ID case and displayed his credentials. "My name's Schilling and I'm the Director of Field Operations at the Intelligence and Security Agency. Now answer the question, please."

The sergeant consulted his monitor. "Nobody except the medical staff is allowed in her room without prior authorization."

"Add me to the list. Jason Collier as well. Nobody else without clearing it with me first."

"Uh, no disrespect, sir, but you're a civilian and I can't ..."

"Then call whoever you need to, but make it happen."

"Yes, sir."

Jason Collier appeared at Peter's elbow. "They've got Kate in a guarded room on a floor set aside for VIP patients. She's listed in stable condition. Monica Lindsey's critical and in the ICU. The doctor will meet us upstairs."

Peter nodded. "Lead the way."

They exited the elevator on the sixth floor and proceeded down a long hallway. An MP stood outside a door at the end of the corridor. As Peter tried to move past him, he stepped back to block the way.

"No visitors allowed, sir. Doctor's orders."

"And where can I find him?"

Before the guard could reply, the door opened and a stocky man in a white physician's coat stepped out into the hall. "What's going on here? Who are you?" he asked, directing his gaze at Peter.

"Peter Schilling. I'm with ISA. In case you're not aware of it, your patient works for us."

"She's not working for anybody at the moment, and she just had a dose of morphine that will knock her out for a while. Come with me."

He led them to a consultation room which proved to be sparse even by military standards. A bulletin board affixed to one wall provided the single interruption in an otherwise unbroken expanse of white paint. A metal table surrounded by four straight-back chairs comprised the only furnishings.

The doctor closed the door before joining Peter and Jason at the table. "I'm Dr. Crenshaw. Lt. Col. Crenshaw if you want to be picky, but we don't pay much attention to rank when it comes to treating patients."

"How is she?" asked Peter, taking out a notepad and pen.

"Since she's not military, I'm not supposed to discuss her condition with anyone except family."

"Do you see any family around here? I'll go through channels if you prefer, but I guarantee you'll be ordered to cooperate."

Crenshaw held up his hand. "I was only pointing out the legalities. Medical ethics require I do so, but word has filtered down that ISA will be all over this. We'll provide anything you need."

"How badly was she injured?"

"She took a bullet in the side of her abdomen, which exited through her back. It missed all the major organs but nicked an artery, causing significant blood loss. Fortunately, the medics got to her in time. The surgery went well, and she should make a full recovery."

"What about Monica Lindsey?"

The physician sighed and sagged back in his chair. "That's another matter. She was struck multiple times and suffered serious organ damage. We got her into the OR in time to stem the internal bleeding, but she needs further surgery and she's too weak for that right now. I'll go back in if there's no other choice, but she'd probably die on the table. If we can get her through the next forty-eight hours, she'll have a better chance."

Peter jotted a note on his pad. "You have Phillip DeCosta's remains?"

Crenshaw nodded. "His body, what's left of it, is down in the morgue. He never made it out of the vehicle. Between the blast and the resulting fire, there wasn't much left to recover. You have my condolences."

Peter refrained from responding. There'd be time for mourning their losses later. "How soon can Kate be moved?"

The doctor shrugged. "It depends. Moved where? And how?"

"Back to Bethesda naval hospital outside Washington. We'll use a military medevac plane."

"Barring complications, she could be moved as soon as tomorrow. She's past the crisis and stable. With a medical staff accompanying her, it shouldn't be a problem."

"One more thing," added Peter, gesturing at his companion. "This is Jason Collier. He'll be staying with Kate until we get her back home. We still don't know who was behind that attack, and I'm not taking any chances."

"I'll tell the guards. Now, if you'll excuse me, I need to check on our patients."

Peter waited for the door to close before turning to Jason. "Stay alert. That attack came the moment the motorcade arrived at the gate. Those assholes knew the timing down to the minute."

"They had somebody on the inside?"

"It looks that way. The leak was probably on the Saudi side, but we can't assume anything. Nobody talks to her except the medical staff. If the Saudis try to question her, tell them no and call me."

"Got it, boss."

"I've got a meeting over at base security. Let me know if anything changes."

Upon his arrival at the Riyadh base headquarters, a sergeant escorted Peter to a conference room. Two military officers seated at the table stood as he entered. "We've been expecting you, Director Schilling," said the Air Force General. "I'm Gen. Connelly, commander of the American forces stationed here. This is Gen. al-Samir, the base commander."

"Welcome to Saudi Arabia, Mr. Schilling," said the Saudi officer, extending his hand. "I wish the circumstances were different. We were told to expect a representative of ISA but weren't informed it would be somebody of your rank."

"I was in the region when we got the news," Peter replied as they took their seats. He removed a folder labeled Top Secret from his briefcase. "This is a copy of the preliminary report on the attack, but it doesn't address the underlying issues. What the hell happened?"

"I would think it's obvious," said the Saudi general. "There was an attack by extremists."

"This one happened right outside the main gate of your base."

"They failed to penetrate the perimeter."

Peter was in no mood to be handled. He leaned forward and stared back at the Saudi commander. "They had no interest in assaulting your base. There were only five of them and they wouldn't have made it past the gate. Don't spin this as a successful effort to defend the airbase. They were there to kill my people."

General Connolly held up his hands. "Let's keep this civil, gentlemen. I know you're upset, Director, but it's important that we work together on this."

The Saudi officer sat back in his chair. "I am sorry for your losses, Director, but Saudi lives were lost as well."

Peter took a deep breath to calm himself. "Then we're both searching for the same answers. What have you found so far?"

"Our security people are still looking into it. The attackers were all dead and none of them carried any form of identification. We're attempting to identify the bodies through forensic means, but that may take some time."

"What about weapons?"

"Standard military issue and easily obtained on the black market. The vehicles they used were stolen earlier in the day. That's all we have so far."

"Meaning you have nothing. They parked in full view of your security people, but nobody bothered to check them out. When the shooting started, your guards did nothing. There was no help for the people in those cars until your anti-terrorist unit responded. By then, almost everyone was dead. How do you explain that?"

He paused, waiting for an answer. When none was forthcoming, he asked the key question. "What about the intelligence failure?"

The Saudi general's expression remained calm, but his posture stiffened, and he shifted uncomfortably in his chair. "I'm sorry, but I don't understand."

"They knew the exact time the motorcade would arrive at the gate."

al-Samir's hands balled into fists. "Are you implying that someone within my command was part of this?"

Peter realized he was pushing this man hard, maybe too hard, but he needed answers, not evasions. "You tell me. And if you don't have that information, then please tell me who I should talk to. Your intelligence people are good, General. They'll get to the bottom of it. I just want to be damn sure that what they find out doesn't end up swept under the rug."

"I resent your attitude, Mr. Schilling."

Peter's anger finally boiled over. "And I resent the fact that ISA people are now in the morgue and the hospital. It happened on your watch, General."

The Saudi officer rose from his chair and left the room.

Peter looked over at Connolly. "He knows more than he's saying."

"Of course he does, but I'm sure he's under orders not to talk about it with us. Not yet anyway. This is an enormous embarrassment to both the Saudi military and their intelligence organizations. Until they discover who was behind this, they're not going to say much. And keep in mind that this is their airbase and I need to maintain a good working relationship with him. You're not helping by browbeating him like that."

"No offense, General, but that's your problem. Do you know any more than he does?"

"We have MPs standing guard at the entrance to the base, but that's just a courtesy. The Saudis are in charge and our people follow their lead. In the event of an incident such as this, the guards are instructed to defend the gate and call for support. You may not like it, but they followed their orders to the letter."

"What about the security leak?"

Connelly sighed and spread his hands. "That's a valid question, but I don't think anyone here is going to give you an answer. I'm sure they're hoping the leak came from us, not them."

"The terrorists picked that spot for effect. They not only succeeded in killing Americans, they did it right under the noses of both the Saudi and U.S. military. I want to know who was behind it and how they got their information."

General Connolly leaned forward and lowered his voice. "There is one thing I can tell you. I'm sure al-Samir was speaking the truth when he said there was no identification found on the attackers, but I overheard a conversation between him and the head of base security. One man had a note in his pocket. A note written in Farsi."

Peter stared at the officer. "Iran was behind this?"

The officer shrugged. "Just because one of them might have been

Iranian doesn't mean their government sanctioned the attack. In this part of the world, things aren't always as they appear."

Peter glanced at his watch. "I need to return to the hospital. As soon as the docs give the okay, I'll need a medevac plane to fly Kaitlyn Malone back to Washington. Can you make the arrangements?"

"I'll have my staff take care of it."

"Thanks, General. And tell al-Samir I apologize. Frame it any way you need to."

The general stood to go. "I'm sorry about your losses, Director."

"Yeah. So am I." Peter watched him leave and began stuffing papers back into his briefcase. If Iran was involved, this had suddenly become more than an isolated terrorist act.

CHAPTER THREE

Kate's eyes fluttered open as she slowly awoke from yet another drug-induced nap. Each dose of morphine caused her to drift off to sleep and awake sluggish and disoriented. She reached for the cup of ice water sitting on the tray table but stopped with her hand suspended in midair. A man seated in a chair in the far corner was regarding her with an amused grin. He looked to be in his early thirties with close-cropped brown hair. He needed a shave and his rumpled clothes looked as if they'd been slept in. A shoulder holster was visible under his sport coat.

"Who are you?" she croaked. "And what's so funny?"

He tossed the magazine he'd been reading onto the table beside him. "My name's Jason Collier. I'm your guardian angel for now. Did you know you snore?"

Kate picked up her water and took a sip, letting the cool liquid soothe her raw throat before swallowing. "They assigned me a bodyguard? Whose idea was that?"

"My boss doesn't take chances, and he's not a man you argue with."

"Your boss?"

"Peter Schilling."

It took her a moment to process that, but the resulting realization startled her. "The director of field operations? He sent you?"

"Nope. He brought me with him. We were in Kuwait when we got the news of the attack. My orders are to stay with you while he tries to sort out what happened."

Before she could reply, a sharp knock at the door announced the arrival of Dr. Crenshaw. "You're awake. Good. How are you feeling?"

Kate put the water cup back on the table. "Better. More alert."

He nodded. "We've been weaning you off the morphine. How's the pain?"

"Not bad, as long as I don't move around too much."

He went over to the computer monitor and scanned the display. "Your vital signs have remained stable. I'm going to switch you onto a different medication that'll make you less drowsy. Tell the nurse right away if the pain gets worse."

"How long will I be here?"

"They're flying you back to Washington tomorrow."

"Good. My bed at home is a lot more comfortable than this one."

"I didn't say I was releasing you. You're being transferred to Bethesda. They'll decide when you're ready to go home. My guess is they'll keep you for a few days, maybe a week."

"At least I'll be out of here. No offense, Doc."

He grinned. "In our line of work, we're always glad to see people leave. It means we did our job. There's somebody outside who wants to talk to you if you're feeling up to it."

"Who is it?"

Peter stepped into the room. "I'm Peter Schilling, Kate. I promise I won't be long, but we need to talk."

Crenshaw interrupted before she could reply. "I'll give you fifteen minutes, Director. She needs her rest."

"That's okay," said Kate. "He can stay as long as he needs to."

"Young lady, when you have your medical degree, I'll take your opinions under advisement. Until then, we'll do it my way."

"Fifteen minutes will be fine," said Peter. He turned his attention to Jason. "I've got this for now. Get something to eat and stretch your legs."

"Sure, boss." He smoothed out his jacket as best he could and followed the doctor from the room.

Peter waited until the door shut behind them. "How are you doing?"

"Better," Kate replied. "Have you heard anything about Monica Lindsey? The nurse said she survived, but they won't tell me anything else."

"Nothing specific, but I'm sure they're doing everything they can."

The images of exploding cars flashed through Kate's mind and she forced herself to push those thoughts aside. "Has anyone called my parents?"

"They'll be waiting for you at Bethesda."

Kate's head sagged back against the pillows.

Peter's expression changed to one of concern. "Maybe we should continue this when you've had a little more rest."

Kate shook her head. "I need to know some things. I have questions."

"Me too, so let's get started." He took out his notepad and pen and recounted what he'd already learned of the attack. "Is that more or less accurate?"

"I think so. It all happened so fast. I made it to the trees and used Gen. Haddad's gun to shoot back. I think I got one of them."

"You certainly did. With everything that's been going on, I haven't had time to review your file. You're an analyst, right?"

She nodded.

"How did you end up at ISA?"

She frowned. "Why is that important?"

"I need to know everything about what happened. That includes you. It's part of the process."

Kate reached for the water cup and took another sip. "My degree's in computer science. When I graduated from Purdue, ISA was recruiting people to work in digital forensics. I had offers from the FBI and the Illinois State Police but working for an intelligence agency sounded more exciting. I didn't realize it could get me shot."

"You started out in forensics?"

She shook her head. "I speak fluent Russian and when they saw that on my resume, they set up a different interview. Phil DeCosta hired me as an analyst in the Russian section." She hesitated, fearing the answer to the question she needed to ask. "He's dead, isn't he?"

"Yes. I'm sorry."

Once more, the memory of the noise and flames blocked out everything else. She took a deep breath and forced herself to focus. "Who were they? The terrorists, I mean."

"We don't know yet. Did they say anything?"

"Not until the end. They started shouting at each other that it was time to go, but I guess they didn't make it out before the cavalry showed up."

"They spoke Arabic?"

She nodded. "I'm not fluent by any means, but I understand it pretty well. One of them had an accent. I don't think he was a native speaker. Does it mean something?"

"It might. The Saudis found a note written in Farsi."

Her eyes widened. "The entire trip was about Iran. That's a pretty big coincidence."

"I don't put much stock in coincidence." He closed his notepad. "I think that's enough for now. I'll make sure your folks know you're okay. Once you're back in Washington, we'll talk some more."

Kate watched him go, the analyst in her trying to make sense of what she'd heard. It seemed unlikely that Iran would be behind the attack, but then she remembered where she was. In this part of the world, the improbable often became reality.

Her eyes grew heavy once again, and she settled back against the pillows.

CHAPTER FOUR

General Alexander Kruzov strolled through Zaryadye Park, trying to blend in with the people taking advantage of a warm summer afternoon. He'd abandoned his military uniform in favor of a casual sport shirt and slacks, but still kept a wary eye on those around him. Even the commander of Russia's anti-terrorism task force wasn't immune from the prying eyes and ears of the intelligence services. Anything that gave him a veil of anonymity was worth the effort because this meeting required secrecy above all else.

He paused and leaned against the railing, admiring the view across the Moskva River. Moscow had blossomed after the fall of the Soviet Union, the bleakness of the communist era replaced by optimism. Modern hotels and trendy shops had sprung up everywhere, catering to a burgeoning tourist industry.

The prosperity had crumbled in the wake of Putin's misadventures in Ukraine. Foreign investment had evaporated, replaced by economic sanctions and international condemnation. Businesses closed, unemployment soared, and hotel rooms stood vacant. Putin was gone now, replaced by a new regime. But his legacy remained with no sign that Russian leaders were willing to disavow it.

"Well, my old friend, are you enjoying this beautiful Russian sunshine?"

Kruzov glanced over at the man who joined him at the railing. Dimitri Artisimov might be overweight and balding, but he possessed a keen intellect and an innate ability to cut through to the core of the most complex problems. Roommates at the university, they were both recruited upon graduation. Kruzov entered the army's officer training program while Dimitri had been wooed by the KGB. When the Russian Federation rose from the ashes of the Soviet Union, Dimitri had become a rising star at SVR, the new government's version of America's CIA. As the head of SVR's Directorate R, he oversaw the analysis of everything Russian intelligence collected, from satellite surveillance to intel obtained through a network of spies embedded all over the world.

"A glorious day to be sure, but we're not here as tourists, are we?" Kruzov responded.

"Unfortunately not. Is there anything new on your side?"

Kruzov shrugged. "I keep waiting for someone to come to their senses, but I'm not optimistic. What our leaders are planning borders on insanity. I hope you have better news."

Dimitri lit a cigarette and tossed the match into the river. "I'm afraid not. Early on, I voiced my opposition to the whole thing, perhaps too strongly. I've been left out of several meetings lately, which means they're moving ahead and don't want to listen to the naysayers. Our president is blind to the mistakes of previous administrations and Evgeny Malkin is not a man to cross. Like Putin before him, he's determined to expand Russian influence."

"But the Baltic states are not Ukraine. They are members of NATO. Once again, we're risking war with America, a war there is no certainty we can win. It's madness."

"Surely the generals can see that."

"The ones who were vocal in their opposition were replaced and now oversee training camps in the Siberian wasteland. The rest decided that discretion is the wiser course."

Dimitri took a long drag on the cigarette. "There is a plan to keep America on the sidelines. I know little about it except its code name. They call it Valkyrie."

Kruzov stepped away from the railing. "That was the code word used by the German generals who plotted to assassinate Hitler. They wouldn't be so foolish as to target the American president." His eyes narrowed. "Or would they?"

"It would seem extreme, but reason has taken a vacation these days. Whatever schemes are being dreamed up in the Kremlin, you and I need to focus on the current situation. What about the Defense Ministry itself?"

"Mostly Malkin appointees who understand what happens when you step out of line. There are a few of us who remember what it was like during the Cold War and have no wish to return to those days, but we're outnumbered and powerless to stop this."

They watched a tour boat drift slowly past, its decks largely empty of the tourists who once flocked to Moscow. "Our leaders still chase the futile dream of a Russian empire. Have we learned nothing?"

Kruzov allowed the rhetorical question to pass unanswered. "The attack on the Americans in Riyadh last week came at a seemingly inopportune time. Did that have anything to do with the larger plan?"

Dimitri shook his head. "Not that I'm aware of. It caused some dismay within the agency and the Iranians vehemently denied any involvement, but they maintain less than full control over some of their more extreme elements. I don't think it matters. There was nothing about it that would draw attention to us."

"So, what do we do about this? Nothing?" asked Kruzov, his eyes still following the boat.

Dimitri took a last drag on his cigarette before flicking it over the railing. "I have a plan. It would be a desperate gamble, but there might be no other way."

"What kind of plan?"

Dimitri turned to face him. "How far are you willing to go to put an end to this?"

Kruzov stared into his friend's eyes. "I will never betray Russia. But neither will I stand by and watch misguided politicians take her down the path of ruin. What are you suggesting?"

Dimitri shook his head. "Nothing yet. But I need to know I can count on you when the time comes."

Their eyes remained locked. "There is no one I trust more than you, Dimitri. If whatever you're going to do puts an end to this without risking Russia's sovereignty, then you can count on my support."

"Thank you, my friend. I'll contact you once the details are worked out. And be careful. These are deep waters."

Kruzov watched him walk away with one thought running through his mind. What kind of plan could put a stop to all this?

CHAPTER FIVE

Kate hesitated outside Monica's hospital room. She was only three weeks out of Bethesda herself, and the memories of her stay came flooding back. She shoved those thoughts aside and knocked on the open door. "In the mood for some company?"

The smile that spread across her friend's face was all the invitation she needed. Kate dropped her bag onto a chair and went over to the bed. Monica had lost weight during her hospital stay and the shadows under her eyes combined with the pale skin and unkempt red hair to give her an almost ghostly appearance. But the sparkle was back in those green eyes and the smile betrayed no trace of the horror she'd survived.

Kate scanned the array of equipment that dripped IV fluids and monitored vital signs. "I'd give you a hug, but I'd hate to knock something loose. They've really got you wired up."

"This is nothing. You should have seen it when I was in ICU. They had me on a ventilator for a week. It was awful."

"You look good."

"Yeah, right."

Kate couldn't hide a grin. "Okay. You look better than I expected. How are you doing?"

"I'll live, something that wasn't a sure thing for a while. When you're on the tipping point of life and death and land on the good side, it's hard to complain about anything. Except maybe the food. I'm still on a soft diet. I'd kill for a medium rare ribeye with a twice baked potato. And a glass of cabernet, a really good cabernet."

"When they let you out of here, dinner's on me. Any idea when that will be?"

"Next week, I hope. They're getting me out of bed and letting me walk around a little, but I wear out pretty fast. I need to get back in the gym."

"One thing at a time, girl. Let's get you out of here before you start thinking about that stuff."

"Enough about me," said Monica. "You're all healed up?"

"Good as new. When I got out of the hospital, I went back home to the farm to recover. Mom's cooking and helping Dad with the chores got me back on my feet. The doc gave me my release two days ago."

"You're back at work?"

"That happens tomorrow. To be honest, I have mixed feelings about it."

"Why?" asked Monica with a surprised expression.

"Everyone's going to make a big deal out of what happened."

"It sort of is a big deal."

"I know. But I killed a man, Monica. He would have killed me, and lots of other people did die, including Phil. You too, almost. I know I did the right thing, but there's more to it than that. I keep seeing his face. He was staring at me when I shot him. I'm not sure that's something I want to be commended for."

"What are you going to do?"

"That job offer from the Hoskins Group is still on the table. They told me I could take all the time I needed, especially after what happened, but I can't stall forever. It would mean a lot more money and a way to put all this behind me. But I'd be moving to New York where I don't know anyone. And I really love my job at ISA. I'm not sure doing risk assessments for corporations operating in remote parts of the world would be as challenging." She hesitated. "Then there's Dan."

"How's that stand?"

Kate shrugged. "We haven't talked since I got shot."

"Not at all? What's wrong with you?"

"While I was in the hospital, visitors were limited to family and a short list of ISA higher-ups. The attack was still being investigated, and they wanted to keep me off the radar. Once the docs let me go, I went straight to Illinois."

"He didn't call?"

Kate looked away. "Almost every day. I never called him back."

Monica's eyes narrowed. "What's going on, Kate? It's not like you to avoid your problems."

"I don't know what to say to him. I'm undecided about the job and I'm unsure of our relationship. And I almost died. It complicates things. It changes your perspective."

"You won't be able to avoid him forever. You work in the same building."

"Yeah." Kate glanced at her watch. "I need to get going. Tomorrow's going to be busy, but I'll stop by the day after. You'll probably be jogging up and down the halls by then."

"I wish. Can I give you some advice? Tell him the truth. And if you really don't know where you stand, tell him that too. Don't leave things hanging. That's not fair to either of you."

Kate grinned. "You should start an advice column. Monica Lindsey's Words of Wisdom."

"Get out of here. I'll be eager to hear how it turns out."

"Yeah. Me too."

Driving back to her apartment, Kate kept replaying Monica's words in her mind. Maybe she was right. Maybe admitting that she needed more time to sort it all out was enough for now. If Dan wanted to push it, that was his problem. And then there was that job offer. Being recruited by the Hoskins Group was both flattering and enticing, but the job that looked so attractive a month ago seemed less so now. If nothing else, the attack in Saudi Arabia reminded her she dealt with actual problems the world faced. Doing intel analysis in the corporate world seemed trivial by comparison. Still, a $40,000 raise was nothing to dismiss out of hand.

Kate parked in front of her building and let herself into the lobby. A good long run might be just the thing to clear her mind. She was gradually regaining her conditioning, and while she wasn't all the way back yet, she was getting close. When she unlocked her door, however, she got an unwanted surprise.

Dan Grissom looked up from the magazine he'd been flipping through and flashed the boyish smile that always made her heart pump a little faster. "Welcome home."

"Dan. What are you doing here?"

"You gave me a key, remember?" He placed the magazine on the coffee table. "I heard you got back last night. Why didn't you call?" He stood and moved toward her, hesitating when he saw her step away.

She couldn't dodge this any longer. "I didn't know what to say. We had that fight before I left for the Middle East, and I didn't want to risk another until I sorted some things out."

"I tried to see you at Bethesda. I wasn't on the approved list of visitors."

"That was ISA's decision. They slapped a security tag on what happened in Riyadh and that meant I had to stay under wraps for a while. I got the flowers you sent. They were beautiful. Thank you."

"I wanted to tell you how sorry I was about that argument. You were right. I overstepped. When I found out you'd been released, I came over to talk it out, but you weren't here."

"I went back to the farm to recover. I got all the emails and texts you sent, but I wasn't ready to deal with it."

"And now?"

She shrugged. "You want an answer, but I don't have one. Not yet."

"About moving in together? Let's do a reset and forget I ever brought it up. Or is this about something bigger?"

"I'm not sure about that either." His expression caused her to look away. "Today's Monday. Give me until the weekend and then we'll talk. You've been more than patient and I appreciate that, but I still need a little time. I'm not ready to do this right now."

Before he could reply, the buzzer announced a visitor down in the lobby. Grateful for the interruption, Kate pressed the comm button and stepped back as the screen displayed an image of Peter Schilling.

"Director. This is certainly unexpected."

"May I come up? I need to speak with you."

What could he possibly need to talk to her about before she even returned to work? "Of course." She pressed the button to unlock the lobby door and turned to face Dan.

He gestured at the security panel. "Director? What's going on, Kate?" For all his charms, Dan had a jealous streak that sometimes raised its head at inopportune times.

"It's Peter Schilling."

"The DFO? What's he want? You're an analyst, not a spy. Are you seeing him? Is that why you're keeping me at arm's length?"

"Don't be ridiculous. And please don't make a scene."

"If you're going behind my back, I have a right to know."

Her uncertainty faded in an instant. "Okay, Dan. You want an answer now? Fine. It's over. If I was unsure about it before, I'm not anymore. Now you should go before things get any more awkward than they already are."

A knock announced Peter's arrival. "I mean it, Dan. Just say hello and leave."

She turned to open the door. Peter came in carrying a briefcase but pulled up short when he saw Dan standing in the middle of the living room. "I didn't realize you had company. Is there somewhere we can talk privately?"

"Director, this is Dan Grissom. He was just leaving."

Dan's eyes moved back and forth between her and Peter, and for a moment Kate was afraid he wasn't going to let it go. To her relief, he snatched his sport coat from the back of the sofa and started for the door. "You've changed. I liked the old Kate a lot better."

He stormed out, slamming the door behind him. She watched him go, feeling like a chapter of her life had closed as well.

"It seems I arrived at an inopportune time," observed Peter.

"Actually, your timing was perfect. Why are you here, Director?"

"You can call me Peter. Director is awfully formal if you're going to be working for me. Temporarily anyway."

The statement left her stunned. "Huh? I mean what? I mean …"

"Let's sit down and I'll explain." He nodded toward the door as they settled into armchairs. "How long have you been involved with him?"

Her confusion turned to irritation. "What's that got to do with anything? And with no disrespect intended, why is it any of your business?"

"For the time being, everything about you is my business. If I'm sending someone into the field, I need to know all I can about them. Their strengths, their weaknesses, and their vulnerabilities. It's part of the job."

"The field? What on earth are you talking about?"

Peter leaned forward in his chair. "I need to ask a favor. A high-ranking Russian intelligence officer is defecting. I want you to debrief him."

"Certainly. Who is he?"

"Dimitri Artisimov."

Kate's eyes widened. "He's right at the top of their intelligence hierarchy. He'd be a huge catch."

"At first glance, yes, but people at that level rarely defect. And once it becomes common knowledge, all hell will break loose. Before that happens, I need to know why he's doing this. It's possible he got himself into trouble politically and all he wants is an exit strategy. Or maybe he's been screwing the president's wife and got caught. I have a hard time believing he's doing it for ideological reasons, but we can't rule anything out."

"Does this have anything to do with what happened in Riyadh? That trip wasn't just about Iran, it involved Russia as well."

"The same thought occurred to me. I suppose it's possible."

"Hasn't anyone asked him?"

"He says he'll only talk to you."

"Me? Why?"

"It has nothing to do with you personally. He knows you're our lead analyst for anything pertaining to Russia and says you'll understand the value of what he's bringing us better than anyone else. He's probably right, but I need to make sure it isn't a bunch of bullshit before we grant him asylum."

Kate nodded. "Okay. Where is he?"

"At a safe house in the Paris suburbs."

"Huh? You mean like Paris, France?"

"The ISA liaison at the embassy was attending a soccer game. Artisimov walked up to him and said he wanted to defect. Because of his position with Russian intelligence, this needed to be handled carefully, so Jason Collier is babysitting him until you get there. He was your bodyguard in Riyadh."

"I remember. I'm going to Paris? When?"

"Tonight. An ISA driver will pick you up and take you out to the airfield. There's no time to arrange a commercial flight, so you'll be using an agency jet. Someone will meet you when you land."

"They're expecting me at the office tomorrow. I've got an appointment with Director Linder at 10:00. He's presenting me with a commendation."

"Congratulations."

"I'm not exactly looking forward to it, but I can't not show up."

"I ran this by him, and he agreed it takes priority." He paused for a moment. "I realize this is outside your normal duties, so consider it a request, not an order. You're free to decline. But if you accept, you'll be working for me until we resolve this."

Kate considered the offer. A field assignment was the last thing she expected, but the chance to dip her toe in those waters was too enticing to turn down. "I'll do what I can."

"Good."

Peter placed his briefcase on the coffee table. "Sending our top Russian expert to Paris just as one of their key people is defecting would attract too much attention. I want to keep this off the radar for now, so you won't be using your own passport. I have one for you in the name of Carla Fremont. It's an established cover that won't be questioned. The passport will give you diplomatic status and allow you to bypass customs when you arrive."

"Why do I need to do that?"

"Because of this." He removed a holstered pistol from the briefcase. "You showed in Riyadh that you can handle one of these. Where did you learn to shoot?"

"Farm kids grow up around guns. When I moved into an apartment my junior year of college, Dad bought me a Sig Saur pistol for protection and made damn sure I knew how to use it. No matter where I've lived since, that Sig is always in the drawer beside my bed. When that attack happened, I didn't even think. I grabbed the general's sidearm and did what I had to."

"The weapon's only a tool. You kept your head, and that's why you survived."

Kate picked up the pistol. Out of habit she made sure the safety was on and the chamber was empty. "It's the same model as mine. How did you know?"

"I had your apartment searched while you were in the hospital," he answered, raising his hand to cut her off before she could respond. "ISA people were targeted in Riyadh. It's even possible that taking out a specific individual was their goal. I don't rule things out or leave any stone unturned, so I needed to learn all I could about you. Nothing was taken, nothing was disturbed, and you were never suspected of anything. I was merely being thorough. In this job you have to be."

Kate stared at him.

"This world doesn't work by the rules you're used to," he continued. "What we do is driven by necessity and the willingness to take full advantage of any opportunity that turns up. The niceties of normal life are irrelevant."

The analyst in her could see his point, but it was her life they were talking about, and he was an intruder in it. She placed the weapon back on the table. "Why do I need a gun, anyway?"

"As a precaution. Once the Russians realize Artisimov's missing, they're going to try to get him back or eliminate him. The safe house should be secure, but I don't take chances and I don't send my people into the field unarmed. Do you still want to do this?"

She nodded. "You're not sending me to France to be a spy. I'm simply an analyst on a field trip. I can handle that."

"Good. I'm also giving you another passport under a different name and a driver's license and credit card to go with it. They're only for emergencies. Don't use them unless you have to."

"So, I'm to get what I can from him and come home. If what he has is valuable enough, does he come with me?"

"No," he replied. "Although the French are an ally and a member of NATO, they allow no American bases on their soil. That means we can't get him out on a military plane. Flying him out with you on a government jet would attract attention and involve the use of an airport the Russians have access to. A commercial flight is entirely out of the question. To further complicate things, the French are currently negotiating a deal that would restore their access to Russian oil and natural gas, so we can't assume they'll be willing to expedite a politically explosive defection. It'll take a couple of days to come up with a viable extraction plan, but I want you back here as soon as possible. Learn what you can and let Jason take it from there."

"Then I better get packed. Is there anything else?"

"I don't believe so."

"Aren't you going to wish me luck?"

"This is the field, Kate. If it comes down to luck, you're probably screwed already."

"Yeah. Right." She escorted him out feeling like Alice when she stepped through the looking glass.

CHAPTER SIX

Kate paused as she stepped down onto the Orly Airport tarmac, unsure where to go. The ISA pilot walked up behind her. "The diplomatic terminal's through there," he said, pointing to a door marked Entrée Diplomatique. "If they ask, tell them you're staying at the embassy."

Once inside, Kate displayed her passport to the woman seated at the desk. She scanned it into her computer and handed it back with a sunny smile. "Bienvenue en France, Ms. Fremont. Enjoy your stay in our country."

"Merci. I'm looking forward to it."

She emerged onto the sidewalk to find a short, stocky man leaning against a black sedan. He waved her over and displayed an embassy badge. "Carla Fremont? Welcome to France. Just the one bag?"

"Plus my backpack. I'll keep that with me."

He placed her duffle in the trunk and opened the rear door for her. In awe of the fact that she was actually in Paris, she spent the drive staring out the window hoping for a glimpse of the Eiffel Tower. But as they drove north from the airport, another thought crept into her mind.

Kate leaned forward in her seat. "This car has diplomatic plates?"

"Yes, of course."

She turned and looked out the rear window. If the Russians were looking for Artisimov, they might be interested in where embassy cars were going. "Can you tell if we're being followed?"

"I drive diplomats to meetings and official functions. They said you were ISA. Shouldn't you be able to tell?"

"I'm sort of new at this."

She scanned the vehicles behind them. It was a busy freeway, and the early morning traffic was heavy. "Get off at the next exit and head for the center of the city."

"Anyplace in particular?"

"The Eiffel Tower."

"Traffic will be a mess down there."

"Good. Drop me off as close as you can and go back to the embassy. What's the address of our destination?"

He handed her a slip of paper. "What about your luggage?"

"I'll take my backpack with me. The duffle stays with you."

Once on the street, she mingled with the crowds, trying her best to blend in. Maybe she was being paranoid, but it wouldn't hurt to play it safe.

A café across the street gave her an idea. She entered through the front door and spotted a sign marked Toilette. Shutting herself in a stall, she took the Sig from her backpack and put it in her jacket pocket. She left the cafe through the rear and followed the alley to a side street where she hailed a taxi. "Le Louvre, si vous plait."

She exited the vehicle at the museum and walked south for two blocks before flagging down another cab. She gave him the address of the safe house and settled back in her seat. It probably meant nothing, but at least she'd thought like an intelligence operative instead of acting like a tourist.

The cab deposited her outside the house. She rang the bell and waited impatiently for an answer.

"You're late."

She turned and found Jason Collier standing behind her. "Very subtle, Jason. Shouldn't you be inside with Artisimov?"

"I slipped out the back door when I saw the cab. You should have gotten out a couple of blocks away instead of drawing attention here."

"Sorry. I'm not up on my spy craft. Can we go inside?"

Jason closed the front door behind them as a balding man in a rumpled suit walked out from the kitchen. "It is her?"

"Yeah. Dimitri Artisimov, Kate Malone."

The Russian regarded her curiously. "I know you by reputation. The photograph in your dossier does not do you justice."

His English was fluent, although heavily accented. "Dubroye ootro, Dimitri. Kak vy pozhivayetye?" Kate used the formal greeting. It would be a good idea to start off on the right foot.

"Nichyego." He switched back to English. "You speak like a native, but your accent is from the south. Most Americans sound like they're from Moscow."

"My mother's parents emigrated from Sochi. They lived with us when I was a child and never learned much English. I grew up speaking to them in Russian."

He nodded. "That explains much."

"Excuse me?"

"By all accounts, you are intelligent and excel as an analyst. But now I find you to be beautiful as well. How could such a woman not be Russian?"

Kate ignored the attempt at byplay. "I'm here because you wanted to talk to me, so let's keep this on a professional level, okay?"

"As you wish."

Kate went over to the front window and looked out at the street. "Jason, I think maybe we should find somewhere else to be."

"Why? My orders are to wait here with him until they decide how to handle this. You're the amateur here. Let me do the thinking, okay?"

"Will you shut up and listen for a minute? Someone at the embassy sent an official car with diplomatic plates to pick me up."

Jason's annoyed expression changed to one of surprise. "What?"

"I had the driver drop me off in the city and did my best to make sure I wasn't being followed. But if the Russians caught up with the car and realized I wasn't in it anymore, wouldn't they have intercepted the driver to find out where I was going?"

"Nice work, Kate." He took out his phone and made a call. "Put me through to Ken Rosenthall. Tell him it's Jason Collier."

He glanced over at Kate. "Ken's the ISA station chief in Europe. Ken? Did the driver who picked up Kate Malone show up back at the embassy?" There was a momentary pause. "Kate's fine. She realized somebody screwed up and got here on her own. We're going to relocate right now. I'll call you after."

He hung up the phone and swore. "You were right. The driver never made it back to the embassy, and he's not answering his phone. Dimitri, grab your coat. We abandon everything and get the hell out of here."

Kate was still watching out the window. "We're too late. A car just pulled up and three men are getting out. What do we do, Jason?"

He looked over her shoulder at the scene on the street. "The tall one is going around back. Dimitri, get in the closet in the back bedroom." He turned to Kate. "Are you armed?"

"Yeah. Peter gave me a ..."

"The back door leads into the kitchen. Shoot anyone who comes through. I've got the front."

"But I ..."

"We don't have time to waste. Move!"

Kate ran to the kitchen and looked for a place that would provide some cover. She moved to a spot against the far wall where the refrigerator would shield her from whoever came through the door. She drew her gun and waited nervously, wondering why she'd ever taken Peter up on his offer.

The sound of shattered glass came from the front of the house followed by three gunshots in rapid succession. She clenched her teeth to keep them from chattering and hoped her quivering knees wouldn't give out on her.

The back door flew open with a crash. A man stepped through

and trained his gun from left to right. Seeing no one, he shoved the table out of his way and moved toward the hallway leading to the bedrooms. Four more shots came from the front of the house.

Kate forced herself to focus. When he turned to enter the hall, she stepped out past the refrigerator and fired one shot. The bullet struck him in the back, but he didn't go down. He staggered to one side and grabbed the door frame for support, dropping the gun in the process.

He turned and looked straight at her, apparently expecting her to finish it. Kate stared back, unable to make herself pull the trigger a second time. Once more, the images of the terrorist attack in Riyadh flashed through her mind. This couldn't be happening. Not again. She belonged back at her desk in Washington, not fending off Russian assassins in Paris.

"Kate!" Jason shouted from the living room. "Get Dimitri. We're leaving."

Dimitri Artisimov stepped into the hallway. "I am ready." He froze when he saw the man sent to kill him.

The Russian agent reached down to retrieve his weapon. The movement kicked Kate's brain back into gear and she fired three more times. The first bullet struck him on the shoulder, causing him to stagger backward against the wall. The next two went squarely into his chest. He slid slowly down onto the floor. She stood over him and watched as blood soaked the front of his shirt.

Jason came in from the living room, bleeding from a wound in his side. He glanced at the dead Russian. "We have to go. The car's parked in the back."

Kate continued to stare at the man lying on the floor.

"Kate! Come on. Snap out of it."

She shook her head to clear it and looked up from the corpse. "Dimitri, do you know him?"

He nodded. "A dangerous man."

"Not anymore," said Jason. "Let's move. We've got to be gone before the cops show up." He handed her the fob. "You'll have to drive."

As they headed for the door, Kate grabbed a dish towel from the rack by the sink. "You're bleeding. Hold that over the wound and apply pressure."

Jason accepted the towel and led them out the back, leaning heavily on Dimitri for support. The car was parked just outside the door. "Turn left at the end of the alley and then right at the light. There's a hardware store two blocks further down. Park behind it."

She followed his instructions, making sure the store shielded them from the view of anyone on the street. "Now what?"

"The license plates that are showing are taped over the real ones. Pull them off and throw them in that dumpster. Give me your phone."

"Why?"

"Just do it and quit asking questions."

She handed it to him and got out to remove the plates. He returned the phone to her as she slid back behind the wheel. "We're heading for a house on the outskirts of the city. I put the address into the phone and all you need to do is follow the directions. Once we're there, pull the car around back."

"How bad are you hurt?"

"It doesn't matter. If I lose consciousness, the app will get you where we're going."

"Why don't we go to the embassy? By now everyone knows we have Dimitri. There's no more need for secrecy."

"The Russians will assume that's where we're going and try to stop us. And someone at the embassy compromised you. That's the last place we want to go. Now drive."

She sighed and started the car. This was turning into one hell of a field trip.

CHAPTER SEVEN

The phone announced the completion of their journey. "Your destination is one hundred feet ahead on your right."

Kate slowed and studied the scene in front of her. A row of small cottages occupied the right side of the street. Across from them was the entrance to a municipal park. Kate scanned the house numbers until she identified the second from the end as their goal and continued around the block to the alleyway. She braked to a stop and turned to the rear seat. "How is he?"

"Unconscious," Dimitri replied.

"Wake him up if you can."

The alley separated the house from a small, decrepit garage. Kate went over and peered through the grimy window. When she turned back to assist Dimitri, Jason was on his feet but looked pale and leaned against the car for support.

He motioned weakly toward the house. "Unless they changed the keypad code, it's 984412."

"There's a car in the garage. What if someone's home?"

"If you knock politely, they won't respond. Just be ready when you go inside."

Kate entered the passcode and heard the lock disengage. She turned the handle and cautiously stepped through the door. The room was windowless, with the only illumination coming from the daylight filtering around her. She fumbled for the light switch but froze when the barrel of a gun was pressed tightly against her temple. A hand reached down and removed the Sig from her pocket.

"Qui etes vous? Qu'est ce vous faiyez la?" asked a female voice.

Kate held perfectly still. "I don't speak French and I wasn't trying to break in. I had the door code. Doesn't that mean something?"

"It means I need to change the code. You still haven't told me who you are." Her English was fluent but spoken with an accent Kate immediately recognized.

"Talia?" Jason's voice came weakly from outside the door. "It's Jason Collier. Can we come in, please?"

The woman shoved Kate away from the door and stepped back with her gun pointed at the entrance. "Come. Keep your hands where I can see them."

Dimitri assisted Jason through the door.

"It's been a while, Talia," said Jason. "I'm sorry to barge in on you, but there are people trying to kill us."

Talia glanced at the blood on his jacket but didn't lower her weapon. "So, what's different from every other time you show up? Who are these two?"

"Kate's my partner for now. This gentleman is someone we're trying to keep safe. His name is John."

"John? Really? You couldn't do better than that? And I hope Kate survives longer than your last partner."

Talia lowered her weapon. "Let's go into the kitchen. You can feed me a bullshit story while I check out that wound." She returned Kate's gun to her. "I'm Talia Levy."

"Kate Malone. You're Israeli."

"Very good. There's some coffee in the cupboard above the sink. Start a pot while I get the medical kit."

Kate spooned coffee into the filter basket while Talia removed Jason's shirt and cleaned away the dried blood. "No exit wound, so the bullet's still in there. It bled a lot. How do you feel?"

"Like it bled a lot. Can you patch it up?"

"I can apply a pressure bandage to slow the bleeding, but this is going to need surgery. I'll set up an IV to get some fluids back into you and give you something to make you sleep for a while. You look like you could use it."

"We don't have time for that."

"Yes, we do," said Kate. "I'm out of my league here, Jason. If you keep passing out, I'm probably going to screw up and all of this will be for nothing. Get a little sleep. I'll call Peter for instructions."

Jason gave Talia a weak grin. "It's her first day in the field and she's already killed a man. I'm not in the mood to argue with her. Besides, she's probably right. Do it."

Kate studied the Israeli agent as Talia tended to Jason's wounds. Black hair cut just below the ears and a total absence of makeup spoke of functionality over fashion, and her assertive manner underscored the intensity that radiated from her every movement. She would not be someone to cross without good reason.

Kate waited until Jason was asleep on the sofa. "So, Talia, I assume you're Mossad?"

The Israeli woman ignored the question. "It's really your first day?"

"Yeah. I'm an analyst who got sent on a routine assignment. Who knew?"

Talia threw her head back and laughed. "Welcome to our world."

"What happened to Jason's last partner?"

"He tried to be a hero. Never a good idea." Talia's gaze moved to Dimitri. "Who is this John you're risking your life to protect?"

"You know I can't tell you. We're only here because our safe house became sort of unsafe. How did Jason know about this place?"

"He and I worked together on a joint mission last year." She glanced over at the sofa. "He must have been desperate. If someone else had been here, this might have gotten ugly."

"We didn't have a lot of options. I should check in with ISA."

"You can use the bedroom down the hall, or you could go out to the garage if you don't trust me. Take the Russian with you. I'll keep an eye on Jason."

Kate looked puzzled. "How did you know he was Russian?"

"I didn't until just now. Not for sure. You need to avoid being manipulated like that."

Once again, Kate realized how far out of her comfort zone she really was. "It was just a lucky guess?"

"He's important enough to warrant ISA protection. His features tend toward Slavic, and he hasn't said a word which means his accent would give him away. Where would such a man be from? The Cold War is over and most of the former Soviet bloc is now part of NATO. The most likely conclusion is that he's Russian, and I just got you to confirm it."

"I guess I have a lot to learn. We'll go out back to make that call. Dimi … I mean John. Come with me."

Once inside the ramshackle garage, Kate found a folding chair for Dimitri and hopped up onto the hood of the car. The original plan was completely blown, and she was going to have to improvise. Conducting this conversation in Russian would ensure that she got her point across.

"Things are going downhill quickly, Dimitri. With Jason injured and my being thrown into the deep end, I'm not sure how we're going to get you out of France. I'm about to make a call to my boss. He'll want to be certain this is all worthwhile."

"He knows who I am and what my knowledge is worth."

"Maybe, but the situation has deteriorated. He might decide to cut his losses. Giving him some idea of the value of your information could tip the scales in your favor."

"Then I would no longer have any leverage."

"You don't need to tell me everything or go into detail. Hold back as much as you like, but give me some idea of what's at stake."

He stared at the dirt floor for a moment. "You're aware of our new intelligence arrangements with Iran?"

"That's old news."

"The exchange of information is not the extent of it. Russia will soon move troops onto an Iranian airbase. Those forces will be armed with weapons which will cancel out Israel's strategic advantage in the region."

Kate stared at him. "Nuclear weapons? Has the Russian leadership lost their minds?"

"They will be small-scale tactical missiles and Russian forces will remain in total control of them, but their presence will even out the balance of power and allow Iran to pursue certain goals in the region. Those goals will work to Russia's benefit as well."

"How?"

"Our leadership has plans to realign alliances in Europe. Tipping the scales in the Middle East is part of the overall strategy. I'll give you the rest once we're on U.S. soil."

The implications of this were enormous, but the analyst in her still focused on the details. "They're assuming we'll just let this happen?"

"They think that will be the case. I believe our leaders have miscalculated in assessing American resolve. If this turned into open warfare, Russia would suffer greatly. I cannot stand by and let that happen."

"How much can you give us?"

"I know many of the details of our plans for Iran and the strategy to realign Europe. I can give you the identities of the key players in both Russia and Iran." He hesitated. "You should also know that not everyone is on board with this. There are those who think as I do, and I can put you in contact with them. Is that good enough?"

Kate gave a resigned sigh. "Yes, Dimitri. I'd say that's good enough."

Kate was about to take out her phone when the door opened. "Jason's awake and wants to talk to you," said Talia.

"You said he'd sleep for a while."

"I gave him a low dose because of the blood loss. Evidently it wasn't enough. Have you made your call yet?"

"No. How much of that did you overhear?"

"My Russian's not great, but he mentioned Russia and Iran in the same sentence. That means Mossad will be interested in what he has to say."

"We're taking him back to Washington," said Kate. "Deciding who we share his information with is above my paygrade. Actually, almost everything is above my paygrade. Let's go back inside."

Jason was sitting up on the sofa when they came into the living room. The IV was still in his arm, but he appeared more alert.

"Feeling better?" asked Kate.

He shrugged. "Did you call Peter?"

"Not yet. I was having a chat with ... John."

"I heard you call him Dimitri," said Talia. "There's no further need to pretend."

Kate regarded her suspiciously. "Jason, how well does Talia speak Russian?"

"Badly. Why?"

"She overheard me talking with Dimitri. Some of what he said is sensitive, to say the least."

Jason's eyes moved to the Israeli agent. "Talia?"

"I know your boss. Call him. I have a proposal."

He regarded her carefully before looking back at Kate. "Make the call and put it on speaker."

She dialed a number and placed the phone on the coffee table. Peter answered on the first ring. "Kate? What's the status?"

"Things are a mess. Russian agents attacked the safe house."

"Is Jason with you?"

"Yeah boss, I'm here. Somebody at the embassy set Kate up. She figured it out, but they must have gotten the location out of her driver."

"How bad was it?"

"The house is shot to hell. We left bodies behind."

"Where are you now?"

"At a place Talia and I used when we needed to lie low."

"Talia? Talia Levy?"

Talia leaned toward the phone. "Hello, Peter. They're safe for now, but Jason's injured and needs medical attention."

"What about you, Kate? How are you holding up?"

"Never mind me," said Kate. "What do you want us to do?"

Several seconds of silence led Kate to wonder if they'd lost the call. Peter's voice finally came back on the line. "With Artisimov defecting, the Russians are probably going to appeal to the French government. That will complicate things. The French won't let Artisimov out of the country until they decide how to proceed. They may even conclude it's in their best interest to turn him back over to the Russians. We must act fast, but getting you all out of France won't be easy. I'll take the first flight I can. Can you hold out until then?"

Jason started to respond, but Talia held up her hand. "Peter, it will be several hours before you arrive. There will still be no plan in place, and the Russians will not stop looking for them. I can offer your team a way out of the country, but the destination will be Tel Aviv."

Another long silence. "And if I agree?"

"You can meet us there. Jason will be treated in a proper hospital and Dimitri will stay in Kate's custody. No one will question him until you arrive, but Mossad gets to be in the room when you debrief him."

"Jason, what do you think?" asked Peter.

"Kate's the only one who's spoken with Dimitri about any of this."

Kate's head jerked up in surprise. They were leaving this up to her? "I can't go into it on the phone, Peter, but it's probably something we'd end up sharing with Israel anyway. We absolutely can't risk losing Dimitri, so getting him away from the Russians is the most important thing right now." She glanced over at the Israeli spy. "But I don't know Talia. Can we trust her?"

"Her priority will always be what's in Israel's best interest," replied Peter. "But if getting Dimitri out of France is just as important to her as it is to us, then she's our best option."

"Then I say we take her up on the offer. I've only been in France for a few hours, but I can't wait to get the hell out of here."

"Alright then. Talia, they're in your hands. I'll send you my ETA once I'm in the air."

Kate hung up her phone and glanced over at Jason. His eyes were drooping again, and he laid back against the sofa cushions. "I'm still a little groggy. Work it out with Talia, Kate. You can trust her."

Kate sighed and regarded the Israeli. "So, what's the plan?"

"Have you heard of a company called Bartek International?"

"I don't think so."

"It's a financial consulting company based in Munich. The business is legitimate, but behind the scenes, it's a front for handling funding and logistics for Mossad operations in Europe. The company owns a plane."

"How is this going to work?"

"There's a small airfield about thirty miles south of the city. It's used mostly by local aviation enthusiasts, but it can handle a private jet. The plane will file a flight plan listing its destination as Cannes with a stop here to pick up passengers. Since the flight from Paris to Cannes is domestic, we won't have to deal with customs or immigration."

"But we fly to Israel instead?" Kate considered that for a moment. "Won't that be a dead giveaway that Bartek isn't what it seems? You'll be compromising a valuable asset."

"Very good, and you're correct. Subtlety always works best. An inflight medical emergency will require the plane to divert to the nearest large airport, which in our case will be Geneva, Switzerland. The flight path to Cannes practically takes us right over the city."

"We'll be out of France, but still have to go through Swiss customs. There'll be a paper trail."

"Not if we don't get off the plane. An ambulance will take one of the flight crew to the hospital complaining of chest pain. While we're on the ground, the pilot will file an amended flight plan with Tel Aviv as the destination. No one will question it."

Kate marveled at the beauty of it. A totally reasonable sequence of events that in no way hinted at its actual purpose would be their ticket out of this mess. "You've done this before."

"Or variations of it. One never knows when the need will arise."

"Why are you in France in the first place?" asked Kate.

Talia gave her a sharp look and Kate realized the question was probably outside the bounds of accepted protocol.

"The details are classified," the Israeli spy finally replied. "But the underlying reasons should be obvious. As a result of our war against Hamas, many terrorist organizations such as Hezbollah and the various militias supported by Iran moved their leadership and organizational control to Europe in an effort to evade the wrath of our defense forces. Hunting them down and disrupting their operations became a matter better handled by Mossad than the military."

"And we're forcing you to abandon your mission."

"No. You have actually expanded its scope. Iran is the puppet master and uses all of these groups as proxies. If Dimitri can shed any light on the internal workings of those relationships, it could help our cause immensely. But right now, we have more immediate problems to deal with."

"How quickly can you set up the extraction?"

"I can have the plane on the ground within three hours."

"Then let's do it."

CHAPTER EIGHT

Kate prepared a simple lunch of canned soup and crusty bread while Talia made the arrangements for their escape. Dimitri paced back and forth across the kitchen, muttering under his breath in Russian.

"Relax," said Kate in the same language. "We'll be out of here soon."

He stopped his pacing and faced her. "I thought I was defecting to you, not Mossad."

"You are."

"We're going to Israel. Tel Aviv is not Washington. I think maybe I made a mistake."

"Would you prefer to go back to Moscow? You know what's waiting for you there."

"I have your assurance that your country remains our ultimate destination?"

"That's my understanding. But if we're going to get out of France in one piece, Israel has to be our first stop. Be patient."

"An easy thing for you to say. You'll return to your safe little office when this is over. My future is not so clear."

She threw the bread knife down and turned to face him. "Easy? You think any of this is easy? I killed a man this morning. Do you know what that feels like? I'm on the run from Russian agents, the

French police, and God knows who else. I have to place my trust in an Israeli spy I only just met, and all you do is complain and dangle little pieces of information so we won't dump your ass in the street for SVR to find. This better be worthwhile, Dimitri, or I swear that Russian agent may not be the only man I shoot today."

Talia came into the room, phone still in hand. "What's all this? What is he saying?"

"He's being a jerk."

"He's scared. So are you. It goes with the territory, but you can't let it get the better of you."

"Maybe that works for you and Jason. I'm not a spy."

"You are today. You better start thinking like one if we're going to make this work."

Kate let out a long sigh. "Yeah. Just don't tell me it's easy. Is everything on schedule?"

"We leave for the airfield immediately after we eat."

Since the police might have issued an alert for Jason's car, they moved it into the garage and used Talia's Peugeot for the trip. Kate was in the front passenger seat while Jason and Dimitri sat in the back. Jason was running a fever, which meant infection was setting in, but the nap had helped some and he seemed more alert.

The area surrounding the airfield was heavily wooded, with little traffic on the surrounding roads. Everything was working in their favor until they came around the last curve. A police car sat just inside the entrance. Talia swore in Hebrew and kept driving until they reached an intersection. She pulled into a parking lot and turned to face the others. "I've used this airfield many times and there's never been a police presence. They knew we were coming."

Jason sat up straight, visibly trying to rally. "You made all the arrangements. I'm not saying you sold us out, but someone you've been in contact with must have. No one else could have known our plans."

A thought occurred to Kate. "Uh, Jason, that may not be entirely true."

"What are you talking about?"

"Somebody at the embassy tried to arrange for me to lead the Russians to Dimitri. That means there's a security problem on our side."

He shook his head. "Nobody in Washington or at the embassy knew we were coming to this airfield. Peter knows we're trying to get to Israel, but even he doesn't know the plan."

"Hear me out," Kate continued. "He's making a sudden unscheduled flight to Tel Aviv, probably using a government jet. If the Russians have a source inside U.S. intelligence, then the trip's going to attract some interest and it wouldn't be much of a leap to guess we're the reason for it. The logical assumption would be that we're trying to get to Israel, and the only way to do it is by plane."

He pointed back down the road. "But that's not Russians back there. It was a marked police car."

"SVR can't have unlimited resources in France. Especially after we killed three of their men this morning. I don't know how many airfields in the area can accommodate a corporate jet, but I'm betting there are too many for them to cover alone. Peter said Russia is probably spinning this as a kidnapping of one of their officials. What if the French government is buying it? That would explain the cops being there."

"She may be right," said Talia. "The bigger question is what to do about it."

"We could drive to Cannes to meet the plane there," suggested Kate.

Talia shook her head. "It's a ten-hour trip and the longer we stay in France, the worse our chances are of getting out. That plane is our only realistic shot at a clean escape. Otherwise, we go back to the house and hope nobody figures out where we are. Eventually, either ISA or Mossad will come up with a way to extract us, but that could take days."

They sat in silence until Talia suddenly jerked upright and popped the trunk. "We'll use the Trojan horse method. There's a heavy blanket and two empty suitcases in the trunk."

Kate looked puzzled. "What good does that do us?"

"Dimitri and I hide in the trunk. Jason gets on the floor of the back seat with the blanket over him and suitcases piled on top. You'll drive. When you pull up to the gate, it will look like you're alone in the car. How many people have seen you since you arrived?"

"Only the driver who picked me up and the man I shot at the safe house."

"Then all they have is the name you used when you arrived. I assume it was a cover."

"Yes. Carla Fremont. But Peter gave me another one for emergencies."

"Good. You'll use that one. Put on an act like you're a spoiled rich girl flying to Cannes to meet her boyfriend. Flirt like hell and make them focus on you instead of the car. A sexy blonde will divert men's attention faster than anything else."

Kate looked doubtful. "Jason?"

"This can work. Sex can be just as effective a tool as a gun. You're not going to get in bed with them, but you can give them the impression you're the kind of girl who might. More than one agent has gotten themselves out of a dire situation by taking their clothes off. All you have to do here is flirt. Undoing the top couple of buttons on your shirt will help too."

Kate sighed in resignation. "Okay, but there better be a stocked bar on that plane."

When she pulled up to the airfield entrance, one of the uniformed officers motioned for her to stop. He walked up to the driver's door. "Papiers, si vou plait."

Kate gave him a big, sunny smile. "I don't speak French. I'm an American. Do any of you speak English?"

"Passport, please."

She handed it over and continued to smile while he checked the name against a list on his clipboard. "How long have you been in France, Ms. Hancock?"

"Only a couple of days." She gave him another smile and an opportunity to look down her shirt.

"You're here to meet a plane?"

"It's an airport, right? Or did I miss a turn? I get so confused by the signs. Anyway, my boyfriend sent the plane. I'm meeting him in Cannes. He's French, so you don't need to worry about anything."

Kate could see the other two cops grinning, but this one's eyes never moved far from her breasts. "Please step out of the car."

"Sure." She opened the door and got out. "Do you want to frisk me or something?"

She could tell he did, but he motioned toward the rear of the car instead. "Open the trunk."

Kate felt a moment of panic. "Are you going to search my luggage? Did I do something wrong?"

"Just open it."

She laid a hand on his arm. "Well, we might have a teensy problem. My boyfriend and I like to indulge in some things that make the party better, if you know what I mean. We don't sell anything, so it's not like we're criminals. We just like to have a good time. But if you look in the trunk, then you'll have to do your duty and I'm sure there are more important things for a handsome officer like you to be doing than busting someone like me."

She gave him a wink. "Maybe you could let me get on that plane?"

"Put your hands on the hood of the car and spread your feet apart."

"Why?"

"If there's nothing illegal on your person, then I've got no need to search the car."

"Oh my, that's great."

He patted her down, taking his time and doing a very thorough job. His hands went everywhere while she gritted her teeth and waited for him to finish.

When he was done, he put his hand on her ass and looked over at the other two. "Either of you want to double check my work?"

They both laughed and shook their heads. "Vous etes un cochon, Claude," said the one in plainclothes. "You're a pig."

"So my wife tells me." He patted the seat of her jeans. "Go see your rich boyfriend. I envy him."

Kate forced a smile. "Why thank you, officer. You have a nice day."

She got back in the car and drove toward the hangar, parking out of sight of the gate. She popped the trunk and retrieved her weapon from under the driver's seat. Despite his condition, Jason had a grin on his face as she helped him out of the back of the car.

"It wasn't funny, Jason. That asshole put his hand between my legs. I need a hot shower and a stiff drink." She turned to face Talia and Dimitri. "And if anyone is even thinking about making a smartass remark, I'll remind you I have a gun. Now let's get on the damn plane."

The jet began its taxi out to the runway as soon as the door shut behind them. Kate buckled herself into a comfortable leather seat and glanced over at Jason. "How're you doing?"

When he didn't respond, she took his hand and felt for a pulse, heaving a sigh of relief when she found one.

"The fluids I gave him aren't doing the job," said Talia. "He needs whole blood." She put her palm against his forehead. "And the fever's worse."

"Will he make it to Israel?"

"He's tough. But he's not going to be of any help to you for a while. It looks like you'll be flying solo."

Kate settled back in her seat. "Great. Just great."

CHAPTER NINE

Peter was packing his computer bag when the desk phone rang. Despite the temptation to let it go to voicemail, he picked up the handset. "Schilling."

"The director would like to see you." Ella Kinsmore was Carl Linder's executive assistant, and a summons from the seventh floor could not be ignored.

"I'll be right there." He took his sport coat from the hook by the door and headed for the elevator.

"You can go on in, Mr. Schilling," said Ella, looking up from her computer as he arrived. She took her duties as gatekeeper seriously and nobody walked straight into the boss's office without her consent.

"Peter, come in," welcomed the director. "You know both Warren and Susan, I'm sure."

Warren Sinclair stood and extended his hand. "It's been a while, Peter."

The senior senator from New York's distinguished appearance and engaging smile frequently graced the nightly news programs. He projected an air of assurance that inspired the confidence of both his constituents and his colleagues in the Senate. As a graduate of the Air Force Academy and a former fighter pilot, he had the respect of the military as well. In his position as chair of the Senate Intelligence Committee, he was routinely read in on ongoing operations.

"It has, Senator, and I'm okay with that. No offense, but I'm perfectly happy having Director Linder deal with the committee."

Sinclair grinned. "An honest man. You wouldn't do well in politics, Peter."

"No sir, I wouldn't. Susan, how are things at our sister agency?"

The CIA Director glanced up from the leather-bound notepad resting on her lap. Susan Reardon's severe expression and abrupt manner conveyed a no-nonsense approach to her job, and her reputation backed that up. She was not someone to be taken lightly. "Hello, Peter. I'm glad you could join us."

He doubted that was true. The relationship between ISA and the CIA was tricky. The roles of the two agencies overlapped, but while CIA's charter prohibited them from operating domestically, ISA had no such restrictions. The resulting tension contributed to a less than optimal working relationship.

Peter took a seat on the sofa. "May I ask what this is about?"

"Susan asked for this meeting," said Carl. "I'll turn the floor over to her."

She set her notepad down on the coffee table. "I asked Warren to be here because ISA is engaged in an outrageous attempt to circumvent the CIA at a critical moment. Dimitri Artisimov defected, and you didn't tell anyone?"

"The situation's not that clear cut," said Carl. "He approached our liaison in Paris requesting asylum. We're still sorting it out."

"Where is he now?"

"Still in France at a secure location. I assure you all, steps have been taken to ensure his safety."

"CIA should take the lead on this. I'll dispatch some people immediately. Your team can stand down once mine arrives."

"There are other factors at play here," Carl replied. "Artisimov requested that the CIA stay out of the process. He was quite insistent about it. I'm not sure why he feels that way, but the last thing we need is for him to stop talking. May I ask how you became aware of this in the first place?"

"An embedded source in Russia got word to us overnight."

Peter admired his boss's adept handling of the situation. Artisimov had made no such request. Carl was an old hand at dealing with the inter-agency jealousies and political maneuverings that plagued the intelligence community, and he wouldn't need any help with Susan. Instead, Peter watched her closely, looking for anything that might give him a clue as to why she brought Sinclair along.

"What else did your source tell you?"

"Nothing I'm willing to discuss here." She drummed her fingers against the arm of her chair. "I understand Kate Malone was sent to debrief him."

Peter's expression never changed, but his mind raced. This entire thing had taken a sudden and unexpected turn.

"Then you're misinformed," Carl responded calmly. "Kate's still on medical leave. She hasn't set foot in the building since the attack in Riyadh."

Sinclair inserted himself into the conversation before she could reply. "I assume President McAllen is aware of this situation?"

"Of course," replied Carl. "I informed him right away, but we all know he has neither interest in nor patience with the details of intelligence operations. I'll give him a report after Artisimov has been debriefed. A copy will be provided to both of you as well."

"I insist that CIA be allowed into this," said Susan. "The matter is too important to be handled by ISA alone."

Sinclair settled back in his chair. "As the chair of the committee, I want the best outcome possible. Making sure Artisimov will talk is the overriding priority here, but I must be honest and say I understand Susan's concerns."

"As do I," said Carl. "But I think this is too big an opportunity to squander. For whatever reason, Artisimov is insisting the CIA sit this one out. Once he's on U.S. soil and completed an initial debriefing, he'll be made available to whoever wants to talk to him. For now, however, I think it's best to humor him."

Sinclair nodded. "I'm satisfied for the moment, but I'll expect updates as things progress. And the CIA is to be kept in the loop as well."

"Certainly."

"Warren, I think …" Susan began.

"I get where you're coming from, Susan. But I believe the best course is to let ISA carry the ball for now. You can take this to the president, but my recommendation won't change. Carl, I meant what I said about keeping us informed. I hope to hear something soon."

"Absolutely. Thanks for coming, Susan. You too, Warren. Ella will show you out."

"That was enlightening," observed Peter as the door closed behind them.

"In what way?" his boss replied.

"She knew Kate went to talk to Dimitri. She used an airtight cover and nobody outside ISA was aware of where she was going or why. The story about an asset inside Russia was a load of crap."

"You think she has a source here instead?"

"I wouldn't put it past her. She's ambitious."

Carl laughed. "This is Washington. Everyone's ambitious. She may have come up through the ranks of the intelligence community, but she's a politician at heart and her ambitions are not modest."

"She brought Sinclair along to apply additional pressure."

"That was one reason, but I think she has a bigger agenda. She'd like to attach herself to his coattails. There are rumors he's planning a run for the White House. If he's elected president, I think she sees herself in a West Wing office as National Security Advisor."

"She better tread lightly then. Sinclair's nobody's fool and he'll resent being manipulated."

"Warren has chaired that committee for the past six years and the last thing he wants is a civil war in the intelligence community, especially if he's considering a run for the presidency. As long as I could make a solid case, he wasn't going to rock the boat. Any word from Kate yet?"

"Yes, and it's not good. The Russians discovered their location.

Kate and Jason got Artisimov out, but it was messy. Jason took them to a Mossad safe house."

Carl straightened in his chair. "Did you authorize that?"

"It was the only option available. You remember Talia Levy? She's making arrangements to get them out of France, and I'll meet them in Tel Aviv. But we've got a problem here too."

"You think the leak in Paris and Susan's knowledge about Kate's trip are related?"

Peter shrugged. "We shouldn't ignore the possibility."

"Susan Reardon may be a lot of things, but I refuse to believe she'd actively undermine an ongoing operation of this importance. She'll bitch about being left on the sidelines and try to use her influence to gain an advantage, but sabotage the mission itself? Absolutely not."

"Normally I would agree, but the alternative is that we have two leaks, one to the CIA and one to the Russians. I think it's much more likely there's a connection."

"What do we do about it?"

"Nothing for now. It's all speculation. But we need to be careful."

Carl nodded. "When do you leave for Israel?"

"Right away. Mueller will mind the shop while I'm gone."

"How's he working out?"

Peter hesitated. Nick Mueller was new to ISA and the circumstances of his arrival were unusual. Carl had made him Peter's number two with no prior consultation, something that would ordinarily never happen. Nick was reputed to have been a rising star at NSA. Something derailed his career, but nobody seemed willing to talk about it. That fact alone spoke to the serious nature of the infraction, but also to the level of influence brought to bear. Mueller's father was a retired Admiral and a close friend of the president. Instead of being out on his ass, Nick was provided with a soft landing at ISA. Strings had been pulled and while Peter didn't know why, he had a deep-seated distrust of things that didn't fit neatly into place.

"So far it's been fine, but I'd still like to know how he got here."

Carl picked up his phone. "Keep me informed of any developments."

Peter recognized a dismissal when he heard one. "Yeah. Sure."

He returned to his office to find Mueller waiting for him. The expensive haircut, the carefully tailored suit, and a condescending attitude all spoke of money and privilege. Peter had been trying to not let those things affect his opinion of the man himself.

"How did that go?" asked Mueller as Peter settled into the chair behind his desk.

"Susan Reardon tried to take over the Artisimov defection, but Carl was one step ahead of her. Something on your mind?"

Nick laid a manilla folder on the desk. "This is an update on the attack in Saudi Arabia. Four of the assailants were Saudi nationals associated with a militant Shiite organization. The fifth was never identified, but based on the note he had in his pocket, we have to assume he's Iranian, which means he was Shiite as well. The Saudis continue to portray this as an attempted blow to the prestige of their armed forces by a disgruntled Shiite minority. The implication is that our losses were collateral damage."

"That's pure bullshit. No one in their right mind is going to assault a military installation in broad daylight with only a handful of people."

"I agree, and I'm sure Saudi intelligence does as well. But it provides a plausible story for public consumption. When anything goes wrong, they always blame the Shiites. It also conveniently solves another problem for them. If they assume the arrival of the motorcade was simply bad timing, then the intelligence leak magically goes away."

Peter tried to rein in his frustration. "Their government may find that explanation convenient, but they have to know the motorcade was the actual target."

"The details of that trip were hardly a secret. Our embassy in Riyadh, the military at the base, and our own intelligence people were all read in. I'm sure the same is true on the Saudi side. And it's one isolated incident, so there's no pattern. We may never know where the leak came from."

"Maybe so, but that can wait. We've got other problems at the moment. There was an attempt to eliminate Artisimov. Our people have relocated, but I need you to check on something. Find out if anyone stationed at our embassy in Riyadh at the time of the attack is now in France. It's a long shot, but maybe we'll get lucky."

"I hate to bring it up, but Kate was there both times. And her expertise as an analyst was Russia. She would have contacts."

"She damn near got killed in Riyadh," snapped Peter.

"I'm just making sure we consider all the possibilities. That's my job. Do you want me to go to Paris?"

"I'll handle it myself. You monitor things here and let me know if anything changes."

Peter watched him leave and sat lost in thought as the door closed behind him. Unanswered questions were piling up, and he didn't like where the whole thing was heading. Security leaks in both Riyadh and Paris were bad enough, but when you added a prominent Russian defector into the mix and threw in Mossad as well, the situation had the potential to spin out of control quickly. And to make it worse, the only functioning agent he had on site was an untrained rookie. Some days, it didn't pay to get out of bed.

He went to the closet to retrieve his go bag. It had been a long time since he'd had to use it, but at least he was still prepared to travel on a moment's notice. This had started out as a simple defection, but his gut was telling him it was only the beginning of something much bigger. And his gut was usually right.

CHAPTER TEN

Upon her return to Langley, Susan Reardon summoned Josh Griswold to her office. "You told me Kate Malone went to debrief Artisimov."

"She did."

"Linder says not. He admitted Artisimov defected, so why would he lie about who he sent to talk to him?"

"I don't know, but I was told it was Malone."

"Told by who?"

Josh knew he had to tread carefully here. "A contact over at ISA. I have no reason to question the accuracy of the information."

"Who is this contact?"

He hesitated. "If this gets messy, do you really want to know the details? I'll look into it, but you need to distance yourself."

Susan threw her pen down onto the desk. "I looked like an idiot in front of Warren Sinclair because your source had his head up his ass. Fix it."

He nodded and left the room. Upon returning to his desk, he picked up the phone. "You need to get your facts straight."

"What are you talking about?"

"Kate Malone. She's still on medical leave."

"She's supposed to be. She's not."

"You're certain?"

"Yeah. What the hell's going on?"

"I'm not sure. Keep me up to date."

Josh hung up the phone and sat staring out the window. Why would Linder lie about it? Something else was going on and whatever it was, it couldn't be good.

He picked up the phone once more. "Meet me after work. We need to talk."

"We shouldn't be seen together." The woman on the other end of the call kept her voice low so as not to be overheard. Emily Nassar set the bar high when it came to caution and secrecy.

"We might have a problem."

The silence on the other end lasted almost ten seconds and Josh began to wonder if the call had dropped. "Drive to Annapolis. There's a bar called Lundeen's."

"That's an hour away."

"And we won't run into anyone we know. Six o'clock." She hung up.

∼

He arrived early and paused just inside the door. She was sitting in a corner booth where she could observe the entire interior of the bar. Her black hair and olive complexion spoke of middle eastern roots, but her English was perfect and her demeanor assertive. He wondered who she worked for, but even thought it would be nice to know how big a hole he had dug for himself, he knew better than to ask. Her sudden interest in Artisimov led him to suspect it was Russia, but it didn't really make any difference.

She frowned as he joined her. "What's so important that you couldn't use the dead drop I set up for you?"

"I think Carl Linder and Peter Schilling suspect they have a mole."

Her frown deepened. "What makes you think that?"

"They lied to my boss about the Artisimov defection. They'd only do that if they thought there was a problem."

"Do they have any idea who it is?"

"I don't think so, but they'll start digging. I'm thinking we should shut things down, at least for now. If he gets caught, then I'm at risk."

"And if you get caught, then so am I. It goes with the territory."

"What should I do?"

"Nothing. Warn him and tell him to be careful, but to continue monitoring the situation. Closing up shop is not an option at this point."

"Why not?"

"That's not your concern. We proceed as planned. Is there anything else?"

He shook his head.

"Then I'll be going. Wait at least thirty minutes before you leave." She stood and walked to the door without looking back.

He ordered a beer and replayed the conversation in his mind. Getting involved with her had been a mistake, not that she'd given him much of a choice. He was going to have to be a lot more careful from now on.

CHAPTER ELEVEN

The sun was setting as the plane rolled to a stop at Tel Aviv's Ben Gurion Airport. An ambulance pulled up, followed closely by a black SUV. The paramedics wasted no time getting Jason onto a gurney while Kate, Talia, and Dimitri climbed into the back of the car. A thin man with silver hair and wire rimmed glasses was seated in the front passenger seat. He turned to face them.

"Kate, this is my boss and the director of Mossad field operations, Jacob Misrahi," said Talia. "Jacob, Kate Malone."

"Shalom, Kate. Welcome to Israel. Your first trip to our country?"

"No, Director, but I always enjoy my visits here. I wish the circumstances were better this time."

He shrugged in acknowledgement. "In our line of work, this is what you come to expect. And please call me Jacob. We tend not to be too formal around here."

Kate watched the ambulance pull away with both the lights and sirens in full operation. "Where are they taking Jason?"

"The Sheba Medical Center. I assure you he'll receive the best care we can provide. Is there anything I can do for you?"

"I had to leave my things behind, and other than a bowl of soup, I haven't eaten anything today."

He smiled. "That we can take care of. Food and a bed are not a problem."

The thought of a meal set her mouth to watering and sleep was long overdue, but those things would have to wait. "Do you have an ETA for Peter Schilling?"

"At least another hour, maybe two. In the meantime, I would like to have some preliminary discussions with your friend here."

Kate's gut tightened. "Talia assured us he would remain in my custody."

Jacob's eyes narrowed. "This is Tel Aviv, not Washington. We enabled your escape from France, not ISA. You are in no position to dictate terms."

"Nobody's dictating anything. I'm just trying not to mess the whole thing up. I'm asking you to honor Talia's agreement and wait for Peter."

Jacob's features relaxed into something that almost resembled a smile. "For someone so new to this, you are not afraid to speak your mind or stand your ground. Given the circumstances, I needed to see what you're made of. You'll do. We will wait."

He'd been testing her and once more Kate realized how far out of her depth she was.

"In that case," said Talia, "we'll go straight to the hotel when we arrive."

Kate hesitated. She was the newbie here, but she still had a job to do. "In light of what happened today, I'm not sure a public hotel is a good idea."

"We call it a hotel," Talia replied. "It's really more like a dormitory. Sometimes our guests need to avoid the spotlight. I'll scrounge up a change of clothes for both of you, and food will be delivered. You can take a shower while I remain with Dimitri. I promise not to question him."

Kate considered the offer. A hot shower, food, and clean clothes sounded heavenly, but she was on her own here. Still, at some point, she was going to have to trust someone. Jason hadn't hesitated to take them to Talia when they were in trouble. If he put that much faith in her, then she could, too.

"That sounds wonderful. Is a cheeseburger and fries possible? Oh wait, that's not kosher, is it? You can skip the cheese."

"Not everyone keeps kosher," said Talia. "Especially in Mossad. In the field, it's almost impossible. Dimitri?"

"I don't suppose you have borscht? If not, a cheeseburger will do."

"Then it's settled."

The drive from the airport to Mossad headquarters took less than twenty minutes. The evening was warm, and the streets of Tel Aviv were busy. Open-air restaurants and sidewalk cafes were bustling with people enjoying the perfect weather. Upon their arrival in an underground garage, Talia ushered them upstairs. The accommodations reminded Kate of her old room in the college residence hall, but it was clean and had a private bath.

Kate emerged from the bathroom just as the food arrived. The shirt and jeans Talia provided fit well enough, and the running shoes she'd been wearing would do for now. Dimitri perched on the edge of the bed, his rumpled clothes replaced by a green nylon jogging suit. He busied himself devouring his burger in large bites. She went to the desk and unwrapped hers, inhaling the wonderful aroma of cooked meat.

"I was just informed that Peter's plane has landed, and he's on his way here," said Talia. "Our presence is requested. You can bring your dinner with you if you'd like."

She ushered them into a conference room on the top floor of the building. Jacob sat at one end of the table next to a woman Kate recognized as Sarah Niminsky. The Executive Director of Mossad was well known within the global intelligence community. She reputedly had no patience with incompetence or with politicians and more than once had been pushed aside, only to be brought back as her more politically connected replacements failed to produce the kind of results she was known for. A second man stood over in the corner, pouring himself a cup of coffee.

Talia handled the introductions. "This is ISA senior analyst Kate Malone, and she's accompanied by this man. He's Russian and his name is Dimitri. I have a pretty good idea who he is, but I'll let Peter address that when he gets here."

Kate stepped forward and extended her hand. "The Director and I met when I was here for an interagency briefing. It's good to see you again, ma'am."

"Shalom, Kate," said Sarah. "Welcome back to Israel."

"Thank you." She turned to the second man as he joined them at the table. He was tall and handsome, with black hair and piercing hazel eyes. He had a smile which Kate was sure had sped up the heart rate of more than a few women. She held his gaze while extending her hand. "And you are?"

"This is David Rifkin," interjected Talia. "David and I sometimes work as a team."

Kate thought she could sense a layer of tension between the two Mossad agents. "So, you're partners?"

David shrugged. "Of a sort. We also used to be married."

A knock on the door announced Peter's arrival, relieving Kate of the necessity of coming up with a suitable response. After another round of introductions, everyone took their seats at the table.

"I'm glad you're here," said Kate. "With Jason in the hospital, I've been trying to manage on my own."

"It sounds like you handled yourself well."

"I killed one man and was groped by another. It's not exactly a day I'll look back on fondly. Maybe we should get down to business?"

"I agree," said Jacob. "This whole thing grew out of an ongoing ISA mission. Why don't we start there?"

Peter gestured toward the Russian. "This man is Dimitri Artisimov."

"Head of the SVR's Directorate R," said Sarah. She glanced over at Dimitri. "He's defecting?"

"Yes, but Kate is the only person he's spoken to about his reasons for doing this. Would it be possible for me to speak with her privately before we discuss this further? We'll only be a few minutes and Dimitri can stay with you."

Jacob nodded. "There's another conference room across the hall."

Once the door closed behind them, Peter motioned her to a chair. "Okay, fill me in."

"Russia is planning on moving troops into Iran to provide a deterrent to Israel. Troops equipped with tactical nukes."

"Did he say why?"

"It's complicated. In the short term, they want to marginalize the U.S. and Israel while establishing Iran as the dominant power in the region. Their real endgame seems to be the resurrection of something resembling the old Soviet Union. I'm not sure how the two things are related, but he says he can give us the details."

"You told me this was something we'd likely end up sharing with Israel. I agree, but this needs to be handled carefully. Mossad may want to keep him here once they find out what he has."

"That's not the agreement I made with him."

"Let me handle it."

"You're the boss." She suddenly realized she was channeling Jason. On some level, it startled her, but it also made her feel like she belonged. When they returned to the meeting room, the Israelis were speaking rapidly in Hebrew while Dimitri stared out the window. The conversation stopped as Peter and Kate resumed their seats.

"Before we begin, I want to establish some ground rules," said Peter. "While I appreciate what Mossad did in getting my people out of France, Mr. Artisimov defected to the United States. He requested Kate take the lead in debriefing him and expected to be going to Washington."

"Would he prefer to be back in Paris with everyone hunting for him?" asked Jacob.

"I am grateful for Mossad's help in this matter," said Dimitri. "And for that reason, I do not object to you being part of this discussion. But I came to them, not you. I want to be clear on that point. And I need some assurance that what happens from here is in their hands, not Mossad's."

"Your final destination will be the U.S.," said Peter. "That is not up for debate."

"Yet here I am." His gaze moved around the table. "Can I trust them to allow that to happen? Mossad's reputation in these things does not inspire confidence. They tend to be rather pragmatic."

Peter turned to the Mossad director. "Sarah?"

She nodded. "We will not detain him. But if this matter is not yet resolved by the time he leaves, someone from Mossad will go with him to ensure we hear what he has to say."

"Agreed. Satisfied, Dimitri?"

"For now, but I must retain some leverage in this. I will give both ISA and Mossad the basic facts of what my government is planning while withholding certain details against a Mossad change of heart. Those I will provide once I am on U.S. soil. Do we understand one another?"

Heads nodded all around the table.

"Very good," said Dimitri. "Where shall I begin?"

"Let's start with Iran," suggested Jacob.

Dimitri straightened in his chair. "At the invitation of the Iranian government, Russia will deploy a military presence to Iran equipped with short to medium range tactical nuclear weapons. They will remain in total control of Russian forces at all times, but their presence will tip the balance of power significantly."

Jaws dropped all around the table. Jacob was the first to speak. "Are they insane? Do they think we will do nothing?"

"The plan was for them to be in place before you found out. Anything you might do after that would risk a nuclear confrontation they believe you would choose to avoid. Other regional military powers such as Egypt and Saudi Arabia would be forced to take a back seat."

"What does Russia gain from this?" asked Sarah.

"Military and political influence in the most oil rich part of the world. The Iranians will also grant us a naval base in the Persian Gulf to oppose the U.S. 5th fleet based in Bahrain. It would leave Iran and Russia in total control of the flow of oil from the gulf."

"I'm surprised they think Iran can be trusted," observed Peter.

Dimitri nodded. "As am I. However, it's a risk President Malkin seems willing to take. My government believes that all Iran wants is to be the major player in the Middle East without having to defer to Israel, the Saudis, or even the United States. I'm not so sure that's actually the case. The divide between the Sunni and Shia branches of Islam runs deep. There is much mistrust and even hatred on both sides, and Iran and Saudi Arabia are the two nations with the military strength to turn that distrust into an open conflict. I would not want to see Russia caught in the middle."

"Your defection is an effort to stop it?" asked Jacob.

He shook his head. "I would not risk my life merely to prevent a regional war."

Sarah leaned forward in her chair. "Even one that could go nuclear?"

Dimitri shrugged. "You see this from the narrow perspective of Israeli interests. Upsetting the balance of power in the Middle East provides a military and economic benefit for Russia, but its real purpose is to cause a distraction. One of several distractions. Iranian intelligence services have much influence over numerous terrorist organizations and there will be an uptick in attacks around the world. Plans are in place to disrupt financial markets as well. It is all intended to muddy the waters before the last piece of the plan comes to fruition."

"And that is?" asked Sarah.

"The destruction of NATO. The cracks in the alliance are already there. Turkey is a Muslim nation that aligned itself with western Europe. It was never a comfortable fit, and the current leadership has begun taking positions more in line with their Arab neighbors. Hungary opposed NATO assistance to Ukraine as well as the addition of Sweden and Finland to the alliance. Their president was a close friend of Vladamir Putin and openly espouses better relations with Russia. And NATO itself has exhibited weakness and lack of resolve. It did not hesitate to take military action in Libya and Bosnia, but failed to rise to the challenge when it came to Ukraine. Some see this as a sign of internal discord."

"And how do the Russian leaders intend to leverage this?" asked Peter.

"Article 5 of the NATO charter states that an attack on any individual member nation will be seen as an attack on all. The strength of that commitment will be put to the test. As you know, the Kaliningrad Oblast is officially Russian territory but is wedged between Lithuania and Poland with no physical connection to the rest of Russia. Forces currently stationed in Belarus will launch an invasion of Lithuania with the stated goal of annexing the southern part of the country to Belarus and thus establishing a land bridge that is no longer under the control of NATO."

"They must know there will be a military response in defense of Lithuania," said Kate. "A strong one."

Dimitri nodded. "But after the chaos of Ukraine, it is thought that some members will choose caution over commitment. Nations such as Hungary, Slovakia, and Romania have direct borders with Russian-controlled regions of Ukraine and will be hesitant to take up arms against us. The cracks in the alliance will deepen and some nations may choose to withdraw their membership entirely. Article 5 will cease to have any real meaning for them, and eastern Europe may find that an alliance with Russia provides more security than one with the West. The Iron Curtain will fall on Europe once again. Even if our efforts to create a land bridge to Kaliningrad fail, the disastrous impact on NATO will, in the eyes of our leaders, result in the rise of Russian influence. They see it as being worth the price."

Peter tapped his pen against the table. "And you're opposed to this?"

"Not at all. I support any effort to extend Russian influence and power. But I fear that in this case, our leaders are overreaching and underestimating American resolve. The military response mentioned by Ms. Malone will be strong, even if not all of NATO supports it. And a war with the West could easily escalate out of control. I made no secret of my opinions on this matter, but nobody wanted to listen.

A war between our nations would be disastrous for Russia, even if we were victorious. That's the reason I took this action. I came to you because I believe that doing this is in the best interest of my country."

"There seems to be an obvious solution to this," said Sarah. "All we have to do is go public about the weapons deployment to Iran. Both Russia and Iran will deny everything, but international scrutiny would force them to back off."

Dimitri shook his head. "It didn't work before, and it won't now. International condemnation of Russian intentions did not deter Putin in Ukraine and it won't influence Malkin either. It could even backfire. I believe they are almost ready to act, and public exposure may only cause them to speed up their timing."

Sarah looked around the table. "So, where does this leave us?"

"Dimitri's right," said Peter. "Going public with no evidence might play right into their hands. We need proof."

Kate followed Dimitri's presentation of the facts closely, and the analyst in her seized upon the one question central to finding a solution. "Dimitri, who is handling the planning and logistics of this? Is it the intelligence community or the military?"

"Intelligence, and specifically SVR. Many in the armed forces are vehemently opposed and several commanders were dismissed as a result. But short of staging a military coup, there's nothing they can do. I can assure you that will not happen."

Silence enveloped the room. Kate had the beginnings of an idea, but she was the least senior person present. Peter said to follow his lead, so she waited to see where the conversation was going to go.

Jacob was the first to speak. "Dimitri, are those weapons already in place?"

"Not to my knowledge, but I can't be sure of that. After voicing opposition to the plan, I was left largely in the dark."

"Then what we decide to do depends on how far things have progressed. Our priority must be to determine the current status. On that point, I am open to suggestions."

Kate saw Peter glance over at her. "Any insights on this, Kate? You're our Russian expert."

The beginnings of a plan had been building in her mind, a plan she wasn't sure she wanted any part of. But she was here to do a job, and she didn't see a better alternative. "No insights, but maybe an idea. ISA has almost no assets inside Iran. Is that true for Mossad as well?"

"None placed highly enough for what we need," replied Sarah.

"Then we need to figure this out from the Russian side. The global intelligence community is relatively small. Anyone who has had contact with me knows me as an analyst. I can go to Moscow in that capacity on the pretense of conducting briefings at the embassy. If Dimitri can provide the names of people inside Russia who oppose this plan and tell me how to contact them, I'll reach out and try to determine where things stand."

Peter shook his head. "I like the idea, but I would never send someone with no training into the field alone for something like this. If you said the wrong thing to the wrong person, you'd find yourself being interrogated in a Russian prison."

"I know, and it scares the hell out of me. But if Russia's the enemy here, at least it's an enemy I know. I speak the language fluently and my job provides the perfect cover. I'm up to speed on the situation and know how their security apparatus works. You won't find anyone better qualified."

"Even if I agreed, you'd need backup."

"Take a step back and look at this objectively, Peter," said Talia. "She's right. I understand your concerns, but she's the ideal person for this. If the director approves, I can be assigned to our embassy as part of their security team. I'll be in Moscow and able to assist if she gets into trouble."

Sarah was drumming her fingers on the table as she listened to the discussion. "I think her idea is brilliant. If ISA lets her go, Mossad can provide the backup, but it won't be Talia. Not in a lead role, anyway. She doesn't speak Russian and we need every edge we can get. I'll find the right agent to accompany her, but this is your call, Peter. She works for you."

He looked over at Kate. "Let's go out in the hall. I want to speak to you privately."

He shut the door behind them and regarded her closely. "Part of me knows this is our best chance, but I don't think you have any idea what you're getting yourself into. Going into Russia as a spy is an extremely dangerous proposition. Even experienced agents would think twice before volunteering for something like this."

"But I won't be going as a spy. Not really. Nobody knows it was me in Paris. They think it was Carla Fremont. This time, I'll use my real identity and have a plausible reason for being there. I'll reach out to a couple of people, learn what I can, and come home. My skillset is a perfect match for the mission."

"But your level of experience isn't. I'm very reluctant to go along with this."

"Do you have a better idea?"

"No. And there's another problem." He glanced back at the closed door. "If we don't take the lead on this, they will. And Dimitri's right, they'll focus on the direct threat to Israel instead of the bigger picture." His gaze moved back to her. "If I saw any other way to accomplish what we're after, my answer would be no. Unfortunately, I don't, and we may not have the luxury of time. You're sure about this? Once we go back inside, we're committed."

She swallowed hard and took the plunge. "I'm sure. Nervous maybe, but I can do this."

When they went back into the room, Talia and David were having a whispered conversation in the corner. All eyes turned to Kate and Peter as they resumed their places at the table.

"Well?" asked Sarah. "What's the verdict?"

"I'll go along with it," said Peter. "But before I give final approval, I want to know who her backup's going to be."

David came over to Kate and extended his hand. "It looks like we're both going to Moscow."

"Then there's something you should know," said Peter. "We had a leak in Paris and I'm not going to take any chances this time. Kate really will conduct briefings for the ambassador and his staff, but no one at ISA without executive clearance will know the real reason she's there. That means I can't use our security people. You're it, David. Whenever she ventures out of the embassy, it's up to you to have her back."

"I understand."

Peter turned to face Sarah Niminsky. "Kate may be new to this, but it's her idea and her mission. David can advise her, and I hope he will, but she doesn't take orders from Mossad. Are we clear?"

There were nods all around the table.

"Good. Dimitri, can you put her in touch with the right people?"

"I anticipated this possibility. Before I left for Paris, I set up a protocol for making contact."

"Then it seems we have a plan. We'll fly home tonight. Sarah, you can assign whoever you like to accompany us. Kate will leave for Moscow in a day or two. I assume David will be at your embassy when she arrives."

Sarah nodded. "He will. Jacob will go to Washington with you and Talia will go to Moscow with David. He'll be Kate's primary backup, but she'll be available in case of emergencies. Don't hesitate to rely on him, Kate. If you run into trouble, he'll know how to handle it."

"Yes, ma'am."

"And I want you to know that Mossad appreciates your willingness to do this. It shows the initiative we look for in our own people. I'm confident you'll succeed."

Kate hoped she was right.

CHAPTER TWELVE

Alexander Kruzov dropped the report onto his desk with a resigned sigh. Dimitri had actually done it. He defected to the Americans, and the failed attempt to eliminate him before he could talk had sparked an international incident.

Kruzov could imagine the holy hell that had to be breaking out over at the Kremlin. But despite the uproar the defection would cause, it wouldn't be enough to bring Malkin to his senses. Not by itself, anyway. The man was obsessed with restoring Russia's former glory and would pay any price to achieve his goal. If Dimitri could spur the Americans into action, the crisis might still be avoided, but only if they listened. That was the key question, and the answer would come soon. Then it would be his turn to stick his neck out. He didn't relish the prospect.

His secretary knocked on the open door. "Sorry to intrude, sir, but Gen. Kresnikov wants to see you in his office."

"Thank you, Elena. Tell him I'm on my way."

Upon his arrival, a young lieutenant escorted him into the inner office. The room was spartan, which matched its occupant's personality. The general was seated behind a desk bare of anything except a laptop and a writing pad. He wore a grim expression as he waved Kruzov to the chair facing the desk. Another man occupied a seat by the window. His graying beard and lack of a uniform marked him as a civilian and it didn't take much of a leap to guess what he was doing here.

"You sent for me, sir?"

"I suppose you've already heard about Artisimov?"

"I just read the report."

"And?"

Kruzov knew he had to tread carefully. "I find it hard to believe. Dimitri's always been absolutely loyal to this country. He didn't rise to a position of such importance without putting Russian interests above all else. What was he doing in Paris, anyway?"

The general grimaced. "That's the question everyone's asking. He told his staff he was going to meet with the ambassador and that the reason for the trip was classified. Our embassy in Paris is unaware of any such meeting. There was some initial speculation that he may have been abducted, but the deception about the trip seems consistent with a planned defection." He gestured at the third man in the room. "This is Pieter Gagarin of the FSB. He has some questions for you."

"I'll be happy to help in any way I can."

His gaze moved to Gagarin. FSB handled the nation's internal security and carried out their mission with a ruthless efficiency. The Russian military maintained a deep distrust of the intelligence services going all the way back to the Cold War when KGB officers inserted themselves into the chain of command with a total disregard for established protocols or military discipline. As commander of the army's anti-terrorism forces, Kruzov had forged a working relationship with them, but that would be of little help if he found himself under their microscope.

Gagarin pulled a notepad from an inside jacket pocket and flipped it open. "I understand that you and Artisimov have a long-standing friendship."

Kruzov nodded. "We met at the university."

"When was the last time you spoke?"

"In person? We went to dinner and a hockey game a month or so ago. We're both fans of HC Dynamo."

"You've had no contact with him since?"

"We've spoken on the phone. He called me on the anniversary of my wife's death to see how I was doing. I believe that was the last time I talked to him."

The security man made a note on the pad. "What about emails or texts?"

Kruzov forced a smile. "I'm sure your people are already digging into them. Is this guilt by association? We were friends, and he defected, so I'm tainted as well?"

Gagarin stared straight at him. "Are you? Tainted, I mean."

"That's a pointless question. I'd deny the accusation even if it were true, but you're more interested in my reaction to being asked than any answer I might give you." He settled back in his chair, trying to project an air of professional competence. "I'm not naïve in these matters. It's your job to look at every possibility, but not everything you see is a plot and not everyone who crosses your path is guilty. Dimitri Artisimov is my friend and if he's crossed a line, he did it without consulting me. I'll stand on my record and answer your questions, but you're looking in the wrong place."

"Did he ever discuss his political views with you?"

"About what?"

"He's on record as opposing the government's plans to reinvigorate the country."

Kruzov leaned forward in his chair. "He never opposed the primary goal. He merely disagreed with the manner in which it will be carried out and stated his opinions openly. That's not treason."

"Maybe not, but defection is. I understand you're leaving for Switzerland in a few days. I find that concerning."

"General Kruzov is attending a U.N. terrorism conference in Geneva," said Kresnikov. "He has an unblemished record of both loyalty and competence, and I see no reason he shouldn't go."

Gagarin looked back and forth between them. "I'm sure you're right, but as Gen. Kruzov himself just pointed out, all possibilities must be investigated. I assume you won't object to someone from our agency accompanying him."

"Not at all, so long as they don't interfere," said Kruzov, trying to keep his voice level. "My staff will make the arrangements."

"Then I think we're done for now." The FSB man put the notepad away. "A defection by someone at Artisimov's level would be a major blow under any circumstances. For it to happen now could be catastrophic. Every precaution needs to be taken. This is a critical point in history."

"We're all aware of what's at stake," said Kresnikov.

With a curt nod, Gagarin left the room. Kruzov waited until the door shut behind him. "I should have seen that coming."

His boss nodded. "Artisimov left you in a bad spot."

"About which I can do nothing. So, unless there's something else, I'll get back to work."

"Certainly. Dismissed."

Kruzov returned to his office, lost in thought. Going to Geneva was already going to be a risky undertaking, and that was before the security services stuck their noses into it. Now it had become infinitely more dangerous. Maybe the Americans would do nothing, and the trip would prove uneventful. He wasn't sure if that would be a good thing or not.

CHAPTER THIRTEEN

Kate gazed out the window of her room at the U.S. embassy, watching a barge on the Moskva River pass slowly under the Kutuzovsky bridge. Moscow had been transformed since the last time she'd been here, and not for the better. The architecture, museums, and history were as wondrous as ever, but the nightlife and restaurant scene was a shell of what it had been only a few years before. The city had not receded into the bleakness of its communist past, but the vibrant optimism was gone now.

She went to her desk and picked up the satellite phone, punching in the number and waiting for the encryption indicator to change from red to green. "Good afternoon, David. I'll be at the south end of Red Square in front of St. Basil's in half an hour."

She replaced the phone in its cradle and took one of several burner phones from the desk drawer. It was imperative that her next call not be traceable or made from inside the embassy. She debated placing her weapon in her purse but decided that maintaining her cover as an analyst overrode the need for any security the gun might provide. That's what David was for. She snatched her personal phone from the top of the dresser and went downstairs to hail a cab.

The drive to Red Square took only ten minutes. Kate bought a cheburek from a street vendor and munched the spicy meat filled pastry as she mingled with the people wandering through the square. Not all that long ago, the square would have been teeming with tourists. On this day, the crowds were smaller and more scattered, but there were still enough people to let her mingle and remain inconspicuous. Minutes later, David walked past her without so much as a glance. Her backup in place, she took out the burner phone and manually dialed a number.

The call was answered on the third ring. "Boris? It's Maria. I was wondering if you might be free for dinner tonight. I was thinking 8:00 or so."

After a moment of silence, a deep male voice answered. "I'm sorry, but you've reached the wrong number."

"My apologies."

Kate hung up and smiled inwardly. It had worked. The names Boris and Maria identified her to her contact. If he hung up, it would mean he considered being seen with her to be too dangerous. But if he said it was the wrong number, she was to meet him tonight at a pre-arranged location. She erased the call log and powered off the phone, wiping it clean of fingerprints and wrapping it inside the bag that had contained the cheburek. The bag went into the first trash can she encountered.

As she strolled east past the multi-colored domes of St. Basil's, she paused beside a park bench and busied herself taking pictures of the majestic buildings surrounding Red Square. David came up beside her, his eyes fixed on the tourist brochure held in his hand. Kate put her personal cell phone to her ear and pretended to make a call. "Stephan, I cleared my schedule and we're a go for tonight. I'm looking forward to it. See you there." She replaced the phone in her pocket and walked away without so much as a glance back at her partner.

Peter had stressed the importance of remaining in character, so she continued to wander about the square taking pictures. After half an hour, she headed toward Zaryadye Park and flagged down another cab. Her first tiny steps into the world of espionage had been a success.

Shortly before 8:00, Kate left the embassy once more. Her blonde hair hung straight to her shoulders and the sky-blue dress showed off her figure and long legs. She wanted to look like a woman ready to enjoy a taste of Moscow's night life. In prepping her for this, Peter had told her that misdirection was often the key to success. The last thing she wanted was to advertise that she was on a mission.

A taxi deposited her at the front entrance of Kask, a pub style restaurant Dimitri had set up as a contact point. She went inside and paused by the door to take in her surroundings. The interior was modeled after traditional British pubs and the dark wood paneling and polished brass fixtures provided an authentic feel. The place wasn't full, but still busy enough to provide the cover she needed.

David sat at the far end of the bar, sipping a beer while watching a soccer game on the TV. Several of the barstools were unoccupied, and she chose the one nearest the door. She ordered a Bloody Mary from the bartender and took a Moscow tour book from her purse, laying it on the bar. The combination of the drink, the book, and an article of blue clothing would identify her to her contact.

Twice men offered to join her or buy her a drink, but neither identified himself as Boris and she politely refused, explaining she was waiting for a friend. After twenty minutes, she wondered if something had gone wrong, but David was still watching the game and seemed unconcerned. She quieted her nerves, sipped her drink and waited.

A short, stocky man approached her from behind. "Is this seat taken?" he asked, placing his hand on the stool next to her. "A beautiful woman should not be drinking alone." She was about to give him the same excuse she gave the others when he held out his hand. "My name is Boris. And you are?"

Every nerve in Kate's body became instantly alert. The voice on the phone had been a deep baritone. This was not the same man. David was watching them in the mirror and as long as he was nearby, she might as well see how this played out.

"I'm Maria. Please sit down."

He ordered a vodka and lifted his glass to her. "How are you enjoying your stay in Moscow?"

Recognizing that he was making this seem like a chance encounter, she played along. "How did you know I was a tourist?"

He tapped a finger on the book. "This, but also your accent. I'd say you're from the south. Sochi maybe?"

"Nice guess. It's been some years since my last visit. A lot has changed."

"Yes, and not always for the better. Are you here for business or pleasure?"

"A little of both." She leaned toward him and lowered her voice. "You know why I'm here. You have something for me?"

He held up his hand. "I hate to discuss business with a lovely woman on an evening such as this. May I buy you dinner? And afterward we could go someplace more intimate. My apartment, perhaps?"

Kate wasn't sure how to handle this. He obviously wanted to get her alone before he'd be ready to talk, but Peter's instructions were to stay within sight of David. She decided she was too new at this to risk going off the plan.

"I'm sorry, but I can't. I'm meeting someone later."

"What a shame. I envy him. Perhaps we could adjourn to that booth over by the wall? These barstools wreak havoc with my back."

She glanced at the empty booth in the corner. It would provide a level of privacy and keep her in David's field of vision. "Sure. Why not?"

She settled onto the wooden seat. Boris, or whatever his name really was, sat across from her and downed the rest of his drink in one gulp before signaling for another. "Just for the record," he said, keeping his voice low, "I would not have trusted you had you accepted the invitation to leave with me. It would have brought your judgment into question."

"You need to be careful, but so do I," she replied. "You're not the man I spoke to on the phone."

"Very good. I'm merely a messenger. The man who sent me is eager to talk to you, but he can't afford to take unnecessary risks. He's involved in this at a high level and needed to be sure this wasn't an FSB trap."

"How do you know it isn't?"

"Because you're new to this. They wouldn't use someone so inexperienced. No offense."

She was tempted to ask how he could be so sure she was a rookie, but decided the question could wait. "When do I meet this person? And where?"

He lifted a cloth napkin from the table and wiped his hands with it before laying it back down. "I just placed a flash drive inside the napkin. It contains information that will assure you of his credibility, along with instructions for making contact. Be sure you follow them exactly because he'll walk away at any sign of trouble. And it must be you who comes. No one else is to be involved beyond the man sitting at the bar."

She glanced at David. "How did you know?"

"You're too new not to have someone watching your back. When I arrived, there were three possibilities. The other two have left."

Her curiosity finally got the better of her. "Why are you so sure I'm new to this?"

He smiled at the question. "The dress. You're an exceptionally attractive woman, but an experienced agent would try to blend in, not stand out. Every man in this bar has been looking at you. That's not a good thing."

He signaled for another round. "Now we should enjoy another drink and act like we're having a good time. Either of us leaving immediately after a whispered conversation would look suspicious."

They sipped their drinks and talked about Moscow, the weather, and nightspots she should sample. She laughed at his jokes and did her best to act like a tourist enjoying an evening out.

When they'd drained the last of their drinks, he lowered his voice once more. "We should leave together and give everyone the impression that we're headed for a night on the town. Once we're away from the entrance, I'll hail you a cab."

He paid the bill and escorted her out. She turned to face him as they rounded the corner of the building. "You were sent to check me out. Except for the dress, did I pass?"

He smiled. "You get a thumbs up. Give Dimitri my regards."

A gunshot came from somewhere behind her. Boris's head snapped backward as blood sprayed across the brick wall behind him. Another bullet whistled past her head so close she could hear its passage before it struck the wall and ricocheted along the sidewalk.

Kate bent low and ran for the corner of the building, bumping into David as he rounded it from the front. He grabbed her by the arm and pulled her past him. "There's a silver Kalina parked down the street. The fob is under the seat. I'll cover you."

"But …"

"Run, dammit!"

Two more gunshots echoed off the buildings as she sprinted for the car. The engine roared to life when she pushed the start button, but she wasn't sure what to do next. Escape was paramount, but she couldn't abandon David. Before she could decide, the passenger door flew open and he scrambled in.

"What are you waiting for? Get us the hell out of here!"

She pulled out into traffic without looking, narrowly avoiding a collision with a passing car. The traffic light at the end of the block mercifully turned green just as she was about to blow through it. She continued for one block before making a right turn, followed by a left into a residential neighborhood.

David pointed to an empty parking place. "Pull over here and shut off the engine."

She did as he asked, trying to force her hands to stop trembling.

"What the hell did you think you were doing back there?" he demanded.

"He said leaving separately would look suspicious. I knew you'd follow us out, so …."

"Not that. Why did you wait?"

"For you, of course," she responded, surprised not only at his tone, but by the question itself.

"You're the primary on this mission. I'm your backup, which means I'm expendable. By waiting, you put us both in danger, not to mention the risk of losing whatever you were able to learn. This isn't a game, Kate. There are no niceties, only necessities."

She looked down at his shirt. "You're bleeding. How bad?"

"It's just a scratch. You're lucky we're both not dead."

It seemed that all her partners ended up getting shot. "I'm sorry, David. I'm not a field operative and I don't understand how this works. I think everyone would be better off if I'd taken Peter's advice and left this to the people who belong in this world."

"Maybe, but you're here now and you can't wish it away." He regarded her with a softer expression. "You made mistakes tonight, mistakes that might have got us killed. But you accomplished what we came for, and in the end, that's all that matters. And I think maybe you're one of the few who do belong. Not everyone has the balls to do this and the talent to do it well. I think you do. No offense."

She smiled weakly. "I'll take it as a compliment. All of it. But what do we do now?"

He thought for a moment. "They're probably going to put a warrant out for you as a witness to the murder of your contact. They may even try to say you pulled the trigger. By running, you've given them an appearance of guilt."

"They tried to kill me, too."

"There's no proof of that. Getting out of Russia is going to be a problem now."

"I've got diplomatic status. They can't arrest me."

"I wouldn't try putting that to the test. Going to either of our embassies is one option, but leaving again without being detained would be a problem. Getting around that would take time we don't have."

"Then where do we go?"

He pulled out his phone and spoke rapidly in Hebrew. Kate

understood none of it but heard Talia's name. After hanging up, he opened the passenger door. "Switch places. I'll drive."

"Where are we going?"

"To a safe house we can use for the night."

He headed north, keeping mostly to side streets. Kate watched out the rear window, but as far as she could tell, they weren't being followed. As they merged into a more traveled thoroughfare, she heard David swear. A police checkpoint blocked the road ahead.

"What do we do?"

"Do you have your alias passport with you?".

She shook her head. "Just the diplomatic one."

"There's a gun under your seat. Follow my lead, but if I say your name, do whatever you have to."

He braked to a stop at the checkpoint, pulling at his jacket to cover the bloodstain on his shirt. A police officer stepped up to the driver's door, motioning David to roll down the window. "ID please," he requested in Russian.

David pulled his passport from inside his jacket pocket and handed it to the cop. "I work at the Israeli embassy. Is something wrong?"

A second officer came to the passenger window. Kate lowered it and gave him the sunniest smile she could manage. He held a photograph in his hand and looked back and forth between it and her. "Passport, please."

She handed it over and waited. He examined it and stepped back, drawing his weapon. "Out of the car and keep your hands in the open."

"As you can see, it's a diplomatic passport. You have no right to detain me."

"FSB issued an alert to place you in custody. You'll need to sort out the immunity issue with them."

The Russian version of the FBI wouldn't care about her status. Not if they connected her to what happened tonight. Once she stepped out of the car, she'd be out of options. David said to follow his lead, so she waited.

"I said get out of the car," the officer repeated.

"Hang on, Kate," said David.

She took the cue and leaned forward and pulled the gun from under the seat. The cop stepped back and drew his weapon as David stepped on the gas. They sped down the street and away from the checkpoint. Kate turned to look behind them as the rear window shattered and a bullet buried itself in the dashboard.

David's eyes never left the road. "Are you okay?"

Kate had been holding her breath ever since David said her name. Now she gripped the gun tighter and slowly exhaled. "I think so."

She looked back, expecting to see a police car in pursuit, but there was no traffic of any sort behind them.

"They must have just set up that checkpoint," said David. "A few minutes later, a second team would have been there ready to give chase. But now we need to ditch the car. We can't drive around with a bullet hole in the window."

"David, they were already looking for me. That cop had a picture. It's only been a few minutes since the shooting. What the hell's going on?"

"I don't know, but right now we've got bigger problems."

He took a sharp left and one block later pulled into the parking lot beside a commuter train station. "Follow me. We need to get somewhere where there's a crowd of people."

Kate shoved the gun into her purse as they ran up the stairs to the train platform. David pulled tokens from his pocket as they boarded the first train to arrive. He was showing no signs of weakness or further bleeding and kept his jacket pulled over the wound. She surveyed the occupants of the car, but no one seemed to pay undue attention to them. Several men let their eyes linger on her and she recalled Boris's lecture about the dress, but no one seemed overly curious or alarmed.

They rode the train for one stop before getting off and hailing a cab to Sheremetyevo airport, where they mingled with the crowds in the baggage claim area. "If they think to check the airport, they'll focus on the ticketing area or the departure gates," said David. "They won't be worried about the people who just arrived."

Once assured they had lost all pursuers, they took another cab to an upscale neighborhood in Moscow's west end.

David had the driver drop them off at a quiet corner and led Kate around to the alley. He stopped outside a metal door and reached behind a trash bin, pulling out a key that had been taped to the rear of the container.

Once inside, they climbed the stairs to the second floor and moved swiftly down the corridor to apartment 203. The key opened this door as well, and they went inside, locking it behind them.

For the first time since walking into Kask, Kate let herself relax.

CHAPTER FOURTEEN

Kate took stock of the apartment. It was small but comfortably furnished and would do until they came up with an escape plan. An open doorway led from the living room into the kitchen, with the bedroom and bath located down a short hallway to her left.

"What is this place?" she asked.

David tossed his jacket over the back of the sofa. "The apartment's leased by an Israeli tech firm but paid for by Mossad. It provides a place to lie low when the need arises." He went to a desk in the far corner. "Check and see if there's anything to eat."

The refrigerator contained eggs, bacon, butter, and juice, along with several plastic bottles of drinking water. The freezer held only a container filled with ice. In the cupboards, she found bread, coffee, sugar, and peanut butter. There was no oven, but a small two burner stovetop occupied part of the counter space and a microwave and coffee machine sat on a table in the corner.

She went back out to the living room. "We'll get by."

He held up a set of keys. "They left us a car. You still got the Glock I stashed under the seat?"

"In my purse."

"Good. That stuff is for you," he said, pointing at a pile of items lying on the desk.

She found an Israeli passport for Rebecca Tobin, as well as a wallet containing a credit card issued in the same name. The wallet held both Israeli and Russian currency.

"Talia left this for us? The food, too? That was fast work."

"The apartment is prepped whenever Mossad has an active operation underway in Moscow. We like to work toward the best possible outcome and be prepared for the worst."

Kate flipped through the passport, stopping to stare at the photo. Instead of her hair being its normal blonde, it was jet black.

"Is there a bottle of hair coloring in with all this?"

"Maybe in the bathroom." He continued rummaging through a cabinet next to the desk. "We'll stay here tonight. Getting out of Russia won't be easy." He straightened up, holding a bottle in each hand. "Vodka or Scotch? I think we can both use a drink."

"Scotch neat. But let me take care of my hair first."

She found a spray bottle for temporary coloring and a pair of scissors in the medicine cabinet. The color would wash out eventually, but further investigation revealed that Talia had left two additional refills. After one last look at herself as a blonde, she went to work. Half an hour later, she emerged from the bathroom as a brunette, her hair two inches shorter and combed back away from her face.

David handed her a peanut butter sandwich and a glass containing two fingers of amber whiskey. "I like your natural color better, but there aren't a lot of blonde, blue-eyed Jews. You'll do."

She took the sandwich from him and wolfed it down, followed by a long swig of scotch. "Yuck. I love peanut butter, and a good single malt is my drink of choice, but they definitely don't go together."

They settled onto the sofa, and Kate took another sip of her drink before leaning back against the cushions. "A lot of questions are banging around in my head, but I'll start with the big one. What the hell happened tonight?"

"I've been asking myself the same thing, but one thing is certain. It wasn't the Russians who shot him. They'd want him alive for interrogation. Whoever killed him didn't care about that."

"But that doesn't make any sense."

He shrugged. "You're the analyst. What does make sense?"

Kate sipped her drink as she tried to work through the problem. "We need to look at the bigger picture and consider all the possibilities. Everything that's happened could just be a string of unrelated events. Riyadh may have been nothing more than an isolated terrorist attack. Tonight's shooting seems to be unrelated to either Russian intelligence or the resistance. Maybe it had to do with something else entirely. And Dimitri's defection would have caused a response all on its own."

"Does that scenario seem plausible to you?"

She shook her head. "No, because I was there each time. That would be one hell of a coincidence."

"I agree. And I don't put much faith in coincidence."

"Then let's assume they're all related. At first glance, Riyadh looks to be an attempt by Shiite radicals to make a political statement by killing Americans. But Shiite extremism in that country is targeted mostly at the Sunni royal family and the government, not us. We think the security lapse was on the Saudi side, and they're saying it came from us. What if that was the actual goal? To stir up distrust between the U.S. and the Saudis just as the Russian troops are due to arrive in Iran. It would muddy up the waters at a critical moment."

"It's possible, I suppose. What about the other attacks?"

"What happened in Paris is clear," said Kate. "Russian intelligence wanted to neutralize Dimitri and they had a source that tipped them off on how to find him. But what happened tonight poses a tougher question. Who would want to kill my contact? We've ruled out the government, and he was working for the resistance."

David considered that for a moment. "Then where does that leave us? It's still three separate events with no obvious connection."

"Yeah. Unless …" She left the sentence unfinished and stared at her drink.

"Unless what?"

"Maybe we're looking in the wrong place. What if it's not the Russians who are masterminding all this? What if it's Iran? They have the resources to set up what happened in Riyadh, and they'd have a vested interest in keeping me from reaching out to the Russian resistance."

"And Dimitri's defection put the entire plan at risk," added David. "They'd want to stop him at all costs. But you realize what this implies?"

Kate nodded. "Iran has a source placed within U.S. intelligence. We've suspected there's a leak ever since Riyadh. Now we know who they might work for."

David chuckled. "The second rule. It never fails to apply."

"What's that?"

"Something they impress on you during Mossad training. The further you dig into a problem, the more complex it gets. Nothing is as straightforward as it seems."

"I can't argue with that. How many rules are there?"

He shrugged. "Who knows? I think they made them up as they went along."

"What's the first rule?"

"Never allow yourself to be personally invested in a mission. It clouds your judgement." He paused. "Believe me, I know."

He saw her watching him and drained the last of his scotch. "Never mind that. Where does this leave us?"

"I think we have to assume Iran's been pulling the strings all along."

David refilled their drinks. "What do you suggest we do?"

Kate glanced over at him. "You're leaving this up to me?"

"That was the arrangement Peter made with Sarah. You don't work for us. If at some point I think you're making a mistake, I'll tell you. If you want my advice, then ask. Outside of that, it's your call. So, I repeat, what's the plan?"

Kate thought for a moment. "Talia will contact us tomorrow?"

He nodded. "Once she has an extraction plan in place, she'll come here."

"We'll fill her in on our theory and she can relay it back to Peter. Our priority at the moment is getting out of Russia in one piece." She pulled the flash drive Boris had given her from her pocket. "What happens after that depends on what's on this." She looked around the room. "But I don't see a computer anywhere."

"That's a problem for the morning."

Kate sipped her drink. "If all this hadn't come up, what would you be doing? I don't mean to pry, I just feel like I dropped in and disrupted everything."

"The Middle East is in chaos. Prior to the Hamas attack on us, things were relatively stable, but that event emboldened others to the point that even shipping through the Suez canal is negatively affected."

He let out a long sigh. "And I have to admit that Israel's response didn't help. The situation was delicate and called for a surgical approach, but the government chose to use a sledgehammer rather than a scalpel. It resulted in thousands of needless deaths and turned the Arab world against us just when we were starting to make some progress in normalizing relations with our neighbors. Mossad is trying to gain inroads, particularly in nations and organizations allied with Iran, but the task is difficult. If your theory about Iran is correct, this may give us a chance to find a way out of the situation. This might the most critical mission I've been on in a long time."

"No pressure there. So, what do we do now?"

He lifted his glass. "We finish our drinks and get some sleep. You take the bed. I'll be fine out here."

She shook her head. "You're the one who got shot tonight, even if it was only a scratch. And my brain's in hyperdrive. Just toss me a pillow and a blanket."

"You're sure? We could both use the bed. I promise to stay on my side."

Kate hesitated. The thought of stretching out in a comfortable place was too tempting to turn down. "Okay, but I'll warn you. I've been told I toss and turn during the night. If I keep you awake, feel free to kick me out."

"You say you toss and turn. Talia swears I snore. With any luck, we won't keep each other awake."

They turned out the lights and adjourned to the bedroom. Minutes later, Kate emerged from the bathroom to find David already asleep. She shook her head in amazement. How could he sleep so soundly after everything that happened tonight?

Kate stretched out beside him and lay awake, staring at the ceiling. No matter how many times she worked through the possibilities, she still came up with more questions than answers. It was past midnight when the pile of worries crowding her mind gave way to exhaustion and sleep came at last.

CHAPTER FIFTEEN

Kate awoke to sunshine streaming through the window. For a moment, she experienced the disorientation of waking up in a strange place, but her momentary confusion was quickly replaced by images of their wild escape through the streets of Moscow. She rolled onto her side, hoping to slip out of bed without waking David. She'd almost made it when a noise from the living room shoved all other thoughts from her mind.

"David, wake up," she whispered, shoving a hand against his shoulder. She snatched her gun from the nightstand and got to her feet.

A knock came from the other side of the closed bedroom door. "Are you two still asleep?"

Kate lowered her weapon. "Come on in."

David stirred and rubbed his eyes. "What time is it?"

"After six and past time for you to be up," snapped Talia as she came into the room. Her eyes moved from Kate to the bed and back again. "I trust you had an enjoyable night?"

"Ignore her," said David. "She knows nothing happened, but she still feels obligated to be the indignant ex-wife. It's an exercise she likes to engage in from time to time."

"And for which you give me plenty of opportunities." Talia

tossed a duffle onto the bed. "This contains clothes for you both as well as personal items. There'll be more in your stateroom on the ship."

"Ship?" asked Kate. "What ship? We're nowhere near a port."

Talia ignored the question. "Get dressed. I'll start breakfast." She retreated to the living room, closing the door behind her.

Kate turned to David. "Do you know what she's talking about?"

"No, but I'm sure we're going to find out. Take a shower and get dressed. I'll take mine after we eat."

When Kate emerged from the bedroom, she found David and Talia sipping coffee at the kitchen table, the tension between them gone for the moment. They both looked up as she entered the kitchen.

"You look good as a brunette," said Talia. "You should consider keeping it, especially when working undercover."

"That's not what I thought I was doing. And keep in mind I'm not a spy."

"You're in a foreign country. You met with an anonymous contact who's working against the government. The police and intelligence services are hunting for you, and I guarantee they consider you to be a spy. If you're going to come out of this in one piece, you better start thinking like one. Now sit down and eat your breakfast."

A plate of eggs, bacon, and toast had been placed in front of the remaining chair. Kate took a seat and dug in. She glanced over at David, who was munching his last bite of bacon.

He grinned at her expression. "I assure you God will have bigger things to hold me accountable for than whether I kept kosher. Besides, I can't resist the smell of frying bacon."

"Rabbi Kertchman wrote us both off as a lost cause years ago," said Talia. "Now can we get down to business? A blue Samara sedan is parked out on the street. I left the fob in the desk yesterday. When we're finished here, you'll drive to St. Petersburg. You should be there by mid-afternoon. Put your weapons in the trunk and leave the car with valet parking at the Kampinski hotel. Take a cab to the Winter Palace where you'll blend in with a tour group from a

Swedish cruise ship docked in the harbor. Since Ukraine, it's the only western cruise line still making ports of call in Russia." She handed a large manila envelope to Kate. "Your papers."

Kate examined the contents. "How did you manage this?"

"With Sweden's new status in NATO, an intelligence relationship has developed. Britain's MI6 reserves a stateroom on every ship that will dock at St. Petersburg in case it might be needed. They also make them available to other NATO members when the need arises. ISA has arranged for Mossad to make use of it. Last night, your information was downloaded onto the ship's computer systems."

"And who are we this time?"

"John and Diane Sullivan of Terre Haute Indiana. There are passports for both of you in that envelope, along with passes for the shore excursion to the palace. There're also cruise ID cards. Those cards will allow you to board the ship when the tour group returns and serve as the key to your stateroom. There are metal detectors placed at the dock, which is why you need to leave the guns in the car. You'll find replacements in your room, as well as clothing and anything else you'll need."

Kate placed the envelope on the table. "And we just sail away? It's that easy?"

"Easy is a relative term. Even the simplest plans can go wrong."

"Why all the different identities?"

"To muddy up the paper trail. The Russians are looking for Kaitlyn Malone. Until you arrive in St. Petersburg, you're Rebecca Tobin, a citizen of Israel. The ship's records show the Sullivans boarded the ship at Southampton three days ago and disembarked at St. Petersburg for the tour. When the tour bus returns, you'll show your cruise IDs and there'll be no questions asked. Go straight to your stateroom and stay there until the ship sails. Once out of Russian waters, you can enjoy yourselves on board for the rest of the evening. The ship will dock at Helsinki in the morning where you'll disembark, supposedly to see the sights and do some shopping. Instead, you'll go straight to the Israeli embassy."

"Will I be going home from Helsinki?" asked Kate.

"That depends on the situation."

David poured himself more coffee. "Have you talked to Jacob or Peter?"

"Both. Dimitri has been forthcoming, and plans are being made to address Iran's intentions in the Middle East. Those plans, however, assume the Russian nukes are not yet in place. They were hoping Kate learned more about that last night."

"I'm afraid not," she replied. "Unless it's on this." She pulled the flash drive from her pocket. "Do you have a laptop with you?"

Talia reached into her backpack and produced a computer, which she placed in front of Kate. "Tell me about the meeting."

"It was a test. They're being careful, and after what happened last night, I don't blame them. He said the information on the real meeting is on here."

The drive contained two documents. One was encrypted and couldn't be opened without the key. The second contained one sentence in plain text typed in Cyrillic script.

Talia leaned over her shoulder. "What does it say?"

"The key lies in the mirror." Kate stared at the screen in frustration. "What the hell is that supposed to mean?"

David drummed his fingers against the tabletop. "What do you see when you look in a mirror?"

"Your reflection," said Kate and Talia in unison. Kate accessed the encrypted file and typed 'reflection' when asked for the key. It failed to open. "Now what?"

"Did your contact say anything that might give you a clue?" asked Talia.

Kate shook her head. "I don't think so."

"You used an alias, right?"

"Yeah. The one Dimitri set up. Oh!"

She tried using 'Maria' as the key, but that failed as well. Kate stared at the screen. She understood the desire to keep the contents of the document secret in case it fell into the wrong hands, but they had gone to too much trouble to give her a puzzle that couldn't be solved. What do you see in a mirror? A sudden and unwelcome thought popped into her mind. She tried once more and when prompted for the encryption key, typed kaitlynmalone.

The file opened. Kate sat back in her chair and stared at the screen. "They knew it would be me. The man Dimitri wants me to talk to knew I'd be the one who came. That explains it."

"Explains what?" asked David with a puzzled expression.

"When Dimitri defected, he asked for me. Nobody else, just me."

"You're ISA's lead analyst for anything to do with Russia," said Talia. "Asking for you would make sense. Did he suggest you volunteer for this?"

Kate shook her head. "But I'm betting if I hadn't brought it up, he would have. What the resistance is doing is incredibly dangerous. They'd want to know who they were dealing with. Dimitri told them to expect me, so they used my name as the encryption key. It provided an additional layer of security because it's unlikely anyone else would figure it out. And it explains why Boris didn't shy away when he realized I'm a rookie. He already knew."

"Did you learn anything last night?" asked Talia.

"Not from Boris himself, but the shooting was a different story. It got me pointed in the right direction." Kate filled her in on her theory about Iran. Talia nodded as she listened. "That makes more sense than anything else we've come up with, but how do we prove it?"

"Whoever wants to meet me may give us what we need."

Talia looked back at the laptop. "Give us a quick translation."

Kate turned her attention to the screen. "The first page contains details about the meeting. Times, identification protocols, things like that. It's taking place at a hotel bar in Geneva on the 20th. That's in four days." She looked up at the others. "But he's not going to show after what happened last night."

Talia shrugged. "Maybe, maybe not. It depends on how much is at stake and how he assesses the risk. If he considers the meeting important enough and if you slip out of Russia cleanly, he might feel it's safe to meet with you. He probably views himself as a patriot trying to save Russia from disaster. Such people are often willing to accept risks they normally wouldn't."

Kate moved to the second page. "He's given us some information to establish his credibility. A Russian advance team is already in place at Tabriz airbase in Iran and new facilities were constructed to house them and the weapons. The missiles are already there but not the warheads. They'll be delivered within the next two weeks. A bunker has been built deep underground to store them and keep them safe in the event of an attack."

"That base is right next to a civilian airport and the surrounding area is heavily populated," said Talia. "The air defense system will be robust. Attacking it will be impossible without risking considerable collateral damage within the civilian population."

David nodded. "I'm sure they're counting on that as a deterrent. But a precision cruise missile strike by the U.S. would set them back months."

Kate shook her head. "They won't take that drastic a step without proof, and this won't be good enough. They'll want hard intel before even considering launching an attack on Iran."

"But now we know we have a little time," said Talia. "I'll pass this along. What else is in the document?"

Kate returned her attention to the computer screen. "The rest of this is mostly a corroboration of what Dimitri already told us."

Talia snapped the laptop shut. "The big question here is whether we can trust this person."

"Dimitri does," said Kate. "That's all I've got to go on. By reaching out to me, he's taking a pretty serious risk. Could it be a trap? I suppose so, but like you just said, some risks are worth taking."

"I agree," said Talia. "We go to Geneva and see what happens."

"You're going with us?"

"Not on the ship. I'll meet you at the embassy in Helsinki. Now you two better get moving if you're going to be on time to meet that tour group. John and Diane Sullivan have a ship to catch."

CHAPTER SIXTEEN

Peter knocked on his boss's door. "Got a minute, Carl?"

Carl Linder looked up from his laptop. "Come in. Any news from Kate?"

Peter took a seat across the desk from him. "I just got off the phone with Talia Levy. Kate went to meet her contact as planned, but it was a setup. She and David managed to escape, but they're off the grid until Mossad can get them out of Russia. You realize what this means?"

Carl emitted a long sigh. "We're back to the security problem."

"Yes. We need to fix this and do it fast. Some of the leaked information was known to only a few people. Most of them are above suspicion for now, but one name stands out. You brought Nick Mueller into ISA and dumped him on me with no warning or explanation."

Peter held up his hand before Carl could respond. "As Director, that's your prerogative and I'm not questioning your reasons. But he was a rising star at NSA until suddenly he wasn't, and if there was a problem over there, it's our problem now. I don't want to go behind your back, but I need answers. There are people I can quietly reach out to off the record, but I'd rather not draw unwanted attention to this."

Carl removed his glasses and placed them on the table. "I took him on because the president asked me to. He and Mueller's father are friends going all the way back to high school and the Admiral asked for a favor. He wanted his son given another chance."

"And you just went along with it?"

"I reviewed the incident report and decided there was nothing serious enough to warrant turning down a presidential request. He's assigned to you because I knew if he screwed up, you'd be all over it."

"You didn't see fit to read me in?"

"I couldn't. The report is classified."

"It's gone beyond that now and we've got a serious problem. Screw the politics. It's an intelligence matter."

"When you sit in this office, those boundaries can get blurred."

Peter nodded. "I understand. If you hear I reached out, don't say I didn't warn you." He got up to leave.

"Wait. Sit down."

He turned to face his boss. "For a lecture on the political realities, or a discussion of what happened?"

"The latter. You're right. We should keep this in house."

Peter returned to his seat and waited as Carl picked up the phone. "Ella? I want no interruptions. Take all my calls and move my meeting with Senator Gutierrez to later this afternoon."

He sat back in his chair and regarded Peter without expression. "If the president ever finds out I let you in on this, I'll probably be tossed out on my ass. This goes nowhere else. Am I clear?"

Peter nodded.

"Mueller headed up a team doing analysis on satellite surveillance of the Persian Gulf region. One of his people screwed up and left highly classified intel on an unsecured server. Nick discovered the mistake, but the person responsible was a friend and he never reported it. Somebody in their IT section caught it and turned them both in."

"The cover up was worse than the security lapse."

"Yes. As far as anyone can tell, the data was never uploaded, but we can't know that for certain. The analyst at fault was fired and Nick would have been as well, but his father intervened with the president. In essence, they covered up the cover up. I was told to find a place for Mueller at ISA, and that's as much as I can say about it. Now, what's behind your interest? Has he done anything to arouse your suspicions?"

"No. But we have a problem and he's the weak link."

Carl spread his hands out on the desk. "I can't confront him without proof he's done something wrong, not when he's got that kind of political cover. You'll need something more solid than just a hunch."

"Maybe there's a way."

"What are you going to do?"

"Do you really want to know?"

Carl sat back with a sigh. "Days like this make me wish I'd taken my father's advice and gone into the family business. I'd have made one hell of a dairy farmer."

Peter's only answer was a grin as he went out the door.

CHAPTER SEVENTEEN

The drive from Moscow to St. Petersburg went without incident. They left the car at the hotel with their weapons locked in the trunk and took a taxi to the Hermitage Museum and the famed Winter Palace, the official residence of the Russian Czars. A group of around twenty people stood outside the main entrance listening to a tour guide.

"That must be the people from the ship," said David. "Wait until they go inside."

Moments later, the guide turned to open the door into the palace and the eager crowd of tourists filed through. As Kate attempted to do the same, a man standing off to one side tapped her on the shoulder. "Your papers, please." He spoke Russian, not English.

Kate thought quickly. If this turned out to be trouble, she didn't know what they could do about it. She tried her best to appear innocent and confused. "I'm sorry. I don't speak Russian."

He repeated the request in English that was far from fluent.

"Oh, of course," she answered, reaching into her pocket. "I have the excursion ticket right here somewhere. Why do you ask?"

"You not with the others. You come from there," he said, pointing toward the parking lot.

"My wife and I took a short walk to stretch our legs," said David. "We've been cooped up on that tour bus most of the day."

Kate handed him the ticket along with her passport. "Did we do something wrong?"

The guard ignored the question and thumbed through the documents before returning them. "Enjoy tour," he grunted, opening the door for them.

"Thank you. Come, dear. I don't want to miss anything."

She gave the guard a smile and led the way toward the double doors at the end of the entrance hall.

"Nicely done," whispered David. "You handled that perfectly."

"Thanks, but I'll feel a lot better once we're on that ship and out at sea."

Kate had toured the palace in the past and never failed to be awed by the grandeur of the setting. Russian history and culture would always hold a special place for her. She knew David was alert to any signs of danger, so she allowed herself to be immersed once more in the glory of Russia's past.

As the tour progressed, Kate became increasingly uneasy. She felt like she was being watched, but a glance around the room revealed nothing untoward. One woman looked away as soon as Kate's gaze settled on her, which probably meant nothing but still left her unsettled. She wondered if she was thinking like a spy or simply being paranoid.

When the tour group boarded the bus for the ride back to the ship, she followed David to seats near the back. "See the woman with the green sweater in the third row?" she said, leaning close to him. "I think maybe she's watching us."

"Why?"

"I don't know. It just feels like that."

"Relax. The ship's a contained environment. It'll be difficult to spy on us without being obvious about it."

Upon their arrival at the dock, everyone filed off the bus and lined up at the gangway. When her turn came, Kate swiped her cruise card and stepped through the metal detector. The operator glanced at her computer screen, matching Kate's face to the picture stored in the ship's computer.

"Welcome back, Mrs. Sullivan. I trust you enjoyed your time ashore."

"Absolutely. It was wonderful. I can't wait for our next stop."

"We're leaving port as soon as everyone's on board. We'll be docking at Helsinki around ten in the morning."

Kate stepped aside and waited for David to pass through the detector. "How do we find our stateroom?" she asked as he joined her by the elevators.

"Talia said it's Cabin 803. We go to Deck 8 and follow the room number signs, just like in a hotel. Have you ever been on a ship before?"

"Never. I hear the food is supposed to be out of this world. I'm starving."

"As soon as we sail, we'll go to the dining room for a good meal and an even better bottle of wine. How's that sound?"

"Heavenly."

Their stateroom turned out to be a suite comprising a living room and a bedroom with an adjoining bath. Kate opened the sliding doors and stepped out onto the balcony. Once at sea, they could relax in comfortable deck chairs and enjoy the scenic panoramas, but at present the view consisted mostly of the boarding dock below. She was about to go back inside when she noticed the woman from the tour bus talking to two men and gesturing up at the ship.

"David, come here a minute."

He joined her at the rail. "What's up?"

"Remember the woman I pointed out on the bus? She's down there talking to those men."

His eyes scanned the dock. "I see her."

As they watched, the woman turned and walked toward the gangway while the men proceeded back up the dock.

"They're leaving," said David. "I'm sure it's nothing."

"But what if it's not?"

"One of the biggest dangers in the field isn't someone with a gun.

It's seeing a threat in everyone and everything around you. It plays games with your mind. If you're right, we'll know it soon enough, but for now I wouldn't waste time worrying about it."

"I guess."

"Come on. Let's go see what they left us."

They explored the bedroom. There were two sets of everyday clothing for each of them neatly folded in the dresser, two backpacks were stacked in a corner, and a selection of personal items had been placed in the bathroom. The closet contained a blazer with matching slacks for him and a casual floral print dress for her. Kate examined the label. "How did they know our sizes?"

"Talia knew what to ask for." He pulled open the bottom desk drawer. "And they left us something else," he exclaimed, laying two automatic pistols on the desktop.

"We don't go through the metal detector when we disembark?"

"Nope." He stretched and kicked off his shoes. "That was a long drive up from Moscow. I'm going to take a nap before dinner. Wake me when we sail."

Kate went out to the living room and took a bottle of water from the mini fridge. She settled into a comfortable chair and let her mind run through the events of the last twenty-four hours. It was hard to believe that just last night she'd gone to Kask, excited by the prospect of meeting with her contact. That excitement was long gone now, but the one bright spot was that in another hour or two they'd be safely out of Russia.

She was still trying to sort it all out when her eyes began to feel heavy. Placing the water bottle on the table, she leaned back and let herself relax. David had been right. A nap sounded like a good idea. She closed her eyes and fell asleep almost at once.

A blast from the ship's horn caused her to come instantly awake. A peek out the balcony door showed a widening gulf of water between the hull and the wharf as they slowly backed away from the dock. She watched as the shoreline drew away from them. Given how this trip had ended, she wondered if she'd ever be able to visit Russia again.

She went to the bedroom to wake David, but he emerged from the bathroom with a towel wrapped around his waist just as she opened the door.

"Oops! Sorry," she said as she hastily backed out. Living in close quarters with a man she wasn't intimately involved with would take some getting used to.

Fifteen minutes later, he joined her in the living room wearing the sport coat over an open neck shirt. "The bedroom's all yours."

"Sorry about walking in on you. I should have knocked."

"We're posing as husband and wife, and we may have to keep it up for a while. When you're sharing a bedroom and bathroom, things like that are going to happen. We need to learn to be comfortable with each other and not worry about it."

Not to mention sharing a bed, thought Kate. "Yeah, I guess. Anyway, it's my turn for the shower. Fix us a drink and I'll be as quick as I can."

She emerged from the bedroom thirty minutes later and joined David on the balcony. His head turned as she stepped through the sliding door from the living room. "Wow." He paused, looking slightly embarrassed. "Sorry, I didn't mean to blurt it out like that."

She laughed and accepted the glass he extended to her. "All compliments gratefully appreciated. And if I remember correctly, you were the one who said we have to get comfortable with each other."

"Then here's to a delicious meal and a peaceful night at sea."

They clinked glasses and Kate sipped her drink. Scotch neat, just as she liked it. She settled into the chair next to his. "How does dinner work? Do we just show up?"

"If we were going to the main dining room, yes. But there are several smaller restaurants on the ship as well. I made a reservation for us at a steakhouse overlooking the bow of the ship. I think we've earned a good meal, don't you? Especially since Mossad is footing the bill."

Dinner provided a much needed diversion from the stress of the past two days. The wood paneled walls, comfortable leather chairs and soft lighting created an intimate setting. David ordered an expensive cabernet sauvignon, which would pair beautifully with their steaks. They toasted their escape from Russia and settled in to enjoy the evening.

When their meal arrived, Kate breathed in the wonderful aromas. Her filet mignon was grilled to a perfect medium rare, and the buttery baked potato and roasted asparagus rounded out a delicious meal.

As they ate, he told her about his childhood in Haifa. His parents were both university professors who stressed education above all else. He'd been more interested in sports than his studies, which resulted in his adolescence being marked by periodic episodes of teenage rebellion.

"Where did you learn English?" asked Kate. "I know they teach it in Israeli schools, but yours is perfect. Talia has an accent, but you don't have even a trace of one."

"College. I went to Michigan. My parents thought studying abroad would expand my horizons. How about you?"

Kate recalled stories of growing up on the farm with cattle and chickens to care for and a never-ending list of chores her father supplied her with.

"It sounds like a lot of work," he observed.

"Yeah, but I loved it. I had a dog and even a horse. Her name was Betsy."

"And yet you ended up at ISA."

"And you at Mossad. How did that happen?"

He shrugged. "When I returned home after college, I served my mandatory military time. After the three years were up, Mossad came calling. It seems I exhibited some abilities they had a need for. What I really wanted was to play soccer. I lettered all four years at Michigan, but wasn't even close to being good enough to play professionally. I took them up on their offer."

"I played soccer in college, too. I even got an invitation to try out for the national U20 team, but I didn't make the cut."

"How do you like living in Washington?" he asked, sipping his wine. "It seems like an odd place to find a farm girl."

"I like it a lot. There's an energy to the city, and I enjoy my job. My real job, that is."

"Is there a boyfriend waiting for you back home?"

"Not anymore. I ended it just before I went to Paris. Why do you ask?"

"At the risk of sounding sexist, it seems unlikely that an attractive and intelligent woman like you would be unattached."

Kate smiled at the compliment. "I have an independent streak a mile wide that most guys have a problem dealing with. That's pretty much what led to the breakup. How about you and Talia? What happened, if you don't mind my asking?"

"We got married when we were in the army. It didn't last long. We're both strong willed and pretty soon the clashes and arguments overcame the attraction. We divorced when I joined Mossad. Talia planned to remain in the army, but a couple of years later I walked into a briefing at headquarters and there she was."

"And they made you a team?"

"Mossad looks for complimentary skillsets when pairing operatives for assignments. We're partners when the situation requires. We make a good team when we're in the field. As a married couple, not so much."

"I can't imagine working so closely with someone I've had a relationship with," said Kate. "It would feel awkward. And complicated."

He shrugged. "If it works, then it works."

When the server presented the check, David charged it to the Sullivan's shipboard account. As they left the restaurant, Kate glanced at the wall clock behind the maître d's station. Almost two hours had passed while they talked and ate.

"How about a walk on the promenade deck before we go back to the room?" David suggested.

"Sure," she responded. "I could use a breath of fresh sea air."

An evening stroll seemed to be a popular idea. Couples walked hand in hand or paused by the rail to admire the full moon as it rose out of the sea. Kate kept expecting to see the woman from the bus, but if she was watching them, she was doing it discreetly.

She breathed deeply, enjoying the crisp evening air. "This is wonderful. A little chilly, though."

David started to remove his sport coat. "I don't need my partner catching a cold."

Kate smiled. "Thanks, but I'm fine. I think the elevators are through there," she said, pointing to a set of sliding doors to their left. "Why don't we go up to the room and have a nightcap before bed?"

"Great idea."

When they opened the door to their stateroom, they found the steward had already been there to turn down the bed. A single lamp in the living room provided a soft light.

Kate went out onto the balcony, admiring the reflection of the moon on the waves while David fixed their drinks. "That was a nice evening," he said as he joined her at the rail.

"Definitely. We needed that. At least I did."

After all the chaos and tension, the intimacy of the evening and a slight buzz from the wine began to have an effect on her. What began as a straightforward mission had become something much more complicated, and she felt like she'd been thrown into the deep end without knowing how to tread water. She was also aware of how living on the cusp of life and death was affecting her libido. Her only life raft was David, and she was suddenly very aware in an entirely new way that he was standing right here beside her. And in a little while, they'd be in the same bed.

"David, I think maybe I'd better sleep on the sofa tonight."

He smiled. "I was thinking the same thing. Only me, not you."

"I know I shouldn't let it all affect me like that, but ..."

"It happens. The danger, the wine, and living in such close quarters can be a powerful combination. You want something or someone to cling to, even for a little while. It happens to everyone, and it's nothing to be embarrassed about. You've got the bed tonight and that's settled, okay?"

She nodded. "Thanks."

"What we're being forced to deal with is the nightmare scenario for a new agent's first mission. I've been wondering when you were going to show some cracks in that professional resolve of yours, and I'm glad it happened here tonight when we're alone and can talk about it."

"It's all so overwhelming."

He nodded. "But I told you last night you have the guts for this."

"Actually, you said I have the balls for it."

He grinned. "Yeah, I did. So, we're good?"

She nodded. "Thanks, David. Thanks for understanding."

"You're welcome. Now we should get ready for bed. I'll get changed and then bedroom's all yours."

Kate watched him go, thinking how fortunate she was to have him as a partner.

CHAPTER EIGHTEEN

Kate rose early, opening the bedroom window and taking in a deep breath of crisp sea air. She went into the bathroom, moving quietly in case David was still asleep. As far as she was concerned, there was no better way to start a morning than with a hot shower, and she stood under the showerhead with her eyes closed as the steaming water washed over her body. Her mission wasn't over yet, not until she met with her contact in Geneva, but at least they were no longer within reach of Russian security. That fact alone lifted a heavy load from her shoulders.

She stepped out of the steamy shower stall and grabbed a towel from the rack. Wrapping it around her, she stood in front of the mirror and studied her reflection. The black hair was going to take some getting used to, as did everything else these days. As an analyst, Kate had always treated intelligence work as an intellectual exercise, fitting pieces of disparate data together like a jigsaw puzzle to create a clearer view of the world. The woman staring back at her had killed one man and seen too many others die. She'd changed identities almost as often as her clothes, and making sure she had a weapon on her person had become as routine as carrying her wallet. Was that the person she wanted to be?

The question begged an answer, but for the moment was irrelevant. A colleague back home had a phrase he used whenever confronted with new or conflicting data. He would look right at her and say, "It is what it is, and don't try to make it into something else." The truth of the saying had never been more appropriate. She'd volunteered for this. Hell, it had been her idea. If it was turning out to be far different from her expectations, there was nothing she could do but keep pushing ahead. The soul-searching questions would have to wait for now.

She went back to the bedroom and dressed in a t-shirt and jeans. Opening the door to the living room, she saw that the curtains over the balcony doors were still pulled shut. The daylight filtering past them provided enough light to see by and she was surprised to see David's blanket and pillow strewn across an unoccupied sofa. She pulled open the curtains, expecting to find him out on the balcony enjoying the sunrise, but the sliding door was locked from the inside and both deck chairs were empty.

The shirt and jacket he wore to dinner hung over the back of an armchair and his shoes still lay where he'd left them, but the khaki slacks were missing. A quick search told her his weapon was gone as well. She went to the stateroom door and opened it carefully. The ceiling lights were still dimmed, and the corridor was devoid of activity.

Kate closed the door, her mind churning. He'd left the stateroom wearing only his pants and taken his gun with him, but why hadn't he woken her? She returned to the bedroom, snatched her weapon from the bedside table, and pulled a windbreaker from the closet. Finding him on such a massive ship would be difficult, but she had to try.

She eased open the stateroom door and stepped out into the hallway. To her left, the corridor ended with the housekeeping storeroom used by the stewards. The opposite end opened onto Deck 8's central foyer where a wide, circular staircase wound its way down through the ship's atrium. The foyer would have been his only option.

She was pulling the stateroom door closed behind her when a red smear on the doorframe drew her attention. The blood hadn't had time to dry, and a similar stain was visible on the carpet. A table placed against the corridor wall held a house phone and a box of tissues. She wiped the blood from the door and scuffed at the stain on the floor until it blended in with the brown carpet. She didn't need the room stewards reporting blood in the hallway.

She crept toward the atrium, keeping one hand on the gun in her pocket. The foyer was unoccupied, but a peek over the railing revealed a group of early risers down on the main deck gathered around the coffee bar. David wouldn't have gone down there clad only in his khakis. A bank of elevators lined the wall behind her, but an examination of the call buttons showed no telltale traces of blood. The trail seemed to end before it even began.

"Damn it, David. Where the hell did you go?"

A door to the left of the elevators was marked with a sign advising passengers not to use the elevators in the event of a fire. It opened onto a narrow staircase that extended all the way down into the bowels of the ship, but it was the landing three decks below that drew her attention. An arm extended out from the edge of the floor and dangled limply over the open stairwell.

Kate ran down the three flights of stairs. A man lay face down on the floor, his neck twisted at an impossible angle. A quick search of the body produced nothing except a holstered 9mm handgun and a wallet containing a Russian driver's license and the equivalent of about fifty dollars. Beyond a broken neck, there were no visible wounds. The blood on the door had come from someone else.

She stood up and considered what to do. There was no way to know if David was the hunter or the hunted. If he was a prisoner somewhere on the ship, the last thing she wanted was an uproar over a dead body and the investigation it would trigger. That could cause his captors to decide to cut their losses and kill him. Even if he was free, he wouldn't want the complications of a ship-wide alert.

Kate wondered if she was thinking this through correctly. With no experience to fall back on, all she had were her gut instincts, and they were telling her she couldn't let this body be discovered until she'd found David.

She opened the door on the landing and stepped into a kitchen.

The room was dark except for the dim light filtering in from the stairwell and the faint glow of the exit signs above the doors. This was not a kitchen used for preparing breakfasts, which made it a convenient oasis for anyone on the run. A storage closet just to her right held a wheeled bin containing freshly laundered tablecloths and napkins. She shoved it aside and went back out to the landing.

It took all her strength to drag the body into the kitchen and stuff him into a corner of the closet. She removed his gun and slid the bin back into place. Until somebody moved it, he was safely out of the way.

Kate considered what to do next. He'd been left on the landing, which meant those involved had been in a hurry. People trying to rush through a crisis often made mistakes. She went to the swinging doors leading from the kitchen to the dining room. The public entrance to the restaurant was on the opposite wall connected to a heavily traveled corridor. A bleeding and half naked man would have raised an alarm by now, so the answer had to lie elsewhere. She turned back to the kitchen, which showed no signs of a struggle. Maybe they hadn't come in here at all, but if they'd continued down the staircase, there was no way to know which deck they were on now.

She noticed a freight elevator at the far end of the room. Instead of a normal door, it had a metal grate that opened vertically. Kate peeked through and saw the car stopped far below her. This was how the kitchen staff accessed the food storage areas down in the ship's hold. She pressed the button and watched as the car ascended the shaft. Upon its arrival, the door slid upwards and she stepped inside.

The single lightbulb set in the ceiling revealed plain metal walls pockmarked with dents where carts and dollies had banged into them. The control panel had only three buttons marked Storage Hold, Han Sing, and Food Court #2. This kitchen evidently served the ship's upscale Asian restaurant, and the same elevator must service a food court on one of the upper decks.

Kate was about to step back into the kitchen when she glanced at the wall beside her. A red stain was smeared across the metal. The elevator had been down in the hold, so Kate pressed the Storage button. The door closed, and the car began a rapid descent. She flattened herself against a side wall, hoping to stay out of sight of anyone who might be present when she arrived.

The elevator came to a stop and the door opened. Hearing nothing, she peeked out. A large open area containing pallets loaded with crates and boxes stretched out in front of her. Crouching low, she pulled the gun from her pocket and hurried from the elevator to a space between two pallets piled high with cases of wine. The recycled air in the hold differed from the fresh sea breezes of the upper decks. It was chilly down here, probably by design. This hold was one big refrigerator.

She kept out of sight while she took stock of her situation. Several other freight elevators lined the walls of the massive compartment, each of which must service a different set of kitchens. A cargo door to her left provided access from the docks. This place was far too large for her to search while trying to remain undetected herself, and David could be anywhere.

She heard faint voices from the other end of the hold speaking a language she didn't recognize. They made no effort to hide their presence, so they were probably members of the crew who worked down here. Still, it wouldn't do to be discovered outside the public areas while carrying a loaded gun. Reluctantly, she decided her only option was to call the Israeli embassy as soon as they docked and enlist Talia's help.

Behind her, the elevator door closed, and the car rose back up the shaft, removing her means of retreat. She looked around, trying to identify another exit route. Using one of the other freight elevators would be risky. She could end up in a kitchen staffed for breakfast and faced with questions she wouldn't want to answer.

A door to her left was labeled with a stenciled image of stair steps and its location so close to the elevator meant it likely was the same staircase she'd been on before. She stayed low as she darted across the floor. Once inside the stairwell, she began the climb up through the subdecks to Deck 8. She emerged into the foyer, which was now populated with people waiting for the elevators and eager for the start of another exciting day. Kate skirted around the crowd, trying not to draw unwanted attention as she made her way to their stateroom.

With the door locked behind her, she went out onto the balcony to think. If David were operating freely, he'd eventually show up back here or at least make contact in some way. But if he were on the run and evading pursuers, this would be the last place he'd come. And if he was a prisoner, she was his only hope. Once they made port, he could be smuggled off the ship in any number of ways, and the chances of finding him would shrink drastically.

With a sudden start, Kate realized the view from the balcony had changed. The endless expanse of blue ocean had been replaced by a shoreline that crept steadily closer. They were heading into port. She went to the bedroom and stuffed a change of clothes into her backpack along with her various passports and the gun she'd taken from the dead man in the stairwell. She took the elevator up to the poolside breakfast buffet and grabbed a ham and egg sandwich and a plastic bottle of orange juice. She wolfed down her breakfast while heading for the embarkation deck.

When the announcement that passengers could now disembark came over the loudspeakers, Kate was first in line. She went down the gangway and paused at the bottom to get her bearings. She spotted a dockside coffee shop with an outdoor patio located across from the ship and found a table where she could monitor the activities at the gangway.

She took out her phone and selected Talia's name from the contact list. The call was answered on the first ring. "How was your night at sea?"

"David's missing."

She related his disappearance and her efforts to find him. "I'm not sure what to do next. I'm watching the activity on the dock, but there's a lot going on."

"Find a cab and come to the embassy."

"But what about David?"

"The mission comes first, and that means we have to get you to Geneva. David can take care of himself. Keep your priorities clear."

Kate fought to keep the anger out of her voice. "So, he's expendable?" She remembered a conversation in Moscow when David had said as much himself. "You can be that cold blooded about this? Well, I can't. If there's a chance he's still on board, I'm getting back on that ship before it sails tonight. And if you don't like it, you can screw yourself."

So much for containing the anger. A brief silence ensued before Talia continued in a softer tone, "You're new to this, Kate. You can't let personal feelings get in the way."

"Yeah, I know. The first rule. David told me."

"Then listen to me. You're inexperienced and working alone. That's a dangerous combination. Dangerous for you and for David as well."

Maybe she was right, but Kate was past caring, and the rules be damned. "Remember what Peter said when I volunteered to go to Moscow? I don't work for Mossad. I understand what you're saying, but I'm not giving up. Not yet. I'll call you later."

She hung up before Talia could respond, taking deep breaths to calm herself. She ordered a double espresso from the waitress and tried to sort through her options. Passengers were leaving the ship eager for a day spent exploring the Finnish capital, but the cargo doors had remained closed. If they started loading or unloading crates and boxes, it would become exponentially more difficult to stop them from getting David off the ship.

An hour went by with no change and she was about to get up and stretch her legs when someone slid into the seat across from her.

"Kaitlyn Malone? You've been difficult to find."

CHAPTER NINETEEN

The woman from the tour bus held Kate's gaze without blinking. Her short auburn hair and sculpted features brought to mind the models gracing the covers of fashion magazines, but her eyes had a hardness to them, even when she attempted a smile.

Kate was alone with no backup for the first time, but she steadied her nerves and held the woman's gaze. "Who are you?"

"The one currently in possession of your partner." Her English was fluent and the Russian accent unmistakable. "He's not saying much, but it doesn't matter. I'll be happy to let him go, provided you take his place."

"What do you want?"

"A conversation. You have become somewhat of a problem. A very annoying one at that. If you come with me, he'll be released. You'll be free to go as soon as we're done talking."

Kate doubted that would be the case. "And if I refuse?"

"Then I'm afraid the Finnish authorities will discover his body floating in the harbor. There is, however, no need for such a terrible outcome."

"I'm not that naïve. We can have our conversation right here, but only after I see him walk off the ship."

"That leaves no incentive for you to give me what I need."

"Then I'm open to suggestions, but I'm not going with you."

"You'd risk his life?"

Kate remembered her argument with Talia. "It goes with the job."

The woman regarded her with a curious expression. "I was told you're an amateur. Apparently, I was misinformed."

The statement set off alarms for Kate. Misinformed by who? "You took him down to the hold. Have him brought up to our stateroom and out onto the balcony. I can see it from here. Once I'm satisfied that he's still alive, you can ask your questions."

"And you'll answer them?"

Kate shrugged. "If I can, but I'm working mostly in the dark. I can't promise I'll have all the answers."

The woman took out her phone and spoke rapidly in Russian. "Bring him up to the rail."

"Fifteen minutes," she said as she put the phone away.

"What part do you play in all this?" asked Kate.

"I'm the one who asks the questions."

Kate decided it couldn't hurt to keep probing. "I'm guessing the dead man on the landing worked for you."

Her eyebrows went up. "You got that far? I don't suppose you know where he is now?"

"There's a kitchen just off the landing. He's in a storage closet behind a laundry bin. Leaving him in the stairwell didn't seem to be in anyone's best interest. Did my partner do that?"

"Unintentionally. He was woozy and stumbled on the steps. Yuri tried to catch him and fell himself."

They sat in silence for several minutes until the woman raised her arm and pointed up at the ship. "There."

David stood between two men. He wore the khakis from last night along with a black t-shirt and leaned heavily against the rail for support.

"How badly is he hurt?"

"He took a blow to the head and may have a concussion. Beyond that, he's fine."

The men pulled David back out of sight. "I held up my end," said the woman. "Now it's your turn. When you were in Moscow, you met a man at Kask. Who was he?"

"He called himself Boris, but that was a code name set up for the meeting. I have no idea who he really was. Somebody killed him before I could find out."

"That was an unfortunate mistake. The man who made it won't be making another."

Kate was stung by the matter-of-fact tone of the response. "And you lost another man this morning. You must be running out of people you can trust."

"That isn't your concern. What did this Boris tell you?"

"Nothing."

"I find that difficult to believe."

"It was a test. The man who was to be my contact sent Boris to check me out."

"And?"

Kate phrased her answer carefully. "I passed. He was about to give me the details of the real meeting when your man killed him, and I've been on the run from the Russian authorities ever since. Now you know everything I do. Are we done?"

"You went to Moscow based on information you were given by Dimitri Artisimov. Don't deny it. It was you in Paris, not some fictional Carla Fremont."

The alarms in Kate's head got louder. This woman had access to information coming from the mole back in Washington. "Yes, it was me. Dimitri told me that Russia is intent on some type of aggressive action, but held back most of the details while he bargained for the best deal he could get. I convinced him he had to give us something we could corroborate. He provided the contact protocols for my meeting with Boris and said I'd learn what it was about then. Except I learned nothing thanks to your trigger-happy hit man."

"What type of aggressive action?"

If this woman didn't know who sent Boris and was unaware of what the Russian government was up to, it meant she worked for someone else entirely. Her theory about Iran looked more likely by the minute, and it occurred to Kate that she might be the one learning the most from this conversation. "You tell me," she replied with a shrug. "If you knew enough to come after me, then you probably know more than I do. You said killing Boris was a mistake. What kind of mistake?"

"*You* were supposed to be the target. We wanted to prevent you from passing on whatever you'd learned."

Kate fought to stay calm. "What went wrong?"

"He decided to take you both out, and that wasn't his call to make. He assumed you'd panic and freeze, so he shot your contact first. You reacted too quickly and he couldn't finish the job. As I said, we thought you were an amateur. That does not, however, make up for his disregard of my instructions. That's one flaw I don't tolerate."

"So, why didn't you kill me just now and finish what you started?"

"The situation has changed. You've had time to pass along whatever you learned, so killing you no longer serves any purpose. It's possible you might actually be more useful to us alive. Assuming I let you walk away, what will you do next?"

"Shoot you if you give me half a chance."

A ghost of a smile crossed her face. "Then I'll be sure not to."

A jovial voice interrupted their conversation. "Kate, imagine running into you here in Helsinki."

Talia walked up to the table, her right hand inside her jacket pocket. She placed the other on the woman's shoulder and lowered her voice. "If you go for your weapon, you'll be dead before you can get it out of your pocket."

Kate scanned the coffee shop. No one was paying any attention to them, so as long as this woman behaved, they were just three people having a conversation. Their captive never moved a muscle but stared straight at Kate. "Do you think I'm foolish enough to come here without backup?"

"You mean the man with the beard and leather jacket?" Talia replied. "The one over by the customs shed? You'll find him behind that green dumpster, but he's not going to be much help to you anymore. Why don't you tell us who you are and who you work for?"

When no answer was forthcoming, Kate leaned across the table and kept her voice low. "You've got two choices. You can call your men on the ship and tell them to release David, or you can refuse. I'm sure there's more room behind that dumpster if you decide not to cooperate."

"You won't kill me. You've too many questions."

"I wouldn't make too many assumptions if I were you. Let David go, and your men can walk down the gangway and disappear. Refuse, and I'll raise the alarm about him being missing. If that happens, they'll lock down the ship and start a search. Your goons will be trapped on board and be interrogated after they're caught. You can hope they won't say anything you wouldn't like, or we can keep this between us."

Kate looked up at Talia. "She put her phone in her left jacket pocket."

Talia reached in and retrieved it.

"Call your men," said Kate. "Keep in mind that I speak Russian. Do something stupid and there's always that dumpster."

The woman took the phone from Talia. "Pavel, is he still in the stateroom? Leave him and get off the ship. Both of you. I'll explain later."

Kate held out her hand. "Tell him to put David on."

"Are you okay?" she asked when he came on the line.

"Kate? How did you …"

"Later. How bad are you hurt?"

"I got a lump on my head and a headache to go with it. And I'm a little woozy. What's happening?"

"Those men will be leaving momentarily. You're not going to be much help with a concussion. Stay in the room and wait for me. If you need medical help, call the ship's doctor and tell him you fell in the shower."

"How long will you be?"

Kate eyed her captive. "I'm not sure. If the ship sails before I'm back on board, get off at the next port. I'll meet you."

"Kate …"

"I got this, David." She hung up and pocketed the phone.

"You made the wise choice," she said to their prisoner. "Now we'll see how well your men obey. Watch her, Talia."

Kate turned her attention to the gangway. Ten minutes later, the men who had been with David on the balcony exited the ship and walked across the dock.

"Okay," she said, facing her captive once more. "My turn to ask questions. Who do you work for?"

"You can't force me to talk here. It's too public."

"If we have to take you somewhere else, I guarantee you'll talk," said Talia. "If I were you, I'd avoid all that blood and pain."

"You don't work for Russian intelligence or the people who sent Boris," said Kate. "That means you're a wild card. I'm guessing the reason you're here is money. Is that worth dying for?"

"Talking to you isn't worth dying for either."

"Then you're in a tough spot, aren't you?" Kate replied. "What if I offered you a way out?"

For the first time, uncertainty crept into the woman's expression. "Such as?"

Kate pressed her advantage. "Tell us everything you know about this and about who you work for. If it checks out, we'll set you up with a new identity in either Israel or the United States. There'll be no prison time and you get to live."

"You can make a deal like that?"

"Officially, no. But there's a lot at stake here and I have a great deal of leeway. If what you tell us produces results, my government will honor it. Do you think you're going to get a better offer?"

"I don't know if …"

A slender red dart embedded itself in the side of her neck. Her eyes went wide, and she grabbed in vain at the projectile. The drug took effect immediately, and she collapsed onto the floor, her eyes rolling in her head.

Talia grabbed Kate by the elbow and pulled her into the interior of the coffee shop. "Follow me. Now."

"Is she dead?"

"If not, she will be. It depends on how fast the poison works."

Kate took one more look at the body and followed Talia out the back door.

CHAPTER TWENTY

Talia's car was only steps from the coffee shop. She motioned Kate around to the passenger side. "Get in. Quickly.""What about David?"

"He can take care of himself."

Kate looked back at the ship before climbing into the passenger seat. "I should go back on board."

Talia slapped her hand against the steering wheel. "When the pressure was on back there, you handled it like you've been doing it all your life. Don't cave now. Stay focused."

"But …"

"That woman became a loose end and the people we're up against are good at cleaning up their messes. A compressed gas dart gun has a range of up to 75 meters and is completely silent. The shooter could have been almost anywhere on the dock. You weren't the target this time. But if you try to get back on the ship, you might be. Think, Kate."

Kate took a deep breath to calm herself. "Okay. Where do we go?"

"The embassy. We'll figure the rest out from there."

Upon arrival at the Israeli embassy, Talia drove down into an underground garage. "I have to find the Mossad liaison and make some arrangements. I shouldn't be long."

Kate took a seat in the entrance foyer and bided her time by flipping through a Finnish magazine. Ever since Kask, getting out of Russia alive had been her priority, but now she had time to re-evaluate her situation. For the second time in three days, someone had been killed right in front of her, someone she'd been having a conversation with. Bodies were piling up, and this was still far from over. She thought about her office back at ISA and the sheltered approach to intelligence work it provided. What sense did it possibly make to continue with this? But if she turned away and went home, what then? How would she feel if Russia and Iran succeeded? Could she live with that, knowing she might have been able to stop it?

Talia's return interrupted her musings. "May I see some ID, please?" asked the man accompanying her.

"Certainly." Kate rooted through her backpack and presented her passport.

"This is an Israeli passport. Ms. Levy said you're an American."

"Oh. Sorry. I've had to switch identities a few times." She produced her own diplomatic passport. "My name's Kaitlyn Malone and I work for U.S. intelligence. I'm currently part of a joint operation with Mossad."

He nodded. "I received a call from Tel Aviv earlier this morning, but protocol requires the appropriate IDs."

"Of course."

He handed her a visitor pass. "Both of you come with me."

They proceeded down two flights of stairs to a subbasement and along a brightly lit hallway to a conference room. "We call this the bunker," he said, holding the door open for them. "It's our secure communications room."

He gestured at the telephone sitting on the table. "If you need anything, dial 7278. It will ring my phone."

As he closed the door behind him, Kate took in her surroundings. A rectangular conference table surrounded by leather upholstered chairs occupied the center of the room. One wall was lined with TV monitors, all of which were dark. A small table at the far end held a coffee maker and bottles of water. Kate helped herself to one and settled into a chair. "Will anyone be listening?"

Talia pulled out a chair of her own. "The staff knows this goes to the highest levels of Mossad. Nobody's going to risk the wrath of Sarah Niminsky by snooping. And remote monitoring from outside the building can't penetrate this deep. Now, bring me up to speed. What happened on the ship?"

Kate relayed the events of the morning in as much detail as she could remember.

"Do you have any clue who that woman was?"

"No, but I have a pretty good idea who she worked for. She had a dragon head tattoo on the underside of her left wrist. It's used by some Russian organized crime families to signify status, especially when the wearer has gone up against the security services and succeeded."

Talia considered that for a moment. "Mossad refers to Russian organized crime as OPG. It's the acronym the KGB used back in the day."

stands for …"

"Ooskanya Prestupnaya Goreezov," said Kate. "Organized Crime Group. It's the acronym the KGB used for them back in the day. We use it as well."

"But this isn't about a criminal undertaking," Talia continued. "Russian OPG would have no interest in global politics beyond whatever income it might generate. If you're right about her, then she was just a hired gun."

"A hired gun who had to be pretty far up the food chain. Not many wear that tattoo."

"What did she want?"

"Everything I'd found out so far, but I think I learned a lot more than she did."

"Such as?"

"It was her people at Kask, except *I* was supposed to be the target. Somebody didn't want me talking to the resistance. Her trigger man screwed up and shot Boris instead, and since then she's been tracking me to assess the damage. I think they were trying to break into our stateroom when David heard them."

"How much did you tell her?"

"Nothing that matters now. I think we should call Peter and bring him up to speed. Mossad too."

"I agree."

Kate took out her phone and dialed. "Peter, it's me. Before we go any further, is anyone with you?"

"Jacob. We've been waiting for your call."

"Good. I'm at the embassy and Talia's here as well."

"Where's David?" asked Jacob.

"Still on the ship," Talia responded. "They ran into a problem, and he's injured. Not seriously, but we had other things to deal with. Can you arrange to get him off safely?"

"I'll see to it."

"What happened, Kate?" demanded Peter.

She recounted the events of the morning. "Somebody's hiring muscle from the Russian mob. I'm sure it's Iran and they've got a source inside ISA. That woman knew it was me in Paris and the real reason I was in Moscow. Was anyone outside ISA aware of either of those things?"

"Mossad obviously knew about Moscow," said Jacob, "but we didn't know anything about Paris until after the fact."

"People inside ISA knew you were going to Paris," said Peter. "I had to set up the Carla Fremont identity, requisition a weapon for you, and you used an agency jet. Theoretically, everyone outside ISA should have been in the dark, but with so many people aware of the trip, someone may have talked out of turn."

"What about Moscow?" she asked.

"That's another matter. The trip was common knowledge both inside and outside the agency. We wanted it that way so no one would get curious about it. But the list of people who know the real reason is short. Very short."

"Did any of those people know how we were getting out of Russia?"

"Some did."

"Then somebody on that list is the spy."

"Can you prove Iran's behind all this?" asked Jacob.

"Not yet, but it's the only theory that makes sense. The problem is that there's still too much we don't know. Until we figure out who the mole is, I think I should work only with Mossad. There's no other way to make sure we're keeping Iran in the dark."

"You'll be keeping me in the dark as well," said Peter.

"Talia and David will keep Jacob up to date. But anything he tells you must stay confidential. You can't share it with anyone, Peter. Not even the director. If you and I don't talk, then officially you don't know anything."

"There might be hell to pay for this later."

"Not if we succeed. And I don't see another way."

"Kate, you're on your first assignment. I think …"

"We've got this, Peter," said Talia. "Goodbye." She leaned over and disconnected the call.

"You just hung up on my boss," said Kate, glaring at Talia.

"Yes. And I did it before he started giving you orders. Directors want to manage. Field operatives need to react. You were right about everything, but he didn't want to listen. I did you a favor and ended the call."

Kate looked back at the phone. Working outside of ISA had seemed like an easy decision when she suggested it, but now it was real and there was no going back. Talia and David were all she had.

Talia stood up and stretched. "I haven't eaten anything yet today and I'm starving. Let's get some lunch. We need to come up with a plan and I don't do my best thinking on an empty stomach."

∽

Peter stared at the phone as the line went dead. "Damn!" He looked over at Jacob. "Is Talia always that insubordinate?"

Jacob grinned. "She can be strong willed, but she and David are the best we have. You know why she cut the call off, right?"

Peter sagged back in his chair. "So they can keep a free hand. I get it. But Kate's not ready for that."

"I disagree. She lacks experience, yes, but Talia and David will guide her through the nuances. As for the mission itself, I couldn't argue with anything she said. Kate's got an intuitive feel for this. How is it she didn't end up in the field before now?"

"She's a top analyst. When someone's that good at their job, you tend to leave them where they are."

"She belongs in operations."

"I don't disagree, but that's a discussion for another day. Right now, she's been thrown into the fire unprepared and I'm depending on Mossad to get her through it."

Jacob smiled. "I've been doing this a long time, my friend. I spent many years in the field, as did you. I remember what it's like in that fire. You catch the spy. I'll watch over them."

A knock on the door interrupted the discussion. They both looked up as Nick Mueller stepped into the room. "Can I speak with you for a minute, boss?"

Jacob rose from his chair. "I need to make some calls."

Nick waited until he left and closed the door. "You've heard from Kate?" he asked as Peter waved him to a chair.

"Yes."

"And you didn't bring me in for the call? If you don't trust me …"

Peter waved him to silence. "It isn't that. Kate's been under the gun in Europe, and I mean that literally. She's not prepared for that kind of thing and the stress is getting to her. She wanted nobody but me and Jacob on that call, so I indulged her. Don't take it personally."

"Is there anything I should know?"

Peter decided now was the moment to set the trap. "They made it out of Russia, but she's had enough. She'll be flying home tomorrow.

That's a good thing because I think Artisimov's been holding back and I'm hoping she can get him to open up again."

"Maybe I should sit in when she talks to him."

"I'll take that under advisement. Now, if you'll excuse me, I've got an appointment upstairs."

Peter watched him go. The bait was set. Now all he could do was sit back and wait.

CHAPTER TWENTY-ONE

Talia pulled the car up to the curb. "Lunch time. Hungry?"

Kate stared up at the sign. "Seriously? A Taco Bell? We're in Finland. Isn't there some local food we can try? Something you can't get anywhere else?"

"You can't get this in Israel. Mixing meat and cheese isn't kosher, but I love Mexican food. This might not qualify as high cuisine, but it'll do. Indulge me."

They placed their orders at the counter and found an empty booth by the front window. Kate was finishing her burrito when a glance out at the sidewalk stopped her short. "We've got a problem."

Talia dropped her taco. "What's happening?"

"One of the men holding David on the ship just walked past."

"You're sure?"

"Yeah. How many guys wear a tie-dyed t-shirt under a sport coat? How do we handle this?"

Talia looked over at the entrance. "Walk out the front and turn left. There's an alley beside the building. If you're right, he's going to follow you. Lead him around to the back. I'll go out through the kitchen."

"What if it's not just him?"

"We duck back inside and call for help. But if he's alone and thinks you're cornered, then we've got him."

"Shouldn't we call the embassy for backup?"

"If every agent called for help at the first sign of trouble, a lot of valuable intel would never see the light of day. We've got this."

Kate wiped her hand on a napkin and walked to the door. Once outside, she turned left and into the alley. She ran to the back of the building and past the door leading out from the kitchen.

The Russian came around the corner seconds later, a 9mm Glock in his hand. "You're boxed in," he said in heavily accented English.

"That's exactly what I was thinking," said Talia as she came up behind him and placed the barrel of her gun against the back of his head. "Three of your friends have died today. I won't lose any sleep if you're the fourth. Toss the gun away."

It clattered along the concrete, stopping at Kate's feet. Talia took two steps backward. "Empty your pockets and drop everything on the ground. Do it slowly."

Keys, a wallet, some loose change, and a pocketknife fell to his feet.

"Now, raise up your pant legs," instructed Talia. "You don't seem like the type to go around with only one weapon."

He complied, revealing an ankle holster on his right leg containing a small, snub-nosed revolver.

"Grasp the gun by the grip with your thumb and forefinger," she commanded. "Put it on the ground and take four steps backward. Kate, collect the guns and his wallet and go start the car."

Seconds later, Talia and their prisoner emerged from the alley and climbed into the back seat. He had the start of an ugly purple bruise above his left eye, Talia's reminder of the consequences of non-compliance.

"Drive to the embassy," she directed.

Kate nodded. "What do we do with him?"

Talia pulled out her phone and began speaking in Hebrew. When the conversation ended, she shoved it back into her pocket. "Park by the rear entrance. Someone will come out and hand you an envelope."

"Then what?"

"Pull up a map of the city on your phone and drive to the docks. Our destination is a Turkish freighter named the Dizman. It's moored at Pier 7."

"We're leaving on a ship?"

"Not us. Just him. But not before we have an exchange of information."

"I will tell you nothing," said their captive.

Talia smiled. "I think you will. Or would you rather your body be dumped out at sea for the sharks to play with? Either way's fine with us."

His expression made clear which option he preferred. "What do you want?"

"Not yet," said Talia. "Once you're in the cargo hold of that ship, we'll talk, and I can guarantee the captain and his crew won't give a shit what happens to you."

A young woman was waiting for them. "Talia Levy?"

"In the back," Kate replied. "You have something for us?"

She handed a clipboard through the window. "What's this?" asked Kate. "I don't read Hebrew."

"It's a receipt," said Talia. "Damn bureaucrats. Just sign it."

Kate returned the clipboard and accepted a large manila envelope. "Now to the docks?"

"Yes."

Twenty minutes later, Kate braked to a stop beside a wharf-side warehouse. "This is it. That's the Dizman over there." She pointed to a rusty freighter moored to the dock.

"Get out and cover him," said Talia. "If he makes a break for it, shoot him. Okay, asshole. Climb out slowly and step aside."

"How does this work?" asked Kate.

"Mossad maintains a list of ship captains who smuggle weapons and people for Hamas, Hezbollah, and other terrorist organizations. Sometimes we allow them to continue to operate, but only under certain conditions. One is that they make their services available to us as needed. When I called Tel Aviv, I was informed that Captain Terzi and the Dizman were docked in Helsinki."

"Do you speak Turkish?"

"Well enough."

A wooden gangway ran from the ship to the dock below. A man with a week's growth of beard and an acrid cigar protruding from his lips lounged against a railing at the bottom. Talia spoke to him in Turkish. When he gestured for her to go away, she spoke more forcefully, and this time Kate recognized the name Terzi. He seemed uncertain until Talia leaned forward and added something else. Kate couldn't tell what was being said, but the man's eyes went wide. He picked up a handheld radio and spoke rapidly. When he put it back down, he nodded at Talia and motioned them up the gangway.

"What did you say to him?" asked Kate.

"I told him Interpol was aware of the contents of their cargo and I could offer Terzi a deal."

"What's the cargo?"

She shrugged. "How should I know? But Terzi's a smuggler. I'm sure there are things down there he would prefer no one knew about."

They were met at the top by a tall man who was only marginally less filthy than the crewman on the dock. He barked something at them in Turkish.

"Speak English," said Talia. "And we need to talk privately."

"About what?" He glanced at their captive. "You're not Interpol."

"That's correct. I'm Mossad."

The color drained from his face. "Follow me."

He led them along a musty corridor. The paint was peeling from the walls and the only illumination came from the bare light bulbs dangling from the ceiling. "In here," he said, opening a metal door. The room was small and unfurnished. "What is it you want?"

"This man is Russian OPG," said Talia. "We need to interrogate him in a place where no one will bother us. When we're done, he'll be remaining here."

"Alive or dead?"

"That's up to him. If he chooses not to cooperate, you can dump his body overboard after you sail."

Their prisoner turned pale and looked frantically around, hoping for a way out. Talia ignored him. "If he's still alive when we leave, you can do with him as you see fit. You may even be able to sell him back to his owners. This is for your trouble."

She handed him the envelope. "It contains $5,000 in U.S. currency. I'm sure that will buy us an hour in an empty cargo space."

Terzi opened the envelope and inspected the contents. "And then you'll leave?"

"Yes. I don't want to spend any more time in this filthy shit hole than I have to."

Terzi ignored her opinion of his ship. "Come with me."

They descended a series of metal staircases. The stench made Kate want to vomit, but this wasn't the time to show weakness.

"This cargo hold is empty at the moment." He kicked at a rat scampering across the deck and handed Talia a radio. "Call me when you're done." He grinned at the Russian. "I hope he won't bleed too much. My men don't enjoy cleaning up messes."

"Obviously," replied Talia. "You may leave us now. And if I catch anyone trying to eavesdrop, there'll be an even bigger mess to clean up."

He nodded and closed the door behind him. Talia took their prisoner by the arm and fastened his hands behind his back with a plastic cable tie. She marched him over to a stack of three wooden pallets and shoved him down onto them. "Okay, Kate. This is your mission. Find out whatever you need to."

She had never interrogated anyone and wondered how she should begin. On TV, they always did the good cop/bad cop routine. Talia had definitely established herself as the bad cop, so maybe she could play off that.

"What's your name?" she asked their captive, using Russian so that there'd be no confusion over what she wanted.

"I'll tell you whatever you want, but you can't leave me here.

He's not going to go to the trouble of negotiating with my bosses, not after you paid him all that money. He'll cut my throat and be done with it."

"She asked for your name," demanded Talia, advancing with her weapon drawn. Her Russian might not be fluent, but it was good enough for this.

Kate held up her hand. "There's no need for this to get ugly. Not yet anyway. We can talk about what happens to you later. If what you give me is valuable enough, I'll see what I can do, and that's the best I can offer you for now. What's your name?"

"Mikhail."

"Okay, Mikhail. You're OPG. Which organization?"

"Serapov."

It was time to see just how forthcoming he would be. "Is Vladimir still calling the shots?"

"Nyet. He was murdered last year. His son Stefan is in charge now."

"Very good, Mikhail. That was a test. Keep it up and this might end well for you. Your team was sent to find out much I know, correct?"

He shrugged.

"My friend here has a temper," said Kate, gesturing at Talia. "If I were you, I wouldn't test her patience."

His eyes darted toward Talia, and then quickly looked away. "In Moscow, the job was to kill you. When you got away, it became important to find out how much you'd learned. We used our contacts at the Russian port to get four of us onto the ship. A fifth man was to meet us in Helsinki, but he's dead." He glanced at Talia once more. "You killed him on the dock, yes? He was my cousin."

"Let's stay on topic," said Kate. "How did you find out we'd be using that ship to get out of Russia?"

"They had a source, but I know nothing about that."

Kate was certain he was telling the truth. He was a foot soldier in a crime family. The odds that he had access to intel sources would be slim. "The woman I talked to at the port, she was in charge?"

"Natasha, yes."

Kate began ticking the names off on her fingers. "Yuri fell down the stairs and broke his neck. Natasha was killed on the dock and your cousin was supposed to be her backup. He's dead as well, so how many are left?"

"Me and Pavel. We were on the ship watching your friend."

"Who killed Natasha?"

"Pavel. He said he had orders from Stefan to eliminate her if she got caught. She knew too much to be allowed to talk."

"Is that the usual practice?"

He shook his head. "Normally she would have been disciplined personally by Stefan for her failure, but I think he wanted no loose ends to connect us with the client."

Now it came down to the key question. "And who is that?"

Mikhail hesitated and then looked away. "I don't know."

Talia stepped forward and whipped the butt of her gun across his face. "I don't believe you."

Blood poured from a cut on his cheek, and he spat two teeth out onto the floor. Kate swallowed the bile rising in her throat and tried to appear calm. "Let's try that again, Mikhail. Who's paying Stefan for this?"

He licked blood from his lips. "He'll have me killed if he finds out I told you. I don't know who it is for certain anyway."

"But you can make a good guess, can't you?"

"Maybe. If I get off this ship with you, I'll tell you what I know."

"You don't get to set terms. Who is it?"

He shook his head. "Nyet."

Talia jammed the barrel of her gun into his crotch. He screamed in pain, falling off the pallets face down onto the deck. Kate waited until he stopped writhing and his moans diminished to heavy breathing. A rat emerged from behind the pallets and began licking at the blood on the deck.

"The next time it will be a bullet in your knee," said Kate, forcing herself to keep her voice level. "You can't win here, Mikhail. All you can do is suffer a lot of pain and then die an ugly death. Is it worth that?"

He looked up at her. "The day before we got our assignment about you, I was at Stefan's dacha." He paused, sucking in deep breaths. "It was a birthday party for his niece, and I was part of the security. When I got there, he was inside meeting with three men."

He moaned as he tried to sit up.

"You don't know who they were?" asked Kate.

"No, but they looked Middle Eastern, and I heard them talking when they left. They weren't speaking Arabic."

"How would you know that?"

"My girlfriend is from Syria. I speak it a little."

"Could it have been Farsi?"

He shrugged. "Maybe."

"Let's get back to today. How did you know we were at the Taco Bell?"

"I followed you from the dock to the Israeli embassy, and then to the restaurant. Pavel remained near the ship in case you returned for your friend."

"What will he do now?"

"We failed at Kask and again today. Most of the team is dead. He'll report back and hope to survive Stefan's wrath. He doesn't tolerate failure easily."

Kate walked away and motioned for Talia to follow. "What do you think?"

"If Iranian intelligence contracted with the Serapov organization, that would fit your theory. But that assumes those men were speaking Farsi, and that this guy's telling the truth. Not exactly a lock."

"No, but it's more than we had. Iran being behind this makes total sense. They've got a lot at stake."

"I agree, but we need proof."

Kate glanced over at Mikhail. "Which we're not going to get from him. What do we do with him?"

"Just what we said. Leave him."

"He's probably right. Terzi will kill him."

"He chose his path when he went to work for the Serapov's. Whatever happens, it isn't on us."

Kate shook her head. "I can't be that cold about it. Call Terzi."

The captain joined them within minutes. He regarded their bloodied prisoner with a smile. "I trust you got what you wanted."

"That's not your concern," said Kate. "I'm leaving him with you, but I'm going to let his OPG family know where he is. They'll want him back, so if you're going to stay off their shit list, you'll keep him alive. Understand?"

"The five thousand doesn't cover the cost of a passenger."

"It better," said Talia. "Or Mossad may take a much closer interest in your activities. If your ship was to be confiscated, where would that leave you?"

Terzi spit on the deck. "I curse Mossad."

"You and half the rest of the world," she replied. "It doesn't change anything. Make sure he stays breathing. Now you can escort us off this stinking garbage scow."

When they got back to the car, the reaction set in and Kate felt herself start to tremble. "I never thought I'd be capable of something like that."

"Mikhail's a mercenary scumbag who's damn lucky you let him live. The ones we're up against aren't people worth caring about, Kate. They've already tried to kill you once. Sometimes getting information out of them is the only thing standing between success and failure, or even death. In the field, you do what you have to and move on."

"The niceties of normal life don't apply in this line of work," Kate recited. "That's what Peter said before he sent me to Paris. I didn't really understand what he meant until now."

"Forget about Mikhail," said Talia. "We got everything we could, and then you gave him a chance to survive. I wouldn't have bothered."

"Stefan Serapov will probably have him killed anyway."

"But he'll be alive until then. So, what happens now?"

Kate sighed. "I need to think. There has to be a way to stop this."

CHAPTER TWENTY-TWO

Upon their return to the embassy, Kate and Talia went once more to the sub-basement conference room. Talia pulled a chair away from the table and settled into it, watching as Kate paced back and forth, her hands shoved into her pockets and her eyes fixed on the floor in front of her.

"Does that help you think? Or are you just getting in your steps?"

Kate paused and looked over at her. "Sorry. What?"

"Are you getting anywhere?"

"Maybe. But I don't like it. The only person at ISA I've spoken to is Peter, and yet information is still getting back to Iran."

"You think Peter's the mole? I find that hard to accept."

Kate joined her at the table. "Me too. If he were spying for Iran, he'd never have sent an inexperienced rookie to Paris when so much was at stake. Too much could go wrong. But he doesn't operate in a vacuum."

"Anyone specific in mind?"

"Not really, but anyone he shared information with would be at the top levels of ISA."

"Which should make it easier to solve."

Kate shook her head. "Just the opposite. You can't start accusing or even begin looking into those people without something solid to base it on, and right now we've got nothing but a theory."

"Then what's our next step? Do we still go to Geneva?"

"I've been thinking about that. Yes, we still go. But we're going to flip the script."

"Huh?"

"You talked to Peter and Jacob about what was on that flash drive, right?"

"Yes."

"Then we have to assume Iran knows about Geneva. They'll tip off the Russians and it could turn into Kask all over again."

Talia nodded. "I assume that by flipping the script you mean changing the plan."

"Exactly. We'll fly into Bern, where nobody will be looking for us. It's only a short drive from there to Geneva. Then we proceed with the plan, but I won't be going to meet my contact. You will."

Talia's eyes widened in surprise. "He won't talk to just anyone, remember? He's expecting it to be you."

"Think it through. Russia and Iran may have a source, but they don't have all that much to go on. I don't know who my contact is, so neither do they. And they'll be looking for me, not you. You're right, he won't disclose anything to you, but that's okay. You'll explain the situation and arrange a different meeting, one that nobody but us will know about."

"And if he's not willing to do that?"

Kate shrugged. "Then we're no worse off than we are now."

Talia rubbed her hand across her forehead. "This cloak and dagger bullshit gives me a headache. Dimitri Artisimov set the whole thing up. Have Peter tell him that none of this is going to happen the way he planned it, and we need a name. Then we go to Geneva, but nobody goes to the pre-arranged meeting. Not me and not you. We go to him."

"But we decided I can't contact Peter."

"Jacob can."

Kate considered that. It was one thing for Jacob to keep Peter in the loop, but if he appeared to be taking an active role, the mole might start to wonder. "My contact has to be someone fairly high in the government or the military. How many of those types are going to be in Geneva on that day? Call Tel Aviv and ask them to dig into it. If we can narrow the possibilities down to one or two people, then we can go to Dimitri for confirmation. And we won't go through Jacob. I have a better idea."

"Want to share?"

"Not yet. While they're figuring out which Russians might be in play, have them look into Stefan Serapov as well. He might be our best bet for proving Iran's behind all this."

"But you can't go back into Russia. That would be suicide."

"I'm hoping we can find another way. Make the call, Talia. In the meantime, I need to find a quiet place to do some thinking."

"There are some guest rooms on the top floor. I'll let you know when I have something."

∽

Kate came alert at the sound of someone knocking on the door.

"Come in," she called, rubbing the sleep from her eyes.

Talia entered, trailed by David. "Look who turned up." She grinned at the sight of Kate stretched out on the bed. "That's how you do your best thinking? Laying down with your eyes closed?"

"It's been a tough day." She sat up and ran her fingers through her tangled hair. "I haven't even had a chance to shower yet." Her eyes moved to David. "How're you feeling?"

"Embarrassed for letting myself be taken that easily."

"I meant your head."

"Nothing aspirin can't handle."

"Good. What happened?"

He described waking up to voices outside their door and going to investigate. "When I came to, I was somewhere down in the hold."

"They were after me," said Kate. "If you hadn't been sleeping on the sofa, they might have gotten us both. Did Talia fill you in on what's happened?"

He nodded. "It sounds like you had it under control."

"Hardly, but it turned out okay."

"Not to change the subject, but I got a response from Tel Aviv," said Talia. "Maybe we should focus on that."

"That was fast," said Kate.

"You came up here to think almost three hours ago," said Talia, not bothering to hide a grin.

Kate felt herself turning red. "Oh. Uh, what did we find out?"

"Let's go downstairs where no one will be tempted to listen in."

Once seated around the table, Talia pulled out a notepad. "A U.N. anti-terrorism conference is taking place in Geneva this week. The Russian delegation is headed by Gen. Alexander Kruzov."

Kate nodded. "That would make sense. He commands their army's anti-terror forces."

"Yes. It seems he and Dimitri are friends going back to their college days. I think Kruzov is the man you're supposed to meet."

"What do we know about him?"

Talia laid a file folder on the table. "He's in significant debt, as are many of Russia's military officers. The sanctions imposed by the West resulted in serious financial shortfalls. Payrolls were hit especially hard, and his daughters were both attending a university in Germany. He borrowed heavily to keep them there and away from the chaos at home. Maybe we could use that."

"We're not looking for ways to coerce him," said David. "If we're right about him being Kate's contact, then he's already on our side. We just need a way to reach out to him."

Kate continued to scan his dossier. "According to this, he's developed a taste for high end call girls since his wife died. You don't suppose he's got something lined up while he's in Geneva? If he does, she'll be in the same room with him. Alone."

"And we find a way for you to be that girl," said Talia. "I like it."

"I don't," said David. "You'd have no backup at all. It's too risky."

"Do you have a better idea?" asked Kate. "Otherwise, we can all go home and watch it play out on TV. The Cold War all over again, except this time Israel will face a nuclear threat as well."

"She's right," said Talia. "But how do we go about making it work?"

David locked his gaze directly on Kate. "You're sure about this?"

"I don't see another way."

He nodded. "Then let's think it through. He'll be using an escort service, not some random hooker off the street. Every major city has one that politicians and other high-level people can count on for their discretion and the quality of their girls." He took out his phone. "I'll find out who it is in Geneva."

Kate's mind returned to another problem. "And we need to be sure we're on the right track. Do either of you have a burner I can use?"

Talia produced a phone from her bag. "Who are you calling?"

"A friend."

Kate dialed a number and put it on speaker. The call was answered on the third ring. "Hello?"

"Monica? It's Kate."

"Kate? Where the hell are you? You're supposed to be back at work, but nobody's seen you. There're all kinds of rumors."

"Are you out of the hospital yet?"

"Yeah. I'm at home catching up on email and trying not to die from boredom. I'll be starting back part-time tomorrow. What's going on?"

"I can't tell you, but I need a favor. Call Peter Schilling." Kate recited the number for Peter's private cell. "Tell him the original plan is no longer in play. He should ask Dimitri if my contact was supposed to be Alexander Kruzov. He'll know what you're talking about. Emphasize that he can tell no one about this.. Call me back at this number when you have an answer."

"Ask Dimitri if your contact was Alexander Kruzov. Who's Dimitri?"

"Not now. Just call me when you get an answer."

"Got it. Are you okay?"

"I'm fine, Monica. But I need to get off this line. I'll be waiting for your call."

"Who's Monica?" asked Talia.

Kate shoved the phone into her pocket. "My best friend."

"I'm not sure we should bring other people into this."

"She's ISA and was in the car with me in Riyadh. We can trust her. Did you find out anything about the Serapov organization?"

Talia consulted her notes once more. "Not much. It's a criminal enterprise with virtually no presence in the Middle East, but we did come up with something interesting about Stefan's personal life. He has a sister who's distanced herself from the rest of the family. She's divorced but continues to use her ex-husband's last name instead of Serapova."

"And that helps us how?"

"She owns a chain of upscale clothing boutiques. The first one was in Moscow, but she expanded and has shops in several European cities. When the Russian economy started going south under the weight of the sanctions, she moved her base of operations to London. If you want to get to Stefan Serapov, she might be the way to do it."

She hesitated. "And there's something else. Jason Collier died this morning. He survived the initial surgery, but there were complications."

Kate nodded. She'd only known Jason for one day in Riyadh and another in Paris, but the news hit her hard. He was sometimes dismissive and annoyingly condescending, but he'd been her first partner and got her through the chaos of the ambush. Now he was just another death on a constantly expanding list. How many more names would be added before this was over?

David had been having a lengthy conversation on the phone, which ended with him jotting down a name and number on the desk pad. "Geneva is the site for a lot of international conferences, so Mossad put considerable effort into establishing assets there. Sophie Bernard is the madame who services the high-end clientele in the city. Her women are sophisticated, educated, and expensive. I was told she'll be willing to cooperate."

"Then that's our play," said Kate. "But first we need Dimitri to confirm we're on the right track."

The words were no sooner out of her mouth when the phone rang. The screen displayed Monica's number. "Kate, it's me. You were right about Kruzov. And your boss wants to talk to you."

Kate thought for a minute. "Tell him I can't. He'll know why. Thanks, Monica."

"You're going to tell me everything, right?"

"When I can."

She hung up before Monica could begin asking more questions. "That nails it down."

"So, what now?" asked David.

"We go to Geneva."

CHAPTER TWENTY-THREE

Peter stretched out on his office sofa, staring at the ceiling. The trap for the mole was in place, but so far nothing had come of it and time was not on his side. To make matters worse, Kate continued to distance herself. He couldn't blame her given the situation, but a critical intelligence operation was now solely in the hands of an inexperienced operative working with a foreign entity. The whole thing had fallen completely off the rails, and he didn't like it. For someone used to having full control, he now had none.

His desk phone rang, snapping him out of his frustrated musings. "Schilling."

"Sir, the CIA director is on the line and demanding to speak with you."

He came instantly alert. "Put her through."

"Dammit, Peter, you and Carl lied to me."

"Slow down, Susan. What exactly did I lie about?"

"Kate Malone. You denied she had anything to do with the Artisimov defection, but I know she's on her way back from Europe to continue debriefing him. This is outrageous. If I were you, I'd start preparing my resignation letter."

"Susan, there's a piece of this you know nothing about. I suggest we talk. Carl's office in an hour?"

"I want Warren to be there as well. He should hear about your deception firsthand."

"Your privilege. One hour."

He hung up as a smile spread across his face.

~

Susan entered Carl's office trailed by Warren Sinclair, his serious expression offset by her air of triumph. They each took a seat at the conference table across from Carl and Peter.

"I'm sorry it's come to this," she began, bypassing any attempt at pleasantries. "I gave you every opportunity to deal with this openly, but you insisted on ignoring all the normal protocols and locking my agency out of a matter of great national concern."

"If what Susan told me is true, there will be consequences," added Warren. "Deceiving the CIA cannot be condoned or tolerated, nor can lying to the chair of the Intelligence Committee."

Carl held up his hand before either of them could continue. "Before we jump to conclusions and start handing out punishments, there are some things you should both know. We're going to give you an honest and complete briefing, after which we can decide on appropriate actions."

"I can't imagine that anything you say could change the facts," said Susan. "But go ahead. This should be interesting."

"Peter will walk you through it."

Peter glanced down at his notes before beginning. "This started with the Artisimov defection. And you're right, we deceived you on that, but for a valid reason."

"Which was?" asked Susan, her skepticism lacing each word.

"He requested Kate by name. She was the only one he'd talk to. Even though she was still technically on medical leave, I sent her to Paris to find out what this was about. She'd barely arrived when Russian agents hit the safe house in an attempt to retake or eliminate Artisimov. After that, Kate and Dimitri were on the run, and we locked it down. You'd have done the same."

Warren nodded. "I can accept that, assuming you were going to tell us at some point."

"Of course," Carl responded. "But somebody leaked Kate's involvement and made sure she'd be easy to follow to the safe house. It was clear we needed to proceed with caution."

"And have you uncovered the source of the leak?" asked Susan.

Peter nodded. "But I believe this is a bigger operation than just one deeply buried mole."

Susan's condescending expression turned to one of confusion. "I'm not sure I understand."

"You will. Based on what she learned from Dimitri, Kate went to Moscow to reach out to certain people. While she was there, an attempt was made to kill her."

"You used an untrained rookie for a mission like that? Are you mad?"

"Her regular job provided the necessary cover, and she had backup. Kate's been working this as a joint operation with Mossad. What Dimitri brought to us had serious implications for both Israel and the United States."

"Excuse me," said Warren. "Are you saying you read in a foreign agency about an intelligence matter without consulting anyone?"

"It didn't happen like that. Jason Collier took Kate and Dimitri to a Mossad safe house after the attack. There was no other viable option. One of their agents overheard Dimitri talking to Kate. No decision was made by either Carl or me to take this to Israel. It just happened. But while Kate was in Russia, further leaks occurred, and something became clear. The source was somewhere inside ISA because no one outside the agency had been read in."

"Then you should have turned everything over to me immediately," said Susan. "This makes it all even worse, Warren. Surely you can see that?"

"There was a reason we couldn't bring this to you," said Peter. "Wherever else the leaked intel ended up, it was going to the CIA as well. Nobody outside ISA knew what Kate was doing, and she went to Paris using a cover identity. But you, Susan, came storming in here a few days ago knowing all about it. We weren't sure how you found out, but it was clear we needed to proceed carefully. That's why you were kept in the dark."

Sinclair intervened before she could respond. "This mole is still in place?"

"For the moment. We plugged the leak temporarily by having Kate work solely through Mossad. That shut off the flow of information and neutralized the spy. But we still needed to find out how Susan was getting her information and if the mole worked directly for her."

"That's outrageous!" exclaimed Susan. "You're essentially accusing me of being a traitor."

Sinclair waved her to silence. "Let them continue."

"I came to suspect someone on my staff," said Peter, ignoring her outburst. "I told him that Kate was giving up and returning home to resume debriefing Artisimov. It was a lie and absolutely nobody else was let in on it, not even Carl. But you came here today armed with that knowledge."

"I ... I'd never ... There has to be some kind of explanation."

"How did you become aware of the lie I planted?" Peter demanded.

"That's not your concern," she replied defensively.

"The leaks are ending up in Russia and endangering the life of my agent," snapped Peter. "That makes it my concern. Actually, it makes it everyone's concern."

Carl leaned forward in his chair. "You came here making accusations and talking about resignations. Now the situation is reversed. I suggest you come clean unless you want me to take this to the president."

Sinclair nodded. "I agree. Time to put your cards on the table, Susan."

She rubbed her hand across her forehead. "My chief of staff has a contact here at ISA. I don't know who it is."

"Who's your chief of staff?"

"Josh Griswold. And if you think he's spying for Russia, you're wrong. He's been with me for eight years and went through a thorough background check before he got the job." She paused to collect herself. "I was trying to gain an edge, an inside track on something I thought should be CIA's responsibility. I'll admit I used questionable judgement, and what I did might be considered unethical, but that's the extent of it."

"Are you sure about that?" asked Peter.

"I don't know what you're talking about."

"I'm not accusing you of leaking information to Russia. But you made sure an embassy limo picked Kate up at the airport in Paris. It's the only scenario that makes sense. You wanted her to lead your people to Artisimov. She led the Russians there instead."

She turned a dark crimson. "Susan?" inquired Sinclair. "Is that true?"

A barely perceptible nod answered the question. "I only wanted to find out what was going on. But she left the car in a crowded part of the city and my people lost her. They were going to talk to the driver when he returned to the embassy, but he never did."

"Because the Russians intercepted him and got the address of the safe house," said Peter, his disgust coming through with each word. "Four people died that morning because you wanted to turn Artisimov's defection into a political win. To make it even worse, Jason Collier died from his wounds this morning."

"I didn't mean for any of that to happen," she replied weakly.

"And we still don't know where the leak to the Russians is coming from. You may not be the traitor, but information in your possession was being used by the spy. It comes back to you either way."

She straightened in her chair, visibly trying to regroup. "I know, and I'll get some answers. I promise."

"I'm afraid it's gone too far for that," said Sinclair. "You need to step aside, Susan. At least until this is resolved and we have all the facts. If you refuse, Carl won't have to take it to the president. I will. That's not an optimal outcome for anyone."

"Warren, please. I can handle it. I'll make this right."

He shook his head. "I'm afraid that's no longer possible. What you've done can't be condoned as business as usual, and I won't be part of a coverup. It's over, Susan."

She swallowed and turned her eyes to Peter and Carl. "I owe you an apology. It seems you handled this appropriately, and I stepped way over the line. Warren, I'll prepare a letter for the president requesting a leave of absence to deal with a family matter. Is that sufficient?"

"For now. I'm sorry it came to this."

"As am I." She collected her coat and briefcase and left the room.

Warren waited until the door closed behind her. "CIA can't be trusted to investigate themselves. I should probably bring in the FBI."

"Why don't you give us a little time?" suggested Peter. "If the FBI gets involved, the whole thing is bound to go public. There'll be congressional hearings and it'll turn into a field day for the media. It might come to that eventually, but let's avoid it if we can. The leak is plugged for now. We should try to do this quietly."

"I'm sure I don't need to remind you of the political implications," added Carl. "Any ambitions you might have down the road will take a hit if a scandal at CIA becomes public knowledge."

Warren smiled weakly. "I'm way ahead of you. But national security issues can't be ignored. Do us all a favor and clean this up quickly."

Carl waited until the door closed behind him. "I'll authorize a deep dive into Griswold. Beyond that, what's our next step?"

"The flow of information out of ISA is cut off for now, so I want to leave Mueller in place for the time being," said Peter. "We used him to expose Susan without him catching on. He may prove useful again. I want to give Kate a chance to get some answers."

"Your call. Just be careful."

CHAPTER TWENTY-FOUR

Kate walked through the hotel lobby and made her way to the elevators. The Novotel's chrome and glass exterior and modern décor gave it an American feel in a city where the French influence in architecture was everywhere. It was like a little taste of home, and its location close to the U.N.'s offices at the Palais de Nations meant Kruzov had to be staying somewhere nearby.

It was a relief to be off everyone's radar. She'd been on the run in Moscow and Helsinki, but Geneva felt like a safe harbor in a storm. She had to assume Iranian intelligence had learned she was coming here, but Geneva was a large city and the anonymity it provided gave her a level of comfort and security she hadn't felt since arriving in Paris.

She dropped her packages on the bed and was heading for the bathroom when someone knocked on the door. "Service de ménage," called a female voice. "Housekeeping."

"Just a moment." Kate surveyed the room, making sure she hadn't left anything out that might arouse suspicion. Her weapon and various passports were locked away in the room safe, and nothing left in view would attract undue attention. With a nod of satisfaction, she went to the door. A glance through the peephole revealed two women in maids' uniforms. A wheeled laundry bin for collecting used towels and bedding stood behind them.

She unlatched the door. "Good timing. I'm leaving for an appointment and …"

She got no further before the first woman clamped a hand towel over her face. The chemical odor was overpowering, and Kate felt herself losing consciousness as the room swirled around her. The last thing she remembered was being dumped into the laundry bin.

∽

Talia knocked on Kate's door. Getting no response, she tried once more with the same result. They had requested two keys for each room when they checked in and swapped the spares. She pulled Kate's from her wallet and went inside. A quick look around revealed nothing out of place, but a faint chemical odor lingered in the air.

She went back out to the hallway, practically bumping into a maid carrying a stack of towels. "Excuse me. Have you seen anyone else on this floor? Or anything that seemed unusual or out of place?"

"Just another housekeeping crew," the maid replied in heavily accented English. "I told them they were on the wrong floor."

"Were they part of the usual staff?"

The maid shook her head. "Never see them before."

"How long ago was this?"

"Maybe twenty minutes." She pointed down the hallway. "They went that way, toward the elevators. Is something wrong? Should I call down to the office?"

"It's okay. Sorry to bother you."

Talia pulled out her phone and waited until the maid was out of earshot before calling David. "Kate's gone and I can smell chloroform in her room. There were people on the floor posing as housekeeping staff."

"But nobody knows where we're staying."

"That's a problem for later. Right now, we have to find her. Taking her out through the lobby would be way too public. Check the loading dock in the back. See if anyone saw anything. I'll work my way down from here."

She found David waiting for her on the dock. He gestured at a man kneeling beside a dismantled piece of machinery. "He's been working on that trash compactor for the last hour. He says nobody's come or gone."

"I spoke to her on the phone since then," said Talia. "If they couldn't take her out the front and didn't take her out the back, then what?"

"There are other ways out of the building, but they're all equipped with surveillance cameras. The dock would be the easiest way out, so maybe she's still in the hotel."

Talia nodded. "I'll check out the basement. Go to the office and see if any of those doors were activated. We may not have much time."

∽

Kate's return to consciousness was slow and cluttered with images and sounds she could make no sense of. The ceiling fan slowly rotating above her made her dizzy and faintly nauseous. She closed her eyes and took several slow, deep breaths to settle things down. When she opened them once more, the room came into focus, but an attempt to sit up brought on another wave of dizziness, causing her to sag back onto the pillow. She tried to rub her eyes, only to find her right wrist handcuffed to the bed.

"You're finally awake. Good." The voice spoke English with a pronounced Russian accent.

She turned her head toward the sound. A man sat at the writing desk.

"Who are you?" she whispered.

"That's irrelevant. You've been difficult to track down."

Her eyes scanned the rest of the room. Except for the pictures on the wall, it was a duplicate of hers. She was still in the hotel, which meant David and Talia were close by. She looked back at her captor.

His short-sleeved shirt revealed arms free of the tattoos commonly displayed by members of OPG families. "You're SVR."

He shrugged. "As I said, irrelevant. You came to Geneva to meet someone. Who?"

Kate turned her head away.

"Miss Malone, how we proceed is entirely up to you. I suggest you make it easy on yourself."

She looked at the bedside clock. The knock on her door had come almost an hour ago. Talia and David would be looking for her by now, and maybe she could buy them some time if she played this right. "You're too late."

"Too late for what?"

"You're right. I came to meet someone."

He smiled. "Very good. You choose the easy path. Who are you to meet?"

She shrugged. "Your guess is as good as mine."

The smile faded to a frown. "You expect me to believe that?"

"I was given a flash drive in Moscow. It contained the how and when and where. There was nothing about who."

"When is this meeting to take place?"

"Thirty minutes ago, in the bar of the Hotel Bristol. I didn't show, so I'm sure everyone involved is long gone." It was the truth so far as it went. That had been the original time and place for the meeting.

He straightened in the chair. "And I'm supposed to believe that?"

She swung her legs down so that she could sit on the edge of the bed. "The drive was in my right pants pocket. I'm sure you found it."

He picked it up from the desk. "It's encrypted."

"The key is my name. Kaitlyn Malone. All one word, all lowercase. See for yourself."

He opened the laptop lying on the desk and typed in the key. He scanned rapidly through the document, his frown deepening as he went.

Kate watched him carefully. If she could convince him this whole thing was pointless, she might walk out of here. "You can see I'm telling the truth. If you'd followed me instead of kidnapping me, you'd have your answers by now. You screwed up."

He slammed the laptop shut. "You don't know who you were to meet?"

"Not a clue."

He thought for a moment. "Artisimov set this up, correct?"

She nodded. "He put it all in place before he defected."

"You debriefed him?"

"I met him at a safehouse in Paris, but you already know that. He gave me the basics of what Russia's planning, but that drive contains a lot more information than I got from him. Your people hit the safehouse before he could go into detail. After our escape, he was flown to Washington, and I went to Moscow."

Her interrogator glanced back at the laptop. "The man killed at Kask worked at the Ministry of Defense. He gave you the drive?"

"Yes."

"Who killed him? Despite what the police think, I know it wasn't you. You had no reason to want him dead."

Kate's mind raced. Revealing the involvement of the Serapov organization was something to be avoided until she knew more. "I assumed it was you."

His look of uncertainty gave her an opening to divert the conversation. "How did you know I'd be at this hotel?"

"I ask the questions, not you."

"I've told you everything. There's no point to this."

"You got out of both France and Russia without leaving a trace. You're an analyst, not an operative. How did you manage it?"

The question took Kate by surprise. The mole had to know Mossad was involved, but this guy clearly didn't. Iran was being selective about what they passed on to the Russians. An interesting item for later consideration.

"ISA has resources for situations like that."

"You had backup?"

"Of course I did. They weren't going to send me in there alone. Would you?"

"Then you have backup here as well."

"From a distance, but I don't know who it is. We didn't want to spook my contact."

He drummed his fingers on the surface of the desk. "My instructions give me two options. I can choose to terminate you, or I can bring you back to Russia if I think you have additional value. Congratulations. You've earned the right to keep breathing. For now, anyway."

Kate's stomach churned. A return to Moscow would subject her to endless interrogation and would end with a long stay in a Russian prison, or possibly worse.

Her captor stood and knocked on the door to a connecting room. "I need to make a call," he said to the man who opened it. "It might take a while. Watch her."

The second man nodded and closed the door behind his boss. Kate tried frantically to think of a way out. Any opportunity to escape would end once the first man returned. A pad and pen resting on the bedside table gave her an idea.

"I need to use the bathroom or things are going to get messy. Can you let me take care of it?"

The guard looked uncertain and glanced back at the door.

"Please? You'll be doing yourself a favor because he'll probably make you clean it up. What's the harm? You've got that gun and I'm a prisoner."

His eyes roamed over her body. "Be quick. He won't like it if he finds out."

He unlocked the cuffs. She stood and then staggered sideways, grabbing the bedside table for support.

"Sorry. The chloroform left me weak," she said as she palmed the pen.

He came over and rested his hand on her ass. "Maybe later you can thank me for not letting you pee yourself. I can make things easier for you if you cooperate. A sexy American would be a first for me."

Kate straightened. "Sure. Why not?"

He pulled her to him and kissed her, his breath reeking of onions. She waited until he pulled back and then thrust upward with the pen, aiming for the soft spot just above the sternum. With any luck, it would penetrate his trachea.

He reacted quickly and tried to grab her arm but missed and only managed to deflect the blow. The point of the pen struck him on his right cheek and slid up into his eye. He screamed in pain and fell to his knees as blood ran down his face.

She made a dash for the door before his boss could respond to the uproar. Ignoring the elevator, she ran down the staircase to the third floor and sprinted to Talia's room, pounding on the door in desperation. It opened almost immediately, and she fell across the threshold. David dragged her inside as Talia made sure the hallway was empty.

"We have to hurry," said Kate. "They'll know which room I came to once they get a look at the hotel security video. We've got to be gone. Now."

David stuffed a laptop into a duffle along with the weapons, phones, and passports. "Everything else is expendable. Let's go."

They ran down a stairwell and out a fire exit on the side of the building. The drug had worn off and the adrenaline surging through her system had Kate's heart racing. She took deep breaths to calm herself. Several taxis were parked at the curb, and they climbed into the first one in line.

After changing cabs three times, they arrived at a hotel located as far away from their old one as possible. Talia and Kate waited in a corner of the lobby while David booked them into a room. Once inside, Kate collapsed onto one of the matching queen beds.

"What happened?" asked Talia, taking a seat on the other.

"There was a knock on my door. I thought it was housekeeping, but when I opened it, they put the rag over my face and dumped me into a laundry cart. I woke up cuffed to a bed."

"OPG again?"

Kate shook her head. "SVR. How did they find out where we were?"

"Peter knew about Geneva," said David, "so we assume the mole did as well. How they found where we were staying is another question. Have you gone anywhere alone since we got here? Or made any phone calls?"

"No calls. I made a trip to the convenience store down the street this morning. There were some things I needed, but I was only out of the hotel for maybe twenty minutes."

"Did you use a credit card?"

"Yes. The Diane Sullivan one. The identity we used on the ship."

David nodded. "That's it then. That card was registered on the ship for on board purchases. If Iran got into the ship's computer system and figured that out, they'd have passed that bit of information on to the Russians. Once the card was flagged, they knew where you were the moment you used it and the nearest hotel would be the first place they'd check. Never go back to an identity you've already abandoned. This is what can happen."

"How did you get away?" asked Talia.

Kate related the details of her interrogation and subsequent escape.

"Nice work," said David. "But now they have the flash drive."

"I don't think it matters. The meeting was never going to happen and there was nothing else on there the Russians didn't already know. But now they realize how much we know, and that might give them pause." Kate sat up on the bed. "I need a shower. And some clothes. A toothbrush too. That guy's breath stank."

"There's a shop across the street," said Talia. "I'll get what you need."

A hot shower worked wonders and left her feeling like herself again. She emerged from the bathroom wrapped in a towel just as Talia returned carrying two large bags. She deposited them on the bed. "That should be enough to get you by for a couple of days."

Kate flashed a grateful smile and returned to the bathroom with her new wardrobe. She came back out dressed in a tan t-shirt and jeans to find David signing for a room service cart loaded with an array of sandwiches and a large bowl of fruit. Kate selected roast beef on a Kaiser roll and added an apple and a banana. She took a bottled water from the mini fridge and sat on the edge of the bed, tearing into the food like she hadn't been fed in days.

"So, what do we do now?" she asked between mouthfuls.

"This is your call, Kate," said David.

Once again it was up to her, but this time she was ready with an answer. "Quitting isn't an option. Not when we still have a chance and so much is at stake. We came here to approach Kruzov. I don't see any reason to change plans."

"I agree," said Talia. "How do we do this?"

David pulled out his phone. "I have Sophie Bernard's number. Let's see how willing she is to cooperate."

The call was answered on the second ring. "Allo?"

"Madame Bernard. I was given this number by a mutual friend. He said to remind you of that afternoon in Bern."

There was silence on the line for several seconds. "This is not a good time."

"Unfortunately, time is of the essence. My associate and I need to speak with you as soon as possible."

Another silence. "Come to the Four Seasons hotel in one hour. Suite 201." The line went dead.

"She didn't sound happy," said Kate.

"Nobody's ever happy about being coerced by Mossad," replied Talia. "I assume it will just be the two of you?"

"You're the backup this time," said David. "With any luck, Kruzov's arranged for an evening with one of her girls."

∼

The door to 201 opened on the first knock. The woman who answered wore a severe expression. "You are the one who called?"

"Yes. We have Bern in common. May we come in?"

She stepped aside. "What do you want?"

"We're interested in one of your clients. Alexander Kruzov."

"I'm not familiar with him," she responded in a firm voice.

"That's too bad. I'll inform Tel Aviv that you wouldn't cooperate." He turned toward the door.

"Wait. What about Kruzov?"

David smiled. "Better. Does he have an arrangement with you?"

"Possibly."

He stared at her until she finally looked away. "Alright, he's a client."

"He's in the city now. Has he contacted you?"

"I'm afraid I can't discuss that. I'm known for my discretion."

"You'll be known for a lot more than that if you don't cooperate."

She sighed. "He arranged a companion for tonight."

"My associate here is going to take her place."

Sophie gave Kate a careful inspection. "You'll do. He likes brunettes."

"Good," said Kate. "How does this work?"

"Your name is Sharon and you're originally from Canada. Wear something classy. He doesn't like his women to look cheap. He also keeps a low profile. You go to the bell captain at the Intercontinental and ask for Victor Presky. The password is Bolshoi. The arrangement was for two hours. Are you going to kill him?"

"He won't be harmed, and I'll assure him we intercepted your girl without your knowledge. Nobody will guess that you had anything to do with it."

"Be at his hotel at 8:00. Are we done?"

"Yes," said David. "Mossad will take a dim view of any attempt to warn him. If that were to happen, then things will get complicated for you."

"I understand." She looked back at Kate, her eyes roaming over her. "Many of my higher profile clients would enjoy a woman like you, one who is attractive but also intelligent and self-assured. If you ever tire of Mossad, come see me. I assure you the pay will be better. Much better."

"Don't hold your breath."

Talia was waiting when they returned to the hotel. "Did it work?"

Kate nodded. "You're looking at Geneva's newest high-end hooker. We're on for tonight."

CHAPTER TWENTY-FIVE

Kate arrived at the Intercontinental five minutes early. David and Talia were in the bar, and although they wouldn't be much help if she got into trouble upstairs, it made her feel better to know they were close by. The bell captain's station was to her right and a short man in a red uniform looked up as she approached. "May I help you?"

"I'm here to see Victor Presky."

A knowing smile spread across his face. "Of course. One moment." He picked up a phone and spoke rapidly in French before hanging up. "Someone will be down momentarily."

She nodded and strolled through the lobby, stopping to check her appearance in a mirror. Talia had accompanied her on the shopping trip and Kate was unsurprised to find that her sense of fashion didn't extend much past jeans and running shoes. She made a series of useless suggestions while Kate selected an outfit consisting of a skirt and matching jacket worn over a white linen blouse. The skirt came to just above her knees and showed off her long legs to full effect. The ensemble projected sophistication with a promise of something sexy underneath.

A man emerged from the elevator bank and went straight to the bell stand. The captain gestured in her direction. "You asked for

Monsieur Presky," he inquired as he approached. "You have a pass code?"

"Bolshoi."

"Very good. Please come with me."

She followed him to the elevators. They exited on the second floor and proceeded down the hallway. He opened a door and ushered her into the living room of a spacious suite.

"Who do you really work for?" he asked, turning to face her.

Kate's mind raced. Had she somehow been exposed? "My employer exhibits a great deal of discretion in her business dealings. She expects the same from her employees and her clients. I knew your password. Isn't that enough?"

"Remove your clothing."

"Excuse me, but I'm here for Monsieur Presky, not you."

He slapped her across the face. "Whores don't talk back. Or ask questions. Take off your clothes."

"I think there's been a misunderstanding. I'll be leaving, and Monsieur Presky can work this out with Madame Bernard. Please extend my regrets to him."

The door from the bedroom opened, and another man entered the room. Kruzov's picture had been included in the dossier, and this was not him. "That will be all, Pieter. I'll take it from here."

"But my instructions …"

"Are to conduct a security check, not an interrogation. She was going to leave. That's not a threat. You may go."

Kate watched him walk out the door, pushing her confusion aside while trying to maintain some semblance of composure.

"I'm sorry about that," said the newcomer. "There have been some last-minute additions to the security detail and not everyone understands the protocols, especially for something that needs to be handled with the utmost discretion. Please accept my apologies."

Kruzov was a high-ranking officer, which meant his usual security people would be military as well. Last minute additions could only mean that one or more of the intelligence agencies had taken an interest in Kruzov's activities. That was a complication she hadn't foreseen, but even though she dodged a bullet by standing up to Pieter, appearances would need to be maintained. "I still think I should go."

"Please reconsider. A bonus will be paid to you directly for your inconvenience. A payment totally aside from the one to your employer."

Kate pretended to weigh her options. "How big a bonus?"

The man smiled. "A true businesswoman. Half the original fee?"

"And no more physical abuse? Or name calling?"

"Absolutely. But there are security concerns. Please remove your jacket and give me your purse. And pull your skirt up around your waist."

She complied without argument.

"Please turn all the way around."

She did a 360 for him. The sheer, sleeveless blouse could not possibly conceal a weapon, and she was completely exposed from the waist down. He felt the pockets of her jacket and examined the contents of her purse. "Your name?"

"Sharon."

"You're American?"

"Canadian."

"Very good. Monsieur Presky will be here shortly. Please make yourself comfortable."

Kate rearranged her clothing and took a seat on the sofa. Five minutes later the door opened once more, and Alexander Kruzov entered the room. Although not in uniform, he still projected the aura of one used to giving orders. He pulled up short when he saw her, a surprised expression on his face.

"I'm sorry to keep you waiting," he said, regaining his composure. True to Mossad's dossier on him, his English was fluent. He went to the wet bar and took a bottle from the refrigerator. "I suggest we start with a glass of champagne."

He opened the bottle and poured two glasses before joining her on the sofa. He handed one to her and raised his own. "To an enjoyable evening."

Kate raised hers and took a sip.

"Sophie tells me you're in high demand among her clientele. Many request you specifically. I'm eager to discover the reasons you generate such enthusiasm among your clients."

Kate put her glass on the coffee table. "I hope I'm not going to disappoint you, …"

He leaned close and whispered in her ear. "The dark hair threw me for a moment, but I know who you are. Dimitri showed me your picture. There are listening devices placed in here. Play along and stay in character."

He straightened back up. "I seriously doubt you could disappoint any man. Shall we take the champagne and adjourn to the bedroom?"

He leaned close as they passed through the door. "Relax. We're not going to have sex, but we need to convince anyone who might be listening."

She was flying blind, but there was nothing she could do except play along. "May I use the bathroom?"

"Of course, my dear. But please do not undress. That's a task I like to reserve for myself. It's like unwrapping a package on Christmas morning."

He followed her into the bathroom and closed the door. "Are there cameras?" whispered Kate.

"No. Once I knew Russian intelligence had inserted itself into delegation security, I had my people check the suite. They found no cameras, but there are listening devices in both the living room and the bedroom. Removing them would arouse suspicions."

"How do we do this?"

"Follow my lead. SVR is unprepared to take on delegation-wide surveillance on such short notice. They don't have the manpower. If we make this sound like two people engaged in sex, I'm sure they'll decide that your visit is genuine and direct their attention elsewhere. But we have to be convincing."

"I'll do my best. When do we talk?"

"Later."

He quietly slipped back out to the bedroom. "Will you be much longer?" he called.

Kate took a deep breath and went back out. "You said you wanted to start by removing my clothes. This should be fun."

He came to her, placing his arms around her and his lips against her ear. "I'm going to undress you down to your underwear. If we are interrupted for any reason, we can't be fully clothed."

He unfastened the waist of her skirt and let it fall to the floor before lifting the pullover blouse over her head. "Oh my, yes," he said, his eyes roaming over her body. "This will be an evening to remember. Sophie's description did not do you justice, my dear. Why don't you turn down the bed?"

She did as he asked while he removed his shirt and pants, draping them over a chair. He came to her and pulled her down onto the sheets, nuzzling his lips against her ear. "We must make this sound real in the event someone's listening."

She grinned. "Believe me, it won't be the first time I've faked an orgasm."

A loud knock on the bedroom door interrupted them before he could reply. "General. I must come in. It's important."

"I'll be out in a moment."

The door opened and the man who slapped her came in, gun drawn.

"What's the meaning of this?" demanded Kruzov.

"I'm sorry to interrupt, but she's an American agent. Her real name is Kaitlyn Malone, and she escaped custody this morning." He handed Kruzov a photograph. "This picture came in while you were … busy. The one we had before was from our dossier on her. She's naturally a blonde. This one was taken this morning and I recognized her immediately."

Kate waited to see how Kruzov would play this. Would he turn her in to preserve his own safety, or would he take some kind of action?

He looked from the photo back to Kate. "Take her in. And find out what she was doing here."

The security agent came toward her. "Put on your clothes and come with me. If you try anything …"

A red splotch appeared on his chest. His eyes widened and he dropped to the floor. Kruzov stood in the corner holding a silenced pistol. "Grab your clothes. We're leaving. Now."

"But …"

"Quickly."

She gathered her clothing from the floor and followed him to a door on the opposite wall.

"This connects to an adjoining suite. It opens onto a different corridor."

She ran through the second suite and opened its front door just a crack. Another door marked Housekeeping was just down the hall. "Come on," she whispered, pulling him by the arm.

The room turned out to be a storage closet lined with shelves filled with cleaning supplies, fresh towels, and bedding. A metal door about three feet on a side was set into the far wall. She pulled it open and stared down a laundry chute. At the bottom was a cart filled with dirty sheets and blankets.

"Take a look," she said. "It's a two-story fall, but a cushioned landing. Can you do it?"

He peeked through the opening. "Do we have a choice?"

He handed her the gun. Pulling himself up, he slid forward feet first and dropped from sight. Kate tossed their clothes after him and was about to follow him down when the door behind her opened. A man stepped into the room, his gun pointed at her. A week ago, she might have hesitated, but those days were gone now. She raised the silenced weapon and shot him cleanly through the head.

He fell to the floor as she dropped down the chute. She scrambled out of the cart and pulled it away to prevent pursuit. "We're in the basement, but there has to be a way out."

"There," he cried, pointing to a cement staircase leading up to a metal door.

She pulled the blouse over her head. "Give me your phone and get dressed." She dialed quickly. "Talia, I'm in the basement with

Kruzov. There's a door that looks like an exit, maybe out to a loading dock or something."

"Get to the street that runs along the south side of the building. We'll meet you."

Kruzov handed her the skirt. "We need to go now. They'll be here any moment."

They ran up the stairs and out into a dimly lit alley. "This way," she yelled.

A car screeched to a stop just as they reached the street. Talia leaned out the passenger window. "Come on. Get in!"

Kruzov yanked open the rear door and climbed inside as a bullet ricocheted off the hood. Kate turned and fired four rounds blindly up the alley as she backed into the car.

"Go! Go!" she screamed as she pulled the door shut. Another round struck the front quarter panel as David slammed his foot down on the accelerator. Kate kept watch through the rear window. "How did you find a car that fast?"

"We carjacked it from the valet," said David. "And we're going to have to dump it fast."

"Who are these people?" asked Kruzov.

"My backup," she replied. "Now be quiet."

David pulled into a public garage and parked as far from the entrance as he could. Talia took out her phone and spoke in Hebrew. "Okay," she said as she hung up. "This garage is connected to another hotel. We'll be met outside the main entrance in ten minutes."

Kate ignored the stares she attracted as she walked barefoot through the lobby. "Who's picking us up?"

"Someone from the Israeli embassy," Talia replied.

Kruzov stopped dead in his tracks. "Israel?" He turned to Kate. "I thought you were ISA."

She smiled. "I am, but it's complicated. Congratulations, Gen. Kruzov. You've just defected."

CHAPTER TWENTY-SIX

The flight to Tel Aviv took three hours, which Kate spent reviewing everything that had happened since her initial arrival in Russia. Pieces were coming together, but they remained fragments of the bigger picture, a puzzle they were still far from solving.

Upon their arrival at Mossad headquarters, they were greeted by Jacob Misrahi. "I'm glad you all made it back in one piece. And who is this?"

"This is Gen. Alexander Kruzov of the Russian army," said Kate. "I'm sure the name is familiar to you."

Jacob's eyebrows went up in surprise. "We expected you to bring back information, not a high-ranking member of their military."

"Things got a little out of control. Leaving him behind wasn't an option."

"This should be a fascinating story."

"Is Peter here?" asked Kate.

Jacob shook his head. "He knows you want ISA removed from the picture and remained in Washington. I've known him a long time. For him to trust you on this speaks volumes."

Sarah Niminsky was waiting for them in the same conference room where this had all started. Once everyone had taken their places at the table, she looked over at Kruzov. "I know who you are, General. This is a rather startling development."

"For me as well. I would like to begin by saying that while I had no intention of defecting, circumstances left me little choice. Had I let them take Miss Malone into custody, her interrogation would have been harsh and thorough. Nobody can resist indefinitely, and she would eventually have revealed my willingness to cooperate with American intelligence. I chose the most prudent course of action."

"But now that you're here, how far are you willing to go?"

"I believe that trying to prevent this calamity is an act of patriotism and I'm prepared to do what I can to help. I will, however, reveal nothing that is not relevant to the current situation. Is that satisfactory?"

Sarah regarded him closely. "For the moment. Shall we get started?"

"Certainly," Kruzov agreed. "But before we immerse ourselves in this, I must make a request. I have two daughters who will need protection from retribution. Sasha is finishing her graduate studies in Germany. Svetlana is in New York working as a technical translator at the United Nations."

"I'll see to it," said Sarah. "David, why don't you and Kate summarize what's happened since you arrived in Moscow?"

"I'll defer to her," he replied. "She had point on this."

Kate reviewed the events of the last several days, trying to keep her personal feelings and reactions separate from the facts. Sarah looked up from her notepad. "Have you reached any conclusions?"

Kate felt her nerves steady down. As an analyst, she was back on solid ground. "Russia plans to reassert dominance in Europe, and they view their arrangement with Iran to be just one part of the overall strategy. I think the Iranians have a different set of priorities. For them, it's their endgame. The internal resistance in Russia poses a threat to their goals and ISA's involvement compounds the problem. I believe they're determined to put a stop to any attempt to derail the plan. Their recruitment of OPG muscle to prevent me from contacting the resistance is proof of that."

"You consider Iran to be the bigger threat?" asked Jacob.

"Not necessarily, but I think they're going to turn out to be a problem for Russia. We need to exploit that. At some point, putting those missiles in Iran is bound to blow up in Russia's face, and their very presence gives Tehran a free rein to pursue their own agenda. If they push things too far, Israel may find themselves backed into a corner where you'll either need to rely on your own nuclear capability or cave. I don't see Israel ever backing down."

"Never," said Sarah.

"And I don't think Russia wants to be drawn into a Middle East war while they're trying to impose their will on Europe." Kate looked over at Kruzov. "I'm hoping he can shed some light on where things stand."

He nodded. "An advance team in possession of the missiles is in place at Tabriz, but the warheads will not be delivered until the commander of the unit is satisfied with the construction of the facility and the security that's been put in place. I served with him on several occasions, and we harbor similar concerns about the path our leaders are taking. He will drag his feet for as long as he can, but their delivery cannot be delayed indefinitely. I would think they will be in place within two weeks."

Jacob nodded. "At least we now have a time frame. How would you suggest we address this?"

Kruzov sat back in his chair with a heavy sigh. "I have suggestions. You will not like them."

"I'll be the judge of that," said Sarah. "Go on."

"Once the unit is operational, your options become limited. There is a significant civilian presence in the area and an attack on the installation risks a nuclear breach if the warheads become exposed to the atmosphere. A precise cruise missile strike prior to the delivery of the warheads would set everything back, possibly for months. It would give cooler heads a chance to influence events."

Sarah regarded him with a surprised expression. "What you're proposing would lead to a loss of Russian lives."

"There is something in place in the event the need should arise," said Kruzov. "A phone call to the unit commander containing a certain code phrase made one hour before the strike will cause an emergency evacuation drill to be conducted. All personnel will be a safe distance away when the explosion occurs."

"Won't the timing appear suspicious?" asked Jacob. "Your unit commander will be placing himself in a tenuous position."

"In the short term, yes. But if we are successful in stopping this madness, those who put themselves on the line will be rewarded."

Jacob drummed his fingers on the table. "A missile strike is a serious escalation of the situation, and your word won't be enough on its own. Nor will Washington support it. Their current president is a lame duck who'll be out of office after the next election. He won't commit the U.S. to a new Middle East conflict when he already has one foot out the door."

Kate was certain his assessment was correct. They'd need a more practical option, but there were other questions on the table as well. "Does the name Valkyrie mean anything to you?"

Kruzov looked surprised. "Yes. Dimitri mentioned it before he defected. Its goal is to keep America from taking an active role, but I know nothing about it. He claimed to be in the dark as well. However, the name alone raises alarming prospects."

She nodded in agreement. "The assassination of a national leader. Do you think they'd go that far? It's not something they could walk back later."

He shrugged. "On that, I cannot help you."

"Let's leave that be for a moment," said Sarah. "General, where does the Russian military stand?"

"The general staff is vehemently opposed to the plan. The politicians and the intelligence agencies are the ones driving this. Their goal is a new version of the U.S.S.R. no longer weighed down economically by the burden of Marxism, one that can dominate Europe in a way the communists couldn't. The intelligence services, and particularly SVR, are in full support. The resurrection of Russian dominance would mean they might achieve the level of power once held by the KGB."

"But the generals will do nothing?" asked Jacob.

Kate knew the answer before she heard it. Military people followed orders. They might privately express their opposition, but duty was duty.

"Several who voiced their opposition were forced into early retirement or reassigned to meaningless command positions. If they thought there was any hope of political support, a military coup might become possible, but I don't see it as likely. Malkin makes sure the people holding key positions in his government are loyal to him. There is potentially one source of that support, but as things currently stand, he is not in a position to act."

"And that person is?" asked Jacob.

"Vice President Anton Grinkov. He served with distinction in Chechnya and commands loyalty and respect within the military, which is why Malkin selected him. I've known him since we were boys and he feels as I do, but he cannot speak out without repercussions. Malkin would immediately dismiss him."

"Are there any other suggestions?" asked Sarah.

"If President Malkin could somehow be removed from the picture, Anton would assume the role of president. Given assurances that the U.S. and NATO would not try to push an advantage during the ensuing political chaos, he could bring a stop to the madness."

The room went silent. "An assassination?" Jacob finally asked.

Kruzov shrugged. "I told you my ideas would not sit well. I'm simply pointing out one way to address the problem. It's been done before, both by Israel and Washington. It was never formally acknowledged, but we all know it happened."

"I admit our hands are not entirely clean," said Sarah. "But this would require approval at the highest level and would never be considered as a first option."

As Kate listened to the discussion at the table, her mind churned through all she'd learned. Cruise missile strikes and assassinations might work in the short term but would only worsen things down the road. This needed to be handled with a lighter touch.

"There may be another way," she said. "What if we could

pinpoint Iranian intervention into Russian affairs? Point a definitive finger not only at Iran, but at a specific individual?"

"And how would we go about doing that?" asked Jacob.

"By leveraging Stefan Serapov. He took an enormous risk in accepting Iranian money. It had to be enough to make it worthwhile so long as he succeeded, but he didn't. I'm still alive and he learned nothing from me, not to mention losing what I'm sure were some of his top people. Iran is probably squeezing him hard, and if the security agencies ever found out what he's doing, things would get even worse. What if we offered him a way out? He reveals his Iranian contacts, and we lay out the whole thing publicly. Russia would be forced to reassess their relationship with Tehran and rethink their overall strategy. It would buy time for cooler heads like Grinkov to intervene."

Sarah tapped her pen against the table as she considered the plan. "I like it, but how do we pull it off?"

"His sister lives in London. I'll use her as the conduit."

"And if she refuses? She seems to have taken great pains to distance herself from her brother."

"She may hate what he is, but I'm betting she won't let her own brother be thrown to the wolves. And as for him, he's not going to be left with a lot of options. This is our best shot."

CHAPTER TWENTY-SEVEN

David parked their rental across the street from a row of small shops. "That's it," he said, pointing to the second storefront from the left.

Kate examined the clothing boutique appropriately named Zoya's. Its location in the heart of London's Chelsea district ensured an elite clientele not put off by the exorbitant prices.

"This shouldn't take long," she said, opening the car door and stepping out into the street.

A cab driver honked his horn as he passed her from the right. Taking care to look both ways, she crossed to the opposite side and entered the shop.

A fashionably attired woman in her twenties stepped out from behind the counter. "May I help you?"

"I'd like to speak to the owner, please."

"Certainly. She's in the back."

She disappeared through a curtained doorway, returning moments later with a short, impeccably dressed, middle aged woman. She peered at Kate over the top of her reading glasses. "I'm Zoya Orlova. You wish to speak with me."

"Yes," said Kate. "Can we talk privately? It's about your brother."

Zoya's eyes widened. "Watch the shop, Emma. We'll be in my office."

She led Kate back through the storeroom to a spacious office at the rear of the building. "I think you've made a mistake," she began, gesturing Kate toward a chair. "I don't have a brother."

"You may be Zoya Orlova today, but you were born Zoya Serapova," said Kate, using the feminine form of the family name. "Stefan is your brother, whether you acknowledge him or not."

Zoya settled into the chair behind the desk. "Whatever this is this about, I'm afraid I can't help you. Stefan and I are not on speaking terms."

"Do you want to see him in prison? Or worse? He's in a very dangerous situation and I can help. You travel back to Russia frequently. I suggest you make such a trip tomorrow."

"For what purpose?"

Kate handed her a cell phone. "Give this to him. He should call the number set up in the contact list. Tell him I'm the woman from Kask."

Zoya stared at the phone. "That's all? Just give this to him?"

"And tell him what I said. After that, your part is done. Believe me, you don't want to be involved any further than that."

She looked back up at Kate. "I'm not sure I want to be involved at all."

Kate smiled. "I don't blame you, but you'll be doing your brother a favor. He'll owe you."

"I'd rather he didn't. Stefan is a criminal, just like my father. My mother hated the life she had to lead, and when she died, I turned my back on the whole thing. I'll give him the phone, but I want nothing to do with him beyond that."

"I understand." Kate rose to her feet. "Tell Stefan to make the call as soon as possible. Time is short."

She left the shop and returned to the car.

"Well?" asked David.

"She'll do it. She didn't like it, but she took the phone. Now we wait."

Talia leaned forward from the rear seat. "What if he doesn't call?"

"There's too much at stake for him not to," Kate replied. "He'll listen. Whether he does anything about it is another matter, but I don't think he's the type to take a passive approach to anything."

"Look," said Talia, pointing across the street. Zoya Orlova left her shop carrying a large purse and a computer bag. She walked rapidly to a silver Nissan parked at the curb and tossed the bags onto the rear seat before getting behind the wheel.

"Whatever you told her certainly sparked some urgency," said Talia. "I thought she'd be reluctant."

Kate watched as Zoya pulled away from the curb. "She sure sounded that way. Follow her. I want to see where she goes."

The heavy London traffic made tailing the car both easy and difficult. The other vehicles provided the necessary cover, but it was critical to stay close to avoid being cut off by a changing traffic signal. Fortunately, the trip lasted less than a mile and ended at a townhouse on a quiet street in Kensington. Zoya parked in front, took her bags from the rear, and went inside.

David looked up at the three story brownstone. "She's got some money if she can afford this."

"Let's wait a bit," said Kate. "I have a hunch about her."

Fifteen minutes later, Zoya emerged with a roller board and the computer bag slung over her shoulder. She paused on the sidewalk, staring at her phone. Moments later, a car with an Uber decal in the window pulled up to the curb. Zoya climbed into the back seat with her luggage.

"Follow her," said Kate. "But I think I know where she's going."

Several minutes later, the Uber turned up the ramp onto the M4 motorway and headed west. "I was right. She's going to Heathrow."

Talia had reached the same conclusion. "There's an Aeroflot flight leaving for Moscow in an hour and a half," she said, her eyes glued to her phone.

Kate continued to watch the car ahead of them. "I have an idea."

David cut her off before she could finish the thought. "Forget it, Kate. You can't go back into Russia."

"But you can. Do you have your Israeli passports with you?"

They both nodded.

"Israeli citizens don't need a visa to enter Russia. If you can get two seats on the flight, do it. She's a Russian citizen, so she'll be expedited through immigration. You'll lose her there, but her dossier says she has an apartment in Moscow. Have someone from your embassy stake it out until you get there. Watch her, but don't interfere until she's met with her brother and given him the phone. Call me when that happens."

"And then?" inquired Talia.

"Play it by ear. She's in a damn big hurry to get to Moscow, so I suspect she's not as estranged from Stefan as we thought. Find out what you can, but be careful. We need to keep this off everybody's radar."

David nodded. "What about you?"

Kate shrugged. "The only way I can see to stop this is to expose Iran's meddling in Russia. Sowing distrust between those two countries will slow everything down and give the resistance a chance to convince others in the government to put pressure on Malkin. I need to come up with the most effective way to do that."

Talia looked up from her phone. "I got two seats in coach and a reservation at a Moscow hotel in case we need it. We can buy a suitcase somewhere in the terminal to make it look good. So, Kate, if we play this right with the Serapovs, you're saying this will be over?"

"I don't know, but I think it's our best shot."

David pulled up to the departure terminal. "We'll call when we have something."

Kate slid behind the wheel and headed for the Israeli embassy.

CHAPTER TWENTY-EIGHT

Talia parked the car down the street from Zoya's Moscow apartment. "The man watching the place said she went inside an hour ago. If Kate's right about this, something should happen soon."

The words were no sooner spoken when a silver Mercedes sedan pulled up in front of the building. Two men emerged, one going to the front door while the other took up a position beside the car. He looked carefully up and down the street before opening the rear door for a third man who went to the building's entrance.

Talia looked down at the picture displayed on her phone. "That's Stefan Serapov."

They watched as he went up the steps and entered the building.

∽

Kate was having dinner in the embassy commissary when her phone rang. Seeing the number of the burner she gave Zoya, she put the phone to her ear and pushed her chair back from the table. "Yes?"

"This is unexpected," said the Russian voice on the other end.

"I'm sure," she replied in the same language. "I'm in a public place. Call me back in five minutes. We won't want anyone eavesdropping on what we're going to discuss. I advise you to take the same precaution."

She went to her room and waited. In precisely five minutes the phone rang once more. "Okay, Stefan. I'm alone now. Is anyone with you?"

"I'm at my sister's apartment. You told her I was in some sort of danger."

"You are."

"Assuming it's true, why would you care?"

"You mean after you tried to have me killed?"

A long silence ensued. "I don't know what you're talking about."

"I had an interesting conversation with Natasha before her untimely death, and an even more productive one with Mikhail."

"Natasha's dead?"

"Yes. Pavel didn't tell you?"

"They were told not to contact me until they had results."

Kate smiled. Pavel evidently weighed his options and decided disappearing was healthier than going back. "Natasha and Yuri are dead, as is Mikail's cousin. Pavel I know nothing about."

"And Mikhail?"

"If he's still alive, he's on a Turkish freighter called the Dizman. I'm sure you can track it down."

"He knows better than to talk."

"He tried to say as little as possible, but pain is a powerful inducement. He told me he works for you, and I know you're working for the Iranians. They hired you to eliminate me."

Another pause. "That was purely a business arrangement."

Bingo. Her theory was now a fact.

"If the danger you mentioned is about Iranian retribution for failure, I've taken care of that," he said. "I returned their money and offered to track you down for them at my own expense."

"And failed at that as well. This isn't going well for you, Stefan, and unless we reach an agreement right now, it's going to get worse."

"An agreement on what?"

"I want the identity of your Iranian handler. I need his name, his position in their security service, and a way to contact him."

"Giving you that would be suicide."

"If you refuse, then I'll make the Russian authorities aware of your dealings with Iran. You're acting as an agent of a foreign power. That Iran's an ally won't matter."

A longer silence this time, and she waited for the question she knew was coming.

"What are you suggesting?"

"I'm sure you have millions stashed in foreign bank accounts. Do you own a private jet?"

"I have access to one."

"As soon as we're done here, fly to Tel Aviv. The Israelis will expedite your arrival. If what you give me checks out, you'll be set up with a new identity in a country of your choice. You'll be given access to your money and can start a new life. But if it turns out you lied, you'll be sent back to Russia and turned over to the authorities."

Kate knew he wouldn't give in easily. Trying to bargain his way out would be his first instinct.

"Is there room for negotiation here?"

If nothing else, he was predictable. "I'm afraid not. Time is of the essence for both of us. You either comply with my directions or I make that call."

"Then it seems I have no choice at all."

"Very good, Stefan. Now, who is your contact?"

"I only met him in person once and he didn't give me his name, but I like to maintain an advantage. I have sources within the security services. His name is Ali Hammeni, and he's the chief intelligence officer attached to their embassy in Moscow. We used a social media account to leave messages, but he gave me a phone number for emergencies."

He recited the number and the account name for her.

"And your payments?"

"Deposited into a bank account in Dubai. I can give you the number and codes."

"Good. One more thing. How is Iran getting its intel?"

"When Hammeni first proposed our arrangement, he said he had a source in the American CIA. Whether that's true is a question I cannot answer."

"You're sure he said CIA and not ISA?"

"Yes."

A leak at the CIA contradicted everything she thought she knew about the mole. It seemed she still didn't have the complete picture. "Let me give you a piece of advice. I suspect Zoya is actually part of your organization. Her shops would make ideal distribution points for your black market operations. I suggest you take her with you before her involvement becomes known."

"Are we done?"

"For now. You'll be debriefed in Israel."

"I'm not sure whether to thank you or curse you."

"As long as this information is valid, you can do as you please."

The line went dead.

∽

Talia glanced at her watch. "He's been in there for twenty minutes. Do we follow him when he comes out or stay with Zoya?"

"He'll probably go back to his dacha outside the city. I say we stick with her."

The front door opened, and Stefan emerged followed by his sister. They went straight to the car and climbed into the back seat. The two guards got into the front.

"That makes things easier," said David.

A black sedan drove past them and pulled to a stop. A rear door opened slightly as someone tossed a cylinder the size of a rolling pin underneath Stefan's car. The black car sped away.

Seconds later, Stefan's vehicle erupted in a ball of flame and a deafening roar. Windows shattered up and down the block as portions of the façade of Zoya's building crumbled onto the sidewalk. Cars parked nearby were lifted off the ground from the force of the explosion, one landing on its roof in the middle of the street. Pieces of metal and burning debris began falling everywhere, crashing onto the roofs of other vehicles and igniting still more fires. They stared in stunned silence as flames consumed the remains of Stefan's car.

Talia forced herself into action. Going forward was impossible and once the police and firetrucks began arriving, they'd be boxed in. She backed down the street to the intersection, squealing the tires the whole way. Turning the car around, she sped away, putting as much distance between them and the burning wreck behind them as she could.

"Head for the embassy," said David. "I'll call Kate."

∼

Kate was preparing to go back down to her interrupted dinner when the phone rang once more.

"Kate, it's David. Stefan Serapov's dead. Someone tossed a bomb under his car as he and Zoya were leaving her apartment."

"Did you see who did it?"

"The car was already past us before we realized what was happening. I'm sure he has his share of enemies, but I don't think it was a mob hit. The device was sophisticated. It had a huge explosive force and an incendiary component that had to be military. The fire was instantaneous and hot enough to melt metal."

"Iran," said Kate. "Stefan had become a liability. They were tying up a loose end."

"But with him gone, we're back to square one. Again." David's angry tone clearly conveyed his frustration.

"Not this time," Kate assured him. "He called me before they left Zoya's apartment, and I got what I needed. Are you leaving Moscow right away?"

"That would look suspicious, especially considering what just happened. We'll wait until tomorrow. Should we come back to London?"

Kate had been wrestling with how to address the problem of the leak back in Washington. The mole had to be highly placed, but he was only the source of the information, not the conduit. The connection to Iranian intelligence would be buried too deeply to draw anyone's attention, and even if Peter had uncovered the spy within ISA, it wouldn't solve the bigger problem.

"I'm going to ask a favor. A big one. We've been operating off the books. Would you be willing to keep doing that a little longer? Taking down the spy operation is the last piece of this, and I need people I can trust."

The extended silence that followed seemed endless. She held her breath until David finally spoke once more. "You distanced yourself from ISA for valid reasons. Our situation is different. You don't go rogue at Mossad."

Kate's hopes plunged. "I understand. It's okay. I get it."

"No, I don't think you do. What I just said is true under normal circumstances, but that's not what this is. With Israel facing a dire threat, you were the one who figured out the best course of action. And it's personal as well. You put your trust in us when you were in a bad spot and returned the favor when I was taken prisoner on the ship. Israel owes you one. Mossad owes you one, and Talia and I do as well. I think Jacob would agree. If he doesn't, then we'll deal with that later. Count us in."

Kate felt both relief and joy flooding through her and didn't trust herself to speak.

"Kate, are you still there?"

"Yeah. I, uh, I'm not sure what to say. Just saying thanks seems pretty thin."

"Then you can buy us beers when this is over. A lot of beers. What's the plan?"

"I'm still working that out. Today's what? Tuesday? I'll be back in Washington no later than Thursday. Go to the Shoreham Hotel. It's out by Rock Creek Park. I'll meet you there."

Kate hung up and tossed the phone onto the bed. She always thought she understood what friendship and loyalty meant, but that bar had just been raised for her. Now she needed to hold up her end, and that meant turning her focus back to the immediate problem.

If she was going to expose Iran, she needed to plant the seeds of her plan tonight. For the next hour she alternately made notes and paced the floor. With a last nod of approval, she picked up the desk phone and dialed the switchboard.

The Israeli operator answered in Hebrew. "This is Kate Malone. Could we speak English, please?"

"Certainly, Miss Malone. How can I help you?"

"Could you connect me to the embassy's Mossad liaison?"

"Just a moment."

Seconds later, a male voice came on the line. "This is Saul Meier. How can I help you, Miss Malone?"

"I'd like to set up a meeting with Russian intelligence here at your embassy. Would that be possible? You should be there as well."

"For what purpose?"

"Were you briefed on the reason for my being here?"

"Yes. It's a most unusual situation."

"I agree, and I think we can clear it up tomorrow if you'll allow me to invite your counterpart at the Russian embassy over for a chat." Kate held her breath as she waited for his response.

"My instructions are to allow you whatever leeway you need," he finally replied. "This should be an interesting encounter."

"I hope so," she said with a sigh of relief. "Thanks."

She hung up and dialed the operator once more. "This is Kate Malone again. I need the number of the Russian embassy."

"Would you like me to place the call for you?"

"Please."

The call was answered on the first ring. "Hello," said a female voice in fluent English. "You have reached the Embassy of the Russian Federation."

"I'd like to speak to the SVR liaison. I'm with American intelligence and the matter is critical."

"And your name?"

"Kaitlyn Malone."

"One moment, please."

Roughly three minutes passed before a male voice came on the line. "Yes?"

"Do you know who I am?"

"Your name has appeared with regularity on the daily intelligence summary. How can I be sure you are who you claim to be?"

"I escaped an attempt to capture me two days ago while I was in the company of Gen. Kruzov. If you're not already aware of these events, then check it out."

"I'm familiar with the matter. What is it you want, Miss Malone?"

"A chance to sit down with Russian intelligence and lay out what's been happening. There are things going on of which you're unaware. Things that could be disastrous for Russia."

"And why are you suddenly so concerned about my country's welfare?"

"Because it will affect mine as well. It could lead to a war that doesn't have to happen."

"I suggest you come to the embassy so we can discuss this in person."

Kate laughed. "Not in a million years. We can meet at the Israeli embassy at 10:00 tomorrow morning. I'll make the arrangements. Bring whoever you like."

"Israel? Not the U.S. embassy?"

"I'll explain tomorrow. Good night."

Kate hung up with a smile on her face. She was certain there would be a lot of phone calls between London and Moscow tonight. The meeting tomorrow should be very interesting.

CHAPTER TWENTY-NINE

Kate waited alone in the embassy conference room. She was playing way out of her league and knew it, but this was the critical moment if they were going to avoid the threat of global conflict. The politicians, diplomats, and agency directors would not be at the table. It would make this task easier, provided she could present her case effectively.

The door opened and Saul Maier escorted two men into the room. "Gentleman, this is Kaitlyn Malone of the American ISA. Kate, this is Sergei Ostrov. He's the man you spoke to last evening. And this is SVR Executive Director Vasily Kosygin. He took an overnight flight from Moscow to be here for this."

Another man entered the room unannounced. Saul looked surprised but didn't miss a beat. "And this is Ambassador Tielman. We weren't expecting you, sir."

The Israeli ambassador shook hands with the Russians. "When I learned Director Kosygin was here, I decided this might require my personal attention."

So much for the big shots not being involved. Kate took a deep breath and resolved to stay focused.

Saul continued with the preliminaries. "Coffee and water are on the table. Would anyone like anything else? No? Then I suggest we get started."

"Miss Malone, are you here as a representative of your agency?" asked Kosygin as he took a seat.

"Not officially. I'm here to lay out for you what I've learned since my arrival in Paris ten days ago and ask that you take it back to your government. I'm hoping this information will cause your leadership to re-think some strategies currently in place."

"You've been instrumental in the deaths of several of my people and an official from the Defense Ministry. Are you aware that Moscow filed a Red Notice with Interpol seeking your arrest and immediate extradition to Russia?"

Kate's stomach knotted, but she kept her voice even. "No, sir. But my government can demand a hearing before an international court to determine if there's just cause for such action. Until that takes place, a Red Notice cannot be enforced. I hope that by the time we're done here it won't be needed. As for your people, their deaths are regrettable, but I'm sure I don't need to tell you what it can be like in the field."

"Why don't we put that aside and hear her out?" suggested Saul.

"Very well," Kosygin answered. "We can discuss those matters at a later time. You may proceed, Miss Malone."

Kate had her notes in front of her, but she had most of the material memorized. It was important to maintain eye contact with these men as much as possible.

"Almost two weeks ago, Dimitri Artisimov defected. I went to Paris to debrief him, and he summarized for me what Russia is planning for the Middle East and Europe, plans your agency has supported from the start. We couldn't go public because it was uncorroborated intel from a single source. We needed verification. Dimitri told me there is opposition to this plan within both your government and the military, but no one will act without some hope of support. I went to Moscow to contact someone from the resistance movement and determine the status of things."

"I don't know what you're talking about," said the SVR director, rising from his chair. "I'm not going to waste my time with this."

"It's just us here, Director. Take whatever official positions you wish outside this room, but we need to talk this through and reach a common understanding. Your leaders have ambitious plans to restore Russian dominance in Europe. Iran is your partner in this. But there's a lot you don't know."

Kosygin said nothing, but slowly resumed his seat at the table.

Now that she had his attention, Kate pressed her advantage. "Your intention was to put nuclear weapons in Iran to neutralize an Israeli military advantage. For Russia, it was one step in a bigger plan, but Iran saw it as an endgame and intended to leverage their presence. They began acting aggressively to ensure nothing prevented those weapons from being delivered."

"Acting in what way?" For the first time, he engaged her without pretension.

"They penetrated ISA and we're still trying to clean that up. I wouldn't be surprised if they at least tried to get inside SVR."

"Impossible."

"Again, Director, it's just us. And you know better. It's always possible."

He held her gaze without blinking. "Maybe so. And what exactly do you think they're doing?"

Kate tried to keep from smiling. He was going to listen. "They're recruiting OPG organizations to carry out missions for them. On their orders, Stefan Serapov tried to have me killed at Kask. When the attempt failed, they instructed him to track me down and interrogate me. He failed again and paid the price yesterday. I'm sure your people determined the bomb used was hardly the type of weapon common criminals would have access to."

Kosygin looked uncertain. "How would you know this?"

She ignored the question. "I suspect the Serapov organization is not the only OPG family on their payroll, but that's your problem. Now you're wondering if I have proof of all this. Stefan Serapov communicated with his handler through a social media site, but he had a phone number to call in an emergency."

She shoved a piece of paper across the table. "This is the site and the accounts they used. They've probably been taken down by now, but nothing in the digital world ever goes away completely. Your people can find the information. The emergency contact phone number is written at the bottom. His handler was Ali Hammeni. I'm sure you're familiar with him. Iran is not the subservient ally you assumed they would be. They're conducting operations inside your country and planning on taking advantage of your willingness to put those missiles at Tabriz."

She could see his surprise at her knowledge of the location. "Gen. Kruzov was a big help. Israel now has enough evidence to take the issue of the missiles to the Security Council. That level of exposure will draw global attention and put NATO on full alert. I'm sure you can see what all this leads up to. The element of surprise you hoped to achieve is gone and any military venture Russia undertakes in eastern Europe will be met with force."

Kosygin stared at the paper she gave him. "If Iran is doing what you claim, then you may have actually done more for Russia than your own country."

"I'm tired of being hunted by Iran, OPG, and you. I want it to end. If this is beneficial to Russia, then great. My roots go deep into Russian soil. It will always hold a special place for me."

He looked over at the Israeli ambassador. "Ask your government to delay going to the Security Council until I can consult back in Moscow. There may be no need for a public airing of this."

"I'll do what I can. But when it comes to our national security, patience is a rare commodity. Urgency is required here. If those warheads are delivered, there will be an immediate military response. I can assure you the planning is already underway. This must be resolved quickly."

"I'm returning to Moscow at once," replied Kosygin. "I'll brief the president later today. What happens from there is out of my hands, but I will urge a re-evaluation of the situation."

He looked back at Kate. "If your information verifies, the Red Notice will be lifted as will the alerts about you circulating within Russia. I can do nothing about Iran's intentions regarding you."

"I'm working on that."

He smiled for the first time. "I'm sure you are. Please keep the carnage out of my country this time."

Once the Russians had taken their leave, Kate heaved a sigh of relief.

"Well done," said Saul. "What now?"

"That depends on him. Russian politics and power struggles can be unpredictable, and Kosygin's SVR has been behind this from the beginning. I'm not naïve enough to trust him blindly, but there's not much else we can do right now. I'm sure the threat of U.N. exposure will keep those warheads out of Iran, but as for the rest of it, we'll have to wait and see."

CHAPTER THIRTY

The encounter with Vasily Kosygin left Kate drained and in need of some fresh air to clear her head. The embassy was just across the street from Kensington Gardens and the opportunity to stretch her legs and enjoy the sunny morning was too good to pass up. With the Russian security services no longer after her and Iranian intelligence unaware of her current whereabouts, she no longer felt the fear that came with being hunted. She left the embassy with a smile on her face and strolled through the manicured greenery, heading east to where the Gardens merged into Hyde Park.

As she reached the east side of the Round Pond, she was suddenly struck by the feeling she was being watched. On such a beautiful day, there were people everywhere, and identifying someone who might be following her would be difficult. It might only be her imagination, but the past weeks had taught her to trust her instincts.

She crossed the Serpentine on the Carriage Drive Bridge and found a park bench where she could watch the people coming across behind her. One woman stopped in the middle of the bridge, her eyes on Kate. After a moment's hesitation, she turned and went back the way she came.

Kate smiled. Now she was the pursuer. She retraced her steps, her eyes never leaving the woman's back, and followed her toward the southern edge of the park. She paused at the Serpentine Gallery and watched her quarry cross Knightsbridge Road and enter an imposing gray limestone building. Kate didn't need to read the plaque mounted beside the door to know she was looking at the embassy of the Islamic Republic of Iran. They had found her.

She stood beside the pathway, lost in thought. This wasn't the work of the mole. No one back in Washington had any idea where she was. Only Mossad and the embassy staff knew she was in London, but then another thought occurred to her. SVR had known her location ever since her phone call to the Russian embassy last night. Despite Kosygin's denial, Iran had a source inside his agency. She needed to relocate again and do it quickly.

A man strolled toward her, holding a guidebook in one hand and a cup of coffee in the other. He looked like any other tourist, except his eyes never left Kate. He tossed the coffee into a trash receptacle and pulled a small aerosol can from his pocket. She heard the hiss of the spray as she ducked low and ran toward the shrubbery that lined the path. She pulled the gun from her jacket pocket and peeked through the foliage.

A woman lay on the ground retching, her face turning blue as a sudden seizure shook her body. Several people went to her aid, oblivious to the fact that an attempted assassination was taking place. The man stepped around them and continued toward Kate. Despite the public setting, she was out of options. She put three rounds into his chest. He staggered to his right and crumpled to the ground.

Screams echoed through the park as people ran from the scene. Kate left the shelter of the hedgerow and ran toward the dead man, snatching the canister from his hand. Someone shouted for her to stop, but she paid no attention and sprinted toward the north end of the park. She reached the Italian Gardens and crossed Bayswater Rd. at a dead run. Ignoring the screeching brakes and honking horns, she continued north toward Paddington Station.

The railroad terminal was crowded with people, all on their way to somewhere else. Kate mingled with the crowd as she made her way past the statue of Paddington Bear on her way to the east end of the building. She exited beside the taxi stand and slid into the rear seat of the first one in line. The short cab ride back to the Israeli embassy went without incident and she heaved a sigh of relief as she entered the safety of the building.

The woman at the reception desk looked up as Kate came through the door. "Ms. Malone. Ambassador Tielman would like to see you in his office."

Kate nodded. "Tell him I'm on my way."

Moishe Tielman looked up as Kate knocked on the door. "Come in, please. I asked Saul to join us. I hope you don't mind."

She nodded to the Mossad liaison and took a seat across the desk from the ambassador. "Good. I need to speak to you both."

"That was quite a performance you put on this morning. It was satisfying to see Russian intelligence taken by surprise for a change. I don't imagine that happens to Vasily Kosygin very often. You handled it well."

"Thank you, sir. But …"

"I reported back to my government regarding the outcome," the ambassador continued. "Mossad has requested your presence at their headquarters to provide a briefing for their senior staff."

Kate shook her head. "I'm afraid that'll have to wait. I must return to Washington. I'd appreciate it if the embassy would make the arrangements."

"My instructions are to get you to Tel Aviv by this evening," said Saul.

Kate cut him off before he could continue. "I don't take orders from Mossad. I'm grateful for the opportunity to work with your people and especially for your help today, but while the crisis has been contained from Israel's perspective, my situation is still unresolved."

"Russia is removing the Red Notice."

"I'm talking about Iran. They're the ones pulling the strings. They just tried to kill me over in Hyde Park." She pulled the cannister from her pocket and handed it to him. "Be careful with that. It contains some kind of poison gas."

Saul looked from the cannister back to her. "The police activity in the park. That was you?"

"Unfortunately, yes. I killed an Iranian agent before he could use that thing on me. A female bystander was exposed to it."

"How did they find you?"

"My guess is they have a source inside SVR. I'll be happy to brief Mossad leadership via a secure conference call, but it's imperative that I return home as soon as possible. I must insist."

The ambassador and the Mossad liaison exchanged glances. "I think she's earned some leeway here," said Moishe Tielman. "And she's right. She doesn't work for Israel. Not directly, anyway." He turned back to Kate. "We'll get you on a flight this afternoon and Saul can smooth things over with the people back in Tel Aviv. You take my personal thanks with you, as well as the gratitude of my country."

"Thank you, sir."

CHAPTER THIRTY-ONE

Kate stood outside the gorilla enclosure watching its newest addition follow his mother to the pile of bananas and apples stacked beside the waterfall. The young ape climbed onto its mom's back and kept grabbing at the fruit as she tried to eat. She put up with his nonsense until her patience reached its limits and then gently pushed him away. He shrugged off the maternal reprimand and curled up in her lap.

The crowd laughed at his antics, and even Kate had to smile. With one last glance back at the playful little guy, she turned away and continued her stroll through the park. An afternoon spent at the National Zoo provided a much needed reprieve from the tension and stress of her desperate journey through Europe, and the warm sunshine helped dispel her dour mood.

Nobody knew she was back in Washington, and while that provided a certain level of security, it left her alone with her troubles. The mole was still in place. She didn't fully trust Kosygin to do the prudent thing, and Iran clearly wanted her dead. With all that still on her plate, being out in public was a risk. But with a Washington Nationals hat pulled down over her black hair and a pair of sunglasses hiding her blue eyes, she felt secure in her anonymity. She wandered through the grounds, part of her luxuriating in the opportunity to escape the confines of her hotel room, but the rest trying to work through the problems still facing her.

"Hey, Kate, wait up," shouted a male voice from behind her. She froze, wondering who it might be and how to handle it. A guy in his twenties jogged past her and stopped beside a pretty girl pushing a baby stroller. He leaned over and kissed her cheek as they continued along the path.

Kate let out a sigh as she watched them walk away. She longed for this to be over so she could go back to being her old self, someone who didn't see a threat in every shadow. A part of her wondered if that would ever be possible, but she shoved that thought aside and refocused on her problem.

The one thing she wanted most was a weapon. Having a gun tucked into a holster or jacket pocket had become second nature to her, and after everything she'd been through, going unarmed made her feel uncomfortably vulnerable. Getting one through ISA was out of the question. Even if Peter could keep it off the books, he was too close to the mole. Mossad might help, but she had no contacts at Israel's Washington embassy. She'd need Talia or David for that.

Another possibility occurred to her. Her apartment was barely a mile away with the handgun her father had given her tucked away in a bedroom drawer. But somewhere amid the chaos of Europe her keys had disappeared. There was a way around that, but it would mean opening a door she hoped had been shut for good. She pulled out her phone and took a deep breath before making the call. He answered on the first ring. "Hello?"

"Dan? It's Kate."

After a long pause during which she thought the call had dropped, he finally answered. "Kate? Where the hell are you? Are you alright?"

"I'm fine."

"Nobody's seen or heard from you since the day Schilling came to your apartment."

"I've been taking care of some personal business. Look, Dan, ..."

"I'm glad you finally called. That fight we had about moving in together, and then the scene I made when Schilling showed up at your apartment? They caused me to do a lot of thinking."

Kate took a deep breath. This wasn't the time to reopen old wounds. "Dan, listen to me. We can sort all that out later, but right now I need you to do something for me without asking a lot of questions."

A pause. "Okay. Sure. What?"

"Go to my apartment. You've still got a key, right?"

"Yeah. If you want it back, I …"

"There's a gun in a drawer in the bedroom. Put it in a backpack or a computer bag and bring it to the entrance of the Woodley Park Metro Station on Connecticut Avenue at 2:00 this afternoon. Can you do that?"

A longer pause. "You're scaring me, Kate."

"I know, and I'm sorry. Please, Dan?"

"Yeah. Okay. Two o'clock. Can we talk then?"

"No. And please don't push the issue. I'll explain when I can, okay?"

Another pause. "Sure. If you say so. See you then."

"Thanks." She hung up, trying vainly to push the guilt aside. He could access her apartment without attracting attention, and she'd learned hard lessons about putting necessities ahead of everything else.

She bought a hot dog and a bottled water from a concession stand and found an empty park bench. A squirrel waited near her feet, ready to claim any breadcrumbs that might fall to the ground. Kate admired his patience and optimism and wished she could approach her own problems the same way.

Although her instinct was to keep everything at arm's length, some risks needed to be taken if she was going to end the stalemate. David and Talia were willing allies, but they wouldn't have the same kinds of resources they did in Europe. She needed someone on the inside, someone who wouldn't attract unneeded attention. Setting her water bottle down on the bench, she took out her phone once more. "Monica? It's Kate."

"It's about damn time you called. Are you okay?" Her voice sounded much stronger than the last time they'd talked.

"Yeah, I'm good. How about you? Back to normal?"

"Not yet, but I'm getting there. I went to the gym for the first time today."

Kate had to smile. Monica was as dedicated a workout enthusiast as Kate had ever known. "How'd that go?"

"I got on the exercise bike and about died, but it felt good to work up a sweat again. Are you back in town?"

"Yeah but keep that to yourself. You're back at work?"

"Part-time and doing mostly busywork. They promoted someone into Phil's job, but he brought his assistant with him, so they need to find a place to put me."

Kate glanced over at the squirrel. Maybe good things happened if you waited long enough. "I've got an idea about that. Can you meet me at the Shoreham hotel at 5:00? Room 420."

"What's up?"

"I'll tell you then."

"You got it. See you at 5:00."

Kate tossed the squirrel the last crumbs of hot dog bun and headed for the park gate and the walk home to her apartment. She was making a mental list of everything she needed to discuss with Monica when her phone rang.

"Kate, it's me." Dan's voice had an edge of excitement to it. "I'm on my way up to your apartment. Where did you say the thing is I'm supposed to get?"

"The thing? Is someone with you?"

"Yeah. I'm on the elevator."

"It's in the drawer of the bedside table." She could hear the ding as the elevator doors opened.

"Okay. Hang on, I have to find the right key. Got it. Is there anything else you want me to …"

The connection dissolved into a roar of noise before the line went dead.

"Dan? Are you there?" She frantically redialed, but the call went straight to voicemail.

She stared at the phone. "No, no, no." She waved at a passing cab and spent the ten-minute drive rocking forward and back in her seat, her fist beating against her knee.

The driver braked to a stop at the end of her block. "Looks like a fire or something. The street's blocked off."

She shoved a twenty at him and climbed out. A police car parked crosswise in the intersection prevented traffic from entering the street, but it hadn't stopped bystanders from gathering. Every face looked up at the smoke pouring from a window four stories above the street. Her window.

Kate stared at it, wanting to scream in denial, guilt, and pure rage. She sank to her knees and felt tears come. Dan had walked into a killing zone meant for her.

"Bastards. Bastards." She mouthed the word over and over.

"Are you okay, ma'am?" A female police officer looked down at her, a concerned expression on her face.

Kate fought to regain control. It wouldn't do to be noticed here. She got to her feet, her mind racing to come up with a plausible story. "I'm sorry. That's where I was going. That building. My friend lives there. What if …"

"What's your friend's name?"

"Selena Martinez. She lives on that floor." Which was true. Selena lived down the hall and, with any luck, was at work. "How do I find out if she's okay?"

"Have you tried calling her?"

She tried to feign surprise. "No. God, I'm an idiot. Thank you, officer." She walked away, taking her phone from her pocket for effect. The cop started back toward the ruined building.

Kate turned back to face the scene. Dan had to be dead. The bomb would have been placed near the door for maximum effect, and anyone coming through wouldn't have stood a chance. Mercifully, he probably never knew what happened to him. The thought gave her little comfort.

The only thing she could do was go back to her hotel, but the futility of it caused her anger to surge yet again. Somebody would pay for this. Somebody would suffer, and she'd make damn sure she'd be the one delivering the punishment.

She walked all the way back to the hotel, both to calm herself and have some time to think. When she arrived, a tour bus parked by the entrance was disgorging passengers and the lobby had filled with the new arrivals. She made her way around the crowd and was heading for the elevators when a glance at the registration desk stopped her. Talia and David were waiting in line.

They looked up as Kate approached. "We made it," said David with a smile of greeting. "Our flight was diverted because of ..." He paused, his smile changing to a frown of concern. "Kate? What's wrong?"

"Not here. Once you get settled, come to 420. We've things to talk about."

She turned back to the elevators with a sense of relief. She wasn't alone anymore.

CHAPTER THIRTY-TWO

Kate sat at the desk and tried to block out the image of smoke pouring from her apartment window. The intensity of the blast meant Dan's body would have been shredded and the remains burned beyond recognition. She doubted there'd be enough left to identify, which would complicate things for the investigators and buy her some time.

The thought sent another wave of guilt coursing through her. Had she become that cold blooded? She should be mourning him, not clinically analyzing the impact of his death on her situation. She gripped the arms of the chair and forced herself to focus. A time for mourning would come, but right now she needed to think clearly.

The knock on her door jerked her out of her reverie, and she ushered David and Talia into the room. "I'm glad you guys are here. We got a problem."

"The mole?" asked Talia.

Kate shook her head and motioned them to the small sofa beside the window. "Somebody put a bomb in my apartment."

"I thought you were going to stay away from there," said David.

"I wanted my own weapon and asked a friend to get it for me." She stopped, not wanting to let her emotions get the better of her. A deep breath helped steady her raw nerves. "I was on the phone with him went it went off."

Talia winced. "Damn. But you had no way of knowing. It's a tragedy, but not your fault."

Kate closed her eyes to shut out the image of the inferno that must have swept through her home. "It sure feels like it is."

Her phone rang, displaying Monica's number. "Kate? Are you okay?"

"Yeah. You heard? How?"

"Peter. We're on our way to the hotel."

"He's with you?"

"He wanted to know if I'd heard from you. He insisted and I ..."

"It's okay. Ask him to fill you in on what's been happening. It'll save time when you get here. Tell him if he doesn't, I will."

"You can talk to the director that way?"

"I'm way past caring about things like that. Just tell him."

"If you say so. We'll be there soon. Bye."

Kate tossed her phone onto the desk. "We're going to have company. Let's table this until they get here. God, I could use a drink."

"The same thought occurred to us when we landed and the duty free shop was right there," said David, reaching into his backpack. He produced a bottle of single malt and placed it on the desk.

Kate grabbed the ice bucket. "I'll be right back."

Upon her return, David handed her a glass containing two fingers of amber whiskey. "I brought something else as well." He removed a holstered Glock from the backpack.

"You took guns on the plane? How?"

"Not the plane, and not the embassy. We're staying off Mossad's radar for now. They can't order us home if they don't know where we are. When I was here on assignment a couple of years ago, we rented and stocked a storage locker in Arlington. Mossad kept up the lease in case of emergencies."

"Mossad had an active operation inside the U.S.?"

"Your government wasn't the target and I'll leave it at that."

She cradled the weapon in her hand, relishing the sudden comfort it provided. "Thanks. I missed you guys. Being out here all alone was getting to me."

Another knock on the door announced Peter and Monica's arrival. When Kate opened it, Monica's eyes went wide. "What the hell did you do to your hair, girl?"

Kate grinned and gave her friend a hug. "You'll get used to it. I have. Come on in."

Monica's own hair was longer than before and she hadn't gained back all the weight she'd lost, but her green eyes still glistened with the same intensity as always. Kate introduced her to the Israelis while David poured drinks for the newcomers.

"How did you find out so fast?" she asked Peter.

He accepted the glass and took a seat on the bed. "When a bomb goes off in the nation's capital, alerts go out everywhere." He hesitated. "Preliminary reports say someone was inside. Do you have any idea who it was?"

Kate swallowed a gulp of the whiskey to steady herself. "Dan Grissom. You met him at my apartment the day you sent me to Paris. Was anyone else killed?"

"Not that I've heard. That it happened in the middle of the day probably helped."

Kate nodded. "It's what they call a YP building. Young Professional. Almost everyone is single and would be at work during the day."

"Why was he there?"

"I asked him to retrieve my gun from the nightstand," she replied, her voice tinged with the anger she felt. "I never should have done it."

"Don't go there," advised Peter. "Second guessing yourself doesn't help. How are you holding up?"

"When you sent me to Paris, I never expected to end up here. I've watched people die and killed some of them myself. This isn't the person I ever wanted to be, or even one I'm sure I like."

Peter nodded. "It's a normal reaction to a first mission. Coming to terms with everything will take time. Meanwhile, be an analyst again. What is this?"

Kate put the glass down and gestured at the notepad lying on the desk. "I've been trying to work through it. I think there's more going on than we know. A mole is almost always passive. He, or maybe she, collects information and passes it on while doing nothing to draw unwanted attention. Someone like that would be more likely to run if they thought they were in trouble. Planting a bomb would be totally out of character. I think the bomber and the mole are two different people."

"I agree," said Talia. "But there has to be a connection."

"I should bring you up to date on recent developments," said Peter. "The mole at ISA is Nick Mueller, but we've found nothing to connect him to either Russia or Iran. He's been passing information to someone at the CIA."

"Do we know who?"

"Susan Reardon's chief of staff, Josh Griswold, but he checks out clean as well. On the surface, this looks like nothing more than a case of inter-agency meddling. We know it's more than that, but whoever's behind it is doing a damn good job of covering their tracks."

Kate considered that for a moment. "Okay, but why are they leaking information to the CIA director? It makes no sense."

"Misdirection. It's a classic maneuver. At some point, we were bound to realize we had a leak. By letting Susan in on little pieces of it, they diverted everyone's attention and provided additional cover for the spy."

"Tell me about Mueller."

"Nick got in trouble at NSA because an accidental data breach happened on his watch. He never reported it and got caught covering it up. His father used his influence to get him a fresh start at ISA."

"That data breach. Whose fault was it?"

"An analyst working the night shift. Although it was nothing more than a careless mistake, she was fired and moved back home to Seattle. There's no apparent connection to Iran there either."

"Everything always leads to a dead end," said David. "Does Mueller realize he's been found out?"

Peter shook his head. "Not yet. If he's arrested, the spy will simply fade away and we'll never sort this out. We need to find out who it is and do it fast, especially in light of what's happening in Russia. And what's not happening in Iran."

Kate sat up straight in her chair. "What do you mean?"

"Mossad passed along the report of your meeting with Kosygin. Carl wasn't pleased, by the way. He thinks you overstepped."

Kate didn't try to conceal her annoyance. "I didn't know he'd be there. And I don't really care what the director thinks. I was on my own and trying to prevent a crisis. Now what's this about Russia and Iran?"

"Evgeny Malkin has dropped out of sight. He hasn't been seen in public for two days or been mentioned in any government news releases. That could be an indicator that there's been a shakeup. Dimitri knows Kosygin well. He thinks SVR will take advantage of the situation to assert themselves further into the power structure. How far in is the question and right now there's no way to know."

Kate considered that. "So maybe there's been a coup, but we don't know who's in charge now. What's the army doing?"

"Their military raised the alert status of their forces. It could just be a drill, but the timing seems ominous. It could mean they expect an upheaval within the government, but it could also be the start of a buildup to the invasion of Lithuania they've been planning."

"And Iran?"

"By now we hoped to see signs the missile detachment was preparing to leave Tabriz, but satellite surveillance shows no sign of that. We'll keep watching."

Kate got up and paced the room, her hands jammed into the pockets of her jeans. "How did Iran know I was back in Washington?"

Peter shrugged. "They probably didn't. But you were bound to come home at some point. You've been a thorn in their side through this whole thing. And don't assume it was ordered by their government. They can't have many assets here in the U.S. and I don't see them risking exposure for a simple act of revenge."

"Then what?"

"There are rogue elements within both their military and their intelligence organizations, and trying to rein them in is a constant problem for them. It's possible that the spy planted here made an independent decision to take you out. If so, then they've done us a favor."

Kate stopped her pacing and turned to face him, her anger surfacing once more. "What? By blowing up my apartment and killing Dan?"

"He means they think you're dead," said Talia. "That gives us an edge."

Kate resumed her seat and picked up her drink, swirling the remaining whiskey around in the bottom of the glass. She looked over at David who nodded in response to her unspoken question. Talia merely stared at her from the corner of the sofa.

She drained the rest of the scotch. "Thanks for coming, Peter. I'll be in touch."

He returned her gaze with no show of surprise. "Plausible deniability?"

She smiled. "Something like that. There's nothing much you can do officially, anyway. And if this goes badly, I don't want to drag you down into the muck. But before you go, I need to ask two favors. Is there a safehouse somewhere in the Washington area we can use for a few days without ISA knowing?"

"Hand me that writing pad." He jotted rapid notes and passed it back. "That's the address in Arlington. The first string of numbers is the door code. The second string will deactivate the cameras and microphones. And the other favor?"

She looked at Monica. "Are your computer skills as good as you claim?"

"Yes. I almost majored in computer forensics in college, but the thought of spending all day holed up in a basement cubicle changed my mind."

Kate turned her attention back to Peter. "If she's willing, she'll be doing some digging for me at ISA. Make it look official. I don't want to get her into trouble."

He nodded. "Carl's been pushing me to hire an executive assistant. She works for me as of now. You'll call me when you have something?"

"I'll call her."

Once the door had closed behind him, Kate sagged back in her chair. "Well, guys, we're on our own again."

"What's the plan?" asked Talia.

"We need to work on that tonight, and I'll want everyone's thoughts. We'll move to the safehouse in the morning."

"Can I hang out here tonight?" asked Monica. "I want to know what the plan is."

"Yeah. You need to be in the loop. Talia, why don't you order some food from room service and David can pour us another round. I'll get more ice."

Out in the hallway, she stood in front of the ice machine and collected her thoughts. There was one part of this she couldn't tell the others. Once she found the one responsible for the bomb, she was going to kill them. Dan died trying to get back into her good graces and he would not go unavenged. They could take their first rule and shove it.

CHAPTER THIRTY-THREE

"What do you think you're doing?"

Monica looked up from Nick Mueller's computer. He was standing in the doorway, glaring at her with an expression she couldn't quite put her finger on. Anger for sure, but something else as well. Fear maybe?

She stood and extended her hand. "My name's Monica. Monica Lindsey. I'm Director Schilling's new executive assistant. You must be Mr. Mueller."

"Please move away from my computer. Peter said nothing about a new secretary."

Monica ignored the emphasis he placed on the last word. "The position's been open for a while. He didn't want to break in somebody from scratch, but I held the same job for Phil DeCosta before he died. He asked if I'd be interested, and I said yes."

"Come with me."

He led her down the hall to the corner office. Peter shut his laptop as they came in. "Ah! You've already met Monica. Good."

"I wasn't aware we were hiring anyone."

Peter motioned them to the chairs on the other side of the desk. "And I wasn't aware I had to run my decisions past you."

Nick's face turned crimson. "I didn't mean …"

"Phil always spoke highly of her, so when she returned to work, it seemed like a logical choice."

"I caught her at my desk. She was doing something on the computer."

"Yes, at my request. I want her to have access to the calendars and non-classified email of my senior staff. You weren't in the building, so I had someone from IT log her on so she could set it up."

Monica nodded. "It's an effective way to keep everyone connected. I also created a shared folder where you can put any documents I should have access to. And I'd like your phone numbers in case I need to reach you."

Peter spread his hands. "See what I mean? She's efficient, and she knows what she's doing. We're lucky to have her."

From Nick's expression, Monica wasn't so sure he felt the same way. "I was just finishing up when you walked in," she said. "Everything should be good to go."

He nodded in response. "Welcome to the team, then." He turned his attention to Peter. "Unless there's something you need me for, I'll get back to work."

Peter waited until the door closed behind him. "Did you find anything?"

Monica squirmed uncomfortably in her chair. "I'm in an awkward spot here. I work for you, and I hope that's not just temporary. But what I'm doing for Kate means there are things I can't tell you. You heard her yesterday. She wants you out of the loop so she can have a free hand. And you agreed. Please try to understand where that leaves me. I don't want to end up on your bad side."

He nodded In understanding. "You won't. I'm just not used to being shut out by my agents, especially Kate. She had no preparation for this."

"She's changed since Riyadh."

Peter leaned back in his chair. "Yes, she has. I'm not sure she realizes how much."

"Is she going to come back to ISA?"

"That's up to her. I understand what she's doing and why, but some things can't be handled from the outside. You don't need to give me any details, but was there anything on his computer that might give us a leg up?"

Monica hesitated before answering. "Maybe. Nothing specific, but a few things got my attention. I gave myself a lot more access than would normally be necessary, so if IT catches on …"

"I'll cover for you. Tell Kate that if she finds anything that sheds further light on Russia or Iran, I need to know. Those issues will have to be handled at a much higher level."

"I understand. Can I take the rest of the day off? I need to talk to her."

He nodded. "Tell her to be careful."

"I'll pass it along. And thanks for understanding."

∼

Kate answered the phone on the first ring. "Monica. How'd it go?"

"Fine. I'm parked down the street. Can I come up to the house? I'm not sure how this works."

"Leave the car where it is. I'll be waiting."

Monica took off her jacket as she came through the door. "Nice place. But what about the neighbors? Don't they wonder about what goes on here?"

Kate snapped the deadbolt into place. "They think the house is leased for temporary use through an executive service. How did things go at ISA?"

"Everyone assumes you're dead. It's all anyone's talking about."

"Good. That's how it has to be for now."

David emerged from the kitchen. "The new girl. What's up?"

Monica unpacked her laptop and placed it on the dining room table. "I found something interesting. Where's Talia"

"Checking out the area around Nick's apartment building," Kate replied. She pulled a chair over so she could see the screen. "What do you have?"

"I went through Nick's computer. He knows how to be careful, so

I didn't expect to find anything useful. But I may have gotten lucky. He forgot to log out and left the browser open. He was using Google maps to look at a satellite view of a remote area of Virginia. The cursor was right over a building sitting at one end of a clearing in the woods. I made a note of the GPS coordinates and switched to the map view. It's about two hours southwest of here in the middle of nowhere."

She brought the map up on her laptop. "Do you think it means anything?"

David frowned as he studied the screen. "Maybe. Was there anything else?"

"He left a notepad on his desk." She pulled out her phone and displayed a photo. "I took a picture."

Kate took the phone from her. "It's mostly routine stuff."

"Zoom in and check out the note he made in the margin."

She squinted at the image. "EN. Cabin. Noon Sat. You think the building on the map is the cabin from the note?"

"You guys are the experts."

"It's possible. But at least it gives us something to go on. We need to find out who owns that property."

Monica extracted a notebook from her bag. "I did, sort of. I used the GPS coordinates to locate the property in the county records. That stuff's all in the public domain, so it wasn't hard to do. The cabin sits on three hundred acres of nothing except trees, rocks, and hills. The property's been in foreclosure for the past two years, but a couple of months ago a company called Sintran bought it for $50,000."

"Sounds like it went cheap."

"Not when you think about it. The land is too rugged to farm and too remote to be developed. The bank's lucky they got that much."

"What do we know about Sintran?"

Monica glanced down at her notes. "Almost nothing, but that's about all there is to know. It looks to be a front. There's a pretty basic website that doesn't contain much in the way of actual information, and their address is a P.O. box. They hired an attorney to handle the closing, so nobody from the company was directly involved in the transaction. His name is Richard Kozlowski, and his office is in a little town called Holcomb. If they're trying to hide the real identity of the owners, then they're doing a good job of it. But they made one mistake."

"You mean we actually caught a break?"

"Possibly. I checked on that P.O. box. It was paid for with a credit card belonging to Emily Nassar."

Kate jotted down the name on her notepad. "The EN on the note?"

"That's what I thought."

"Nice work." She looked up at the clock on the wall. "David, I think we should drive down to Holcomb and pay this lawyer a visit."

"I was thinking the same thing."

"Monica, call Peter and ask him to see what he can find on Emily Nassar. Don't tell him why, just say I asked."

"Got it. You think she's the Iran connection?"

"Nassar is an Arabic name, not Iranian, but it's worth a shot. Come on, David. We can grab lunch on the way."

~

Kate watched the addresses as David slowly drove down the main street of Holcomb, Virginia. The business district was only two blocks long and contained none of the chain stores that seemed to be everywhere in more populated areas.

"How did they find this guy?" she asked. "This might as well be Mayberry."

They passed a grocery market and a hardware store before Kate spotted their objective. "There," she said, pointing to her right. "208 Main St. But it's a barbershop."

David pulled the Land Rover over to the curb. "Let's see if anybody knows Kozlowski."

The shop was a small operation with only one chair, which was currently occupied by a grizzled mountain of a man whose hair hung to his shoulders. Two other men relaxed on a bench set against the wall. Both were smoking cigarettes despite the No Smoking sign hanging above them.

The barber looked up from the formidable challenge he was about to take on. "You're not from around here."

Kate ignored the small town suspicion of outsiders. "No. We're looking for someone. I was hoping you could help."

"Let me guess," growled the man in the chair. "You're looking for Dickhead."

"If that's Richard Kozlowski, then yes."

"His office is around back," said the barber. "He rents the upstairs apartment as well. If he's not there, check the diner or Casey's. He'll be at one or the other."

"Casey's?"

"The bar down the street. Rick's a better drunk than he is a lawyer."

"Yeah. Thanks."

They walked around to the rear of the building. "An alcoholic lawyer with an office behind a barbershop," said Kate. "What is this?"

"I'm sure they wanted somebody outside the world of mainstream real estate. Keep everything under the radar. It's how they operate."

A sign beside the door proclaimed Richard Kozlowski, Attorney at Law. She turned the handle and went inside.

If a tornado had hit the place, the result would have been the same. All the file drawers stood open, and papers littered the floor. A small safe in the corner had been ransacked, its door removed through the use of power tools which still lay on the floor.

"What the hell?" exclaimed Kate.

David moved to the middle of the room. "Don't touch anything." He continued through a door on the back wall. "Kate! Back here."

It led to a kitchenette containing a sink, a mini-fridge, and a microwave. A man lay face down in a puddle of dried blood, a bullet hole in the back of his head.

"I'm guessing this is Richard Koslowski, former Attorney at Law," said David. He kneeled beside the body. "He's not in full rigor. If he's just going into it, he was killed earlier today. If it's easing off, then it was at least twenty-four hours ago."

He rolled the body over onto its back. Kozlowski's face was purple from the pooling of his blood after death. David began going through his pockets. "Nothing. They took his wallet and phone."

Kate backed out into the office and went over to the desk. "There's an appointment book. He had something scheduled at 9:00 this morning. It's circled in red ink, so it must have been important." She gazed around at the mess. "I don't get it. Why kill him now?"

"They're covering their tracks," said David. "They used him for the real estate transaction, so he knew things. While their operation was ongoing, killing him might have led the police to dig into his recent business dealings, including the sale of the cabin. They couldn't risk drawing attention to themselves, but now they're closing up shop."

"So, we've hit another dead end. Again." She stared out the window. A small, neatly tended garden nestled against the garage.

"He lived here," she said, starting for the door. "The stairs up to the apartment are outside."

The door was unlocked and led into a cluttered but otherwise undisturbed living space. Several days' worth of newspapers littered the coffee table, accompanied by an empty whiskey bottle. The place needed a good cleaning and the furniture had seen better days, but it wasn't trashed like the office.

"They didn't know he lived up here," said Kate. "Maybe we'll get lucky for a change."

They moved through the apartment, touching nothing but looking everywhere. The kitchen counter held a pile of Styrofoam takeout containers and a collection of dirty dishes. Three empty beer cans rested on the table alongside an open package of deli meat which had outlived its expiration date by a considerable margin.

The bed was unmade, and dirty laundry overflowed the basket in the corner, but nothing seemed unusual or out of place. Kate went to the bedside table. Besides a magazine whose cover featured a scantily clad blonde, she found a pile of manila file folders and a notepad. "David, come here."

She pointed to the pad. "Look."

The pad contained a lot of handwritten notes, many illegible. But one stood out.

Sintran P.O. EN. Same woman?

"He was asking questions about Sintran," said Kate. "But same woman?"

"Maybe the person who hired him was a woman, and he's wondering if she was the same one who arranged for the P.O. box."

"He'd already been paid for handling the closing. Why would he care?"

"The whole transaction was cloaked in secrecy and deception," he replied. "It must have aroused his curiosity. Look around this place. He was living pretty much hand to mouth. If he could uncover something worthwhile, maybe he thought he could cash in."

"Blackmail? He obviously didn't know who he was messing with."

"I'm sure he didn't."

Kate leaned over and picked up a cell phone lying on the floor between the table and the bed. "He forgot to take it with him when he went downstairs."

"Bring it and the notepad. We need to leave before someone walks in on us."

David took a hand towel from the bathroom and wiped the door handle clean as they left. At the bottom of the stairs, Kate grabbed his arm. "Wait here a minute."

She went into the office and back to the kitchen. The phone was an older model that still used thumbprints. Taking Kozlowski's stiff hand in hers, she pressed his thumb against the phone. To her relief, it opened. She quickly tapped the settings icon and set the sleep timeout to never. Hopefully, the battery would hold out until she could get it onto a charger. She shoved the phone into her pocket and snatched the appointment book off the desk on her way out.

"Let's get out of here," she said and headed for their car. David wiped down the door handle and followed her out to the street.

Kate glanced back at the barbershop as they pulled away from the curb. "When somebody finally finds the body, the barber's going to tell the police about us."

"Nobody back there has any idea who we are. Even if somebody jotted down the license plate or caught it on a security camera, the car's rented on an untraceable credit card."

As they drove back toward Washington, Kate began going through the contents of the phone. "David, find a place to pull over."

He parked beside a roadside produce stand. "What?"

She held up a picture of a wooden cabin sitting in a wide clearing, surrounded by trees. "That has to be the place. He was there. And then there's this." The next photo was of a woman. It was taken at an odd angle, but her face was clearly visible. "I think this is the person who hired him. He snuck a pic of her while her attention was diverted."

David studied the photo. "The light wasn't great, but if we had something to compare it to, it might be enough for an ID. Is there anything in his notes?"

"His handwriting sucks, and a lot of this stuff is pretty cryptic. As far as I can tell, he was wondering if this woman is the Emily Nassar that rented the P.O. box." She pulled out her own phone. "Maybe Monica turned up something."

She made the call and put it on speaker. "Monica, it's me. Anything yet on Emily Nassar?"

"I was just going to call you. Peter started looking, and he didn't have to look far. There's an Emily Nassar working as an intelligence analyst at CIA. That can't be a coincidence."

Kate stared out the window, her mind churning.

"Kate? Are you still there?"

"Is Nick in the office?"

"Yeah. He's been at his desk all afternoon. I'm keeping an eye on him."

"The time for subtlety is over. You and Peter meet us at the safehouse and bring Nick. I think I know what's going on, and we're running out of time."

David glanced over at her. "What are you doing? We can't tip our hand until …"

"If I'm right and we delay, people are going to die. Monica, make sure Peter understands the urgency."

"Got it. See you there."

She looked back at the picture. *If you're responsible for this, your day of reckoning is coming fast. Dan never knew what happened to him, but you will. I'll make sure of that.*

Kate patted the handgun in her pocket and settled back in her seat.

CHAPTER THIRTY-FOUR

Peter escorted Nick through the front door. "Where do you want him?"

Nick's eyes widened when he saw Kate. "You! You're supposed to be …"

"Dead. Yeah, I know. Sorry to disappoint."

He looked around at the others. "You said we were going to meet someone with information about a mole. What is this? Why am I here?"

"You've been spying on ISA," said Kate. "Now you're going to tell me why and for who."

He turned pale. "I don't know what you're talking about."

"Bullshit. This can be easy or hard. Your choice."

He looked over at Peter. "I'll report this."

"You'll be doing it from a prison cell unless you cooperate. You should weigh your options."

He stiffened his shoulders and tried vainly to project an air of confidence. "I've got nothing to say."

Kate turned to Talia. "Take him down to the basement and secure him. If he gives you any trouble, do whatever you need to."

She was back in minutes. "He's not very comfortable, but he won't be going anywhere. Now, what's going on?"

"Everyone, take a seat," said Kate. "I want to see if you can punch holes in my theory."

She waited while they settled onto the sofa and armchairs. "First, I'm sorry to have to drag you back into this, Peter. I wanted to keep your hands clean, but I think we need to act fast. That means we'll need your help."

He waved her apology aside. "Plausible deniability can be convenient for dodging the fallout, but the job has to get done. Let's worry about that later. Monica filled me in on what you found so far. I assume you have a plan?"

"When you looked into Emily Nassar's file, was there a picture?"

He nodded.

Kate held up the cell phone. "Is this her?"

Peter leaned forward and examined the image. "Yes. Where did you get that?"

"This is Richard Kozlowski's phone. I think he sneaked a pic of the woman who hired him to handle the purchase of the cabin. Now connect the dots."

They all sat in silence, working through the implications of Kate's discovery. Monica was the first to speak. "Nick's been spying for someone at CIA. Susan Reardon said her information was coming from her chief of staff. That may be true, but Emily Nassar works there as well. If we're right and there's a connection, then she purchased the cabin where Nick is supposed to meet someone tomorrow, someone whose initials are EN. It all fits together. If she's working as an agent for Iran, then that explains everything."

"But we can't prove it yet," said Kate. "What have we found out about her?"

Peter pulled out a notepad. "Her parents were Egyptian Christians. Her father was a renowned expert in ancient civilizations and joined the faculty of an Ivy League university. He and his wife became naturalized citizens and raised one daughter, Emily, who was born here. She seems to have been a typical American girl. In high school, she was an honor student and played on the softball team.

After graduation, she remained at home and enrolled in a local college."

"Are there any break points in her timeline?" asked David.

Peter shrugged. "Such as?"

"Maybe you call it something different. A point in time where things changed for her in significant ways."

Peter referred to his notes. "When she was a college sophomore, her parents died in an automobile accident. She accompanied their bodies back to Egypt for burial and stayed for a couple of months. It's understandable. She was an only child with no other relatives here. She wanted to be around family."

"Had she been there before?" asked Kate.

"Yes. They made a trip back every few years when she was growing up."

"What happened after she returned?"

"She put the house on the market and sold off all the furnishings. Then she enrolled at the University of Virginia to finish her degree."

"In what field?"

"Originally her major was English Lit. She switched to Computer Science at Virginia."

David started ticking points off on his fingers. "The girl goes to Egypt. She comes back and cuts off all ties to her old life, moves to a place where nobody knows her, and changes her major to something more useful for a spy. I think the Emily Nassar who returned from Egypt wasn't the same woman who went there. She had her IDs and passport and looked enough like her to pass, but the Emily who came back was an Iranian agent."

Kate nodded in agreement. "David may be right. It's difficult for them to place assets here and they may have seen an opportunity. If so, the real Emily is probably dead."

Monica held up her hand. "Wait a minute. I'm confused. Emily was just a college student. What use was she to them?"

"Nothing at the time," Peter replied. "They were planting a seed. As soon as she established herself in Virginia, she became a sleeper. She completed her degree and began an effort to place herself inside a government agency. Getting hired at the CIA was like striking gold for her. She settled into her new job, did it well, and waited for instructions."

"What we need is proof," said Kate. "And we can start with Nick. Monica, I suggest you stay up here. This could get ugly."

She swallowed hard and shook her head. "If I'm part of the team and want everyone to trust me, then I can't just pick my spots. But if I puke, don't make fun of me. I promise I'll clean it up."

Talia grinned and put her arm around Monica's shoulders. "I heaved my guts out the first time. You get hardened to it."

"Is that really a good thing?"

"Maybe not, but it's a necessary thing."

Nick watched them come down the basement stairs and array themselves in front of him. Talia had placed him on a straight back chair set against a metal support column. His arms were pulled back around the pole and fastened with a cable tie.

He struggled against the restraints. "You can't do this. You have no right."

Kate stood squarely in front of him. "Don't waste your breath talking about rights. Why are you spying for Iran?"

His eyes darted from Kate to Peter. "What's she talking about? Why would I do that?"

Kate pulled a gun from the waistband of her jeans. "We don't have time to coax the truth out of you, and I'm sick of dealing with all the bullshit everyone keeps throwing my way. You're going to tell me what I want to know. If I think you're lying, I'll blow off a kneecap. If you keep lying, I'll blow off the other one."

Nick's face turned deadly white. He looked up at Peter. "You'll let her do this?"

Peter shrugged. "Let her do what? Officially, this isn't happening. You can resist, and she'll still get what she wants. But that will be a bloody and painful process, and afterward you'll be a problem that will need to be disposed of."

Nick flinched as Kate tapped the barrel of her gun on his knee. "Which way is it going to be?"

"She'll kill me." His voice shook with terror.

"So will I," she replied softly. "The difference is that I'm right here in front of you."

He looked away, his jaws clamped tightly together.

"Well then," said Kate, taking aim at his right knee.

Nick tried to pull away from her. "Wait!" The word came out like a pleading scream. "She was blackmailing me."

Kate stepped back and lowered the gun. "Okay. Let's hear it."

"If I tell you everything, I walk out of here, right?"

"If you talk, you get to continue breathing for now. That's the best deal you're going to get."

He swallowed with difficulty. "I'm scared."

"You should be. You said she was blackmailing you. Give us a name. And blackmailing you for what?"

"I only met her once, and I don't know her name. Josh might. He referred to her by her initials. EN."

"Josh Griswold?"

"Yeah. He's Susan Reardon's chief of staff. We play pickup basketball a couple of nights a week and usually go out for a beer afterward. One night I messed up."

"Go on."

"I mentioned the Artisimov defection. Given his position, I assumed he already knew. But he didn't and started asking questions."

"And you told him I was going to Paris?"

He looked away. "Yes."

"What happened after that?"

"A couple of days later, he said someone wanted to talk to me. That Saturday we drove down into the Virginia hills to a cabin in the middle of goddamn nowhere. A woman was waiting for us."

Kate pulled out Kozlowski's phone and showed him the picture. "Is this the woman?"

He nodded. "She wanted me to keep passing information to Josh."

"What kind of information?"

"Any recent intel ISA had on Russia or Iran, and anything I could find out about you. She threatened to let everyone know I told Josh about Artisimov unless I did what she wanted. Another black mark on my record would put an end to my career. Dad wouldn't be able to fix it a second time. What was I supposed to do?"

"Your duty might have been a good choice," said Peter.

Kate didn't try to hide her disgust. "So, your conduit was Josh."

"Yeah. The only time I ever spoke to her was at that cabin. And I thought the stuff I gave them wasn't going anywhere except the CIA. I swear. You have to believe me."

"Your credibility's running on empty. What about Josh? Why is he working for her?"

"He said he was being blackmailed, too."

"For what?"

He shrugged. "He didn't say. I didn't ask."

"You're supposed to go to that cabin again tomorrow?"

His eyes widened. "How did you know?"

Kate ignored the question. "Josh too?"

"He said she wants to talk to both of us." He looked around at the others. "What happens now?"

Peter stepped forward. "For the time being, you stay right here. If you're telling the truth and we're successful in ending this, you'll be able to resign without charges, providing you agree to keep your mouth shut. But if you're still lying, a life spent in prison is the best you can hope for. The alternative would be much worse."

"Last chance," said Kate. "Anything else you want to tell us?"

He shook his head.

"Then sit tight and hope we come out on top."

As she turned away, he suddenly sat up straight in the chair. "Wait. Are you going to go up to that cabin?"

Kate turned back to face him. "Maybe."

"A dirt and gravel road leads up from the county highway. About a hundred yards in, you'll come to a wooden gate with a sign warning against trespassing and a place that's wide enough to turn a car around. The gate's rigged. A wire is attached to its base by a hook. It's connected to a flare gun mounted on a post. If you open the gate, the gun will fire a flare up into the air. Slip the wire off the hook and they won't know you're coming."

"Sounds pretty crude," observed Talia.

"There's no electricity."

Kate patted him on the shoulder, causing him to flinch once again. "You take it easy down here. I'll bring you some water and something to eat later."

Upon their return to the kitchen, Kate turned to the others. "Emily is the Iranian spy. We wouldn't be able to prove it in court, but there's no time for legalities at this point anyway."

Monica resumed her seat on the sofa. "Do we have enough to give it to the FBI?"

"Normally, the answer would be yes," said Peter. "But as Kate said, time is the problem. We'd need to lay everything out for the Bureau, and they'll want to talk to Nick before deciding how to proceed. I don't believe we have that luxury. In this situation, Emily Nassar has two options. The first is to slip away and go home. The second would be to extract a measure of revenge. Based on the attempt to kill Kate, it seems she's choosing the latter."

"I'm not sure I understand."

"She no longer has a source of intel," said Kate. "But she's still an Iranian agent operating inside our borders. She thinks she got her revenge on me. Now she may want to do the same against the U.S."

"A terrorist attack?"

"Maybe. Back when all this started, Dimitri said something was in place to distract the U.S. from what Russia was planning. He called it Valkyrie. I think an attack was in the works even before things started falling apart, and now she may decide to carry it out anyway. It's a possibility we can't ignore. We need to move fast and end this before more people die."

"I made some inquiries," said Peter. "Emily's called in sick the last three days. My guess is she's dropped off the radar to wrap up loose ends. Nick would be one of those. Maybe Josh as well."

"She'll be at that cabin tomorrow," said David. "That's our

chance. And Peter's right. If we turn this over to the FBI, we might end up being too late to stop her."

Kate nodded in agreement. "Then we need to get busy. Monica, bring up the map of the area around the cabin. Use the satellite view so we can see what we're dealing with. Can you project it onto the TV?"

"Sure. Just give me a minute."

They took seats in the living room and studied the images on the screen. "There's only one way in, and that bothers me," said Peter. "That clearing looks to be three or four acres in size with the cabin at the far end from where the path opens onto it. Even if we disable the warning flare, she'll see us coming as soon as we enter the clearing."

"That single entrance isn't just a problem for us, it's one for her as well," said Talia. "If someone raided the place, she'd be trapped. No other way in is the same as no other way out. If she's a trained agent, she wouldn't let that happen."

Kate leaned forward for a closer look. "I don't see anything that could be an escape route."

"Look at the layout," Talia continued, pointing at the screen. "The clearing's near the top of a high hill. The path from the county highway winds its way up and enters the clearing from the west. At the east end is the cabin. Switch to the map view, Monica."

The satellite imagery gave way to a traditional roadmap.

Talia pointed to a spot just east of the cabin. "There's a road at the base of the hill. You can't see it on the visual view because of the trees, but it connects to the highway about a mile farther north. That side of the hill is the steepest part, too steep for a vehicle, but I'll bet there's a footpath that leads from behind the cabin down to that road."

Kate was studying the map. "Suppose you're right about the path. If they're attacked, they slip out the back and make it to the bottom of the hill. But then what? They'd need quick access to a vehicle."

"It's a back road, and the area is heavily wooded," said David. "You could hide a motorcycle with no trouble. Throw a waterproof camo tarp over it and nobody would ever know it was there."

"It makes sense," said Peter, "but how do we find this path?"

"We don't look for the path," said Talia. "We look for the bike. Can you get us a drone with electromagnetic scanning abilities?"

Peter nodded.

"We fly it along the base of the hill. Something containing as much metal as a motorcycle will stand out like a spotlight at midnight."

Kate looked over at Talia. "You and David know more about tactics than I do. How would we do this?"

"Once we locate the path, you and David start up the hill and take up a position in the trees behind the cabin. They're expecting Nick, so we take him and his car. Monica will be dropped off down by the highway so she can watch our backs and warn us if somebody's coming up behind us. Peter and I get out near the top and work our way through the trees to flanking positions. Once we're in place, Nick will drive up to the cabin."

"And then what?"

"I'm sure she plans on killing him. But first she'll make sure he hasn't talked to anyone and get an update on what ISA is planning. They'll go inside. Once they do, Kate and David throw a couple of flashbangs through a window, and we all charge in and secure the scene."

Monica looked puzzled. "What's a flashbang?"

"The technical term is a concussion grenade. It produces a blinding flash of light and a deafening boom, but there's no shrapnel and minimal explosive force. You'd practically have to be standing on top of it to be seriously injured, but anyone who's in the room is going to be blind and deaf for several minutes."

"It sounds too easy," said Monica, a doubtful expression on her face.

Talia nodded. "You're probably right. There's an old military saying that no battle plan survives contact with the enemy. Things won't go as smoothly as I just laid it out, but at least it's a framework we can work from."

"Let's suppose it all goes wrong," said Kate. "What's the exit strategy?"

"You and I hustle back down that path and shoot anyone who tries to follow," David replied. "Talia and Peter will move as far back into the woods as they can. That goes for you too, Monica. Emily's priority will be to get the hell out of there, not hang around as a potential target. Once she's gone, we use Nick's vehicle and follow her."

Kate turned to Peter. "Are you sure you want to be part of this? That goes for you too, Monica. You've both been indispensable, but up to this point it's all been logistics and planning. Now it's going to get real. The three of us have been operating off the grid all along and can just fade away if things go south. You could end up hung out to dry."

"You're here because of me," Peter replied. "I sent an untrained and untested analyst out into the field. My reasons seemed sufficient at the time, but it wasn't fair to you and now you need help. I see no way the three of you could do this alone. Let's just say I owe you one."

"And I spent three weeks in a hospital not sure if I was going to live," added Monica. "She's part of the reason why, and she tried to kill my best friend. She's got some payback coming. I'm in."

Kate couldn't hide the smile that spread across her face. "Thanks, both of you. But don't say I didn't warn you."

"What if Nick refuses?" asked Monica.

"If he's going to avoid prison, he won't have a choice," replied Peter.

Talia was making a list. "We're going to need coms. And weapons."

Peter nodded. "I'll take care of it. When do we do this?"

"They're expecting Nick at noon tomorrow," said Kate. "That's our opportunity, so let's get busy. We have a lot to do."

CHAPTER THIRTY-FIVE

The road at the base of the hill proved to be narrow, and while paved at one time, was now a rutted, pothole strewn obstacle course. David pulled Nick's SUV as far to the side as he could and braked to a halt.

"We should be directly below the cabin. If we're right about the motorcycle, it won't be too far away."

Talia sat in the rear with Nick. "Go find it. I'll stay with him."

The rest of them got out and stretched. Kate looked up at the tree covered hill. Climbing a quarter of a mile of steep incline would not be an easy task.

David opened the cargo hatch and pulled out the drone. It measured eighteen inches with a rotor mounted on each corner. The pale gray color would make it practically invisible to anyone on the ground. He set it down beside the car and placed the control panel on the hood. "Okay, let's see what we can find."

The four rotors began spinning, and the drone slowly rose twenty feet into the air. The device was much quieter than Kate expected, emitting a low hum that was inaudible even a short distance away. David let it hover in place while he made some adjustments on the console, then sent it back the way they'd come, flying as close to the trees as possible. It reversed course at the bend in the road and sailed back toward them, passing overhead and continuing along the tree line. Kate watched the displays over David's shoulder. When the drone reached a point about one hundred feet ahead, one of the graphical readouts spiked and then fell off.

"That's the magnetic display," said David. "I think we found the bike."

"Or maybe an old refrigerator someone dumped there," said Peter.

David maneuvered the drone in narrowing circles until he found the spot with the strongest signal. "That's the place," he said as he gently landed the drone.

Kate rushed to the spot, making her way through the tangled underbrush. "Over here," she cried, pausing by the tree line and pulling a green and brown camouflage tarp from a pair of dirt bikes. She let it drop to the ground and moved further into the trees. A narrow opening in the undergrowth caught her eye.

David came up beside her. "It's even steeper than we thought. Getting to the top will take some time."

"Then we better get started."

He shook his head. "I'd rather know what's up there before we go charging in. Let's get back to the others."

Peter and Monica were waiting by the motorcycles. "The path's there, but it won't be an easy go," said Kate. "David wants a look at the clearing first."

They retrieved the drone and returned to the car. David activated the control panel and the rotors spun once more. He guided it up the hill, staying just above the treetops. Within moments, the clearing came into view on the video display.

An SUV and a pickup truck were parked to one side of the cabin. Two smaller structures stood behind it, backed up against the trees. No one was in sight.

"Two vehicles," said David. "That means Josh is already there. It's pretty much as we expected."

Peter stepped away from the monitor. "I agree. Game on."

He removed a duffle from the back of the SUV and handed them each a small earpiece. "The frequency is pre-programmed. The earpiece acts as both speaker and a voice activated mic. Keep the chatter to a minimum." He gave Monica a handheld radio. "The com link won't extend down to the base of the hill. If anyone comes up that road, you call me on this. Do you know how to use a gun?"

"I'm no expert, but I won't shoot myself in the foot."

Peter looked over at Kate, who nodded. "She needs to defend herself if things go south. But only in an emergency, Monica. Don't go Rambo on us. And when did you learn to shoot?"

"An old boyfriend. Don't ask. And don't worry either. Nobody will even know I'm there."

Peter took a pistol from the bag and handed it to her. "There's a full clip in it so be careful." He began handing automatic assault rifles to the others.

"We want her alive, if possible," said Kate. "But when it comes right down to it, do what you have to. This ends here."

"Talia and I will let you know when we're in position," said Peter. "Nick, when she and I get out of the car, give us five minutes and then drive into the clearing and up to the cabin. Do whatever they tell you. They won't harm you until they're satisfied you haven't talked. That'll give us more than enough time."

"What if he bails?" asked Monica.

"He can't back all the way down that road," replied Talia. "There's too many twists and turns. He'd need to turn around." She stared straight at Nick. "If he tries it, I'll kill him."

"Look, why do you need me at all?" he asked, his voice weak. "Why can't you just assault the place and be done with it?"

"Because people would be killed, including some of us," said David.

"You'll be fine," added Kate. "If they take you inside, we'll use a flashbang to neutralize the scene. If they don't, then Talia will shoot anyone who's outside with you. Either way, it should be over fast. This is how you earn the right to stay out of prison. Focus on that."

Peter checked the action on his weapon. "You two better get started up that hill. Everyone check in once you're in position."

David slung the rifle over his shoulder. "You got the flashbangs?"

"In my backpack," Kate replied.

The trail was narrow and barely wide enough for one person. Kate had expected a zigzag route to make the climb easier, but it went straight up the steep grade, deviating only to avoid obstacles. She finally realized she was looking at it backwards. The path was never meant to be a way to access the cabin. It was an escape route and needed to provide the fastest way possible to the bottom. That it was so narrow actually helped. Branches and small saplings were within arm's reach and provided handholds as they proceeded toward the top.

Surrounded only by dense forest, Kate lost all sense of how much progress they were making. She wiped sweat from her forehead and paused twice to drink from her water bottle. The shade from the trees tempered the July heat and humidity to some extent, but it was still a tough climb.

David held up his right hand and came to a stop. The trail ended about fifty feet ahead of them. They moved into the trees on opposite sides of the path and crept toward the cabin. Near the edge of the clearing, Kate got down on her stomach and inched her way forward until she gained a view of the entire area.

The rear wall of the cabin was featureless except for a single door. Two smaller buildings were nestled against the trees. The door to one of them stood open, revealing the interior of a storage shed. She was about to leave her hiding place when a man exited the second structure, zipping up his fly as he walked toward the back door of the cabin.

"Com check," she said in a quiet voice. "Can everyone hear me?"

"Check," came David's reply. Peter and Talia responded as well.

"We may have a problem," she said. "Neither Emily nor Griswold is in sight, but there's another man here."

"Is he inside the cabin?" asked Talia.

"He is now. There's nobody outside that I can see."

"Then as long as they're all together, the plan should still work."

∼

Monica peeked around the boulder she had chosen as her hiding place. It provided a clear view of the gate and the path leading up to it. The radio squawked softly. "Peter?" she whispered into the mic.

"Yes. Just making sure I can reach you. Stay alert. This shouldn't take long."

"Got it. Good luck."

She placed the radio on the ground beside her gun and looked all around her. The dense undergrowth behind her and the boulder in front shielded her from view. With a nervous sigh, she settled in to wait.

∽

"I'm in position." Peter's voice whispered quietly in Kate's ear.

"Me as well," echoed Talia. "Nick should be entering the clearing about now."

Kate took a deep breath to steady her nerves. Less than a minute later, Nick's SUV drove into the clearing and stopped at the far end. For a moment, Kate wondered if he was going to turn around and make a run for it. "Don't do it," she heard herself whisper. To her relief, the vehicle resumed its slow progress toward the cabin.

"David, cover me and don't let anyone get down that path." She made a quick dash across the open ground to the cabin's rear. She glanced quickly around the corner of the building. Seeing no one, she crept along the north side until she was beneath a window. When the moment came, she'd smash the glass and toss in the flashbang.

∽

Monica heard the vehicle before it came into view. A black Jeep pulled up to the gate, and the driver got out. He wore a tan work jacket and jeans with a black baseball cap pulled low over his forehead.

Monica knew she had to wait until he was back in the car before risking a radio call. He went to open the gate but pulled up short, bending over to examine the base. He straightened up, holding the disconnected end of the trigger wire in his hand. Dropping it, he examined the ground around the gate. His gaze moved to the trees and Monica could finally see his face. Only it wasn't a man at all.

The driver pulled a gun from under her jacket. She stared at the ground and then back at the trees again before returning to the Jeep and climbing behind the wheel.

As soon as she was through the gate, Monica snatched the radio and pressed the transmit button. "You've got trouble coming. Emily's not up there, but she's on her way. And she found the disconnected wire. What should I do?"

"Nothing," came Peter's response. "Stay where you are. And keep out of sight."

Monica put down the radio and picked up the gun. She sat behind the boulder and switched off the safety, wishing she were up top with the others instead of down here by herself. An idea occurred to her, but she couldn't decide if it was stupid or brilliant. She peeked around the rock. If she was going to do this, now was the time. She left the safety of her hiding place and headed for the gate. If she could figure out how to dismount the flare gun, it might give her an advantage.

∼

Kate's earpiece came to life. "Emily's not in the cabin," said Peter. "Monica says she's on her way up. It's your call, Kate."

She didn't need to think about this one. "We're committed. They'll kill Nick if we abort now. I can't see the front of the cabin. What's the status?"

"He just pulled up. Griswold and another man are waiting outside the door."

Kate moved silently toward the front of the cabin until she could peek around the corner. The two men had their backs to her as Nick got out of the car and approached them. "Okay, Josh. Now what?"

"She'll be here soon. Let's go inside."

Kate reached into her backpack for the flashbang, but the second man held up his hand and pulled a radio from his jacket pocket. He put it to his ear. "I understand."

Griswold glanced over at him. "Something wrong?"

"She's on her way up and there might be trouble. I'll keep watch out here. Take him inside."

Josh motioned Nick toward the door. "Come on. We need to talk."

Kate swore under her breath. The plan assumed they'd all be inside the cabin and didn't account for the third man. She keyed her mic. "Talia, if the guard tries to go inside, shoot him. Let me know when Emily shows up."

"What are you going to do?" asked Peter.

"Improvise."

She moved to the rear of the cabin and slowly turned the handle on the back door. It swung open noiselessly and she crept inside. She found herself in a small room set up as a makeshift kitchen containing several coolers, a dozen plastic gallon jugs of water, and a table covered with stacks of canned goods.

She could hear voices out in the front room. Nick had to realize their plan had fallen off the rails. If he decided his best chance of getting out of this was to sound an alert, she'd need to act fast. She moved to the door separating the kitchen from the rest of the cabin. The two of them were standing face to face in the middle of the room with Griswold's back to her.

"What the hell's going on?" asked Nick.

Griswald shrugged. "Relax. She just wants to talk to us."

"There's nothing to talk about. Kate Malone's dead."

"You're sure?"

"That's what everyone's saying. There's nothing more I can help you with."

"Did anyone at ISA catch on to what you were doing? Did Schilling ever seem suspicious?"

"Not that I could tell."

Griswold nodded. "Good. Now there's just one more thing."

He pulled a gun from under his jacket. Nick started backing away. "Wait a minute. What the hell are you doing?"

"I got blackmailed into this the same as you, but I intend to walk away in one piece. And you know too much."

Nick held his hands out in front of him. "Wait. I can still help you. They're here. They're here, I swear."

Josh glanced out the front window. "What do you mean, they're here?"

Kate stepped through the doorway and closed the distance to Griswold in three rapid strides. He turned toward her but was too late to avoid the barrel of her gun as it smashed into the side of his head.

Nick backed into a corner as Griswold crumpled silently to the floor. "I didn't have a choice," he whimpered. "He was going to kill me."

"Shut up. And keep quiet if you want to live through this."

Kate scooped up Griswold's weapon and turned her attention to the room itself. A cabinet standing near the front wall held three AR-15 rifles along with several boxes of ammunition. Spools of electrical wire, needle nosed pliers, small screwdrivers and a soldering iron littered a work bench placed against the far wall. A disassembled cell phone and a dismounted circuit board lay beside them. Everything you'd need to make a detonator for a bomb.

A shelf above the workbench held a collection of manuals, mainly technical, but a blue plastic binder had a taped label with the word 'target' written on it. Kate paged through the contents. It contained both aerial and ground level views of various locations in and around Washington. There were floor plans as well, labeled only by a code which would take time to decipher.

"Emily just pulled into the clearing." Talia's voice had an edge to it. "She's just sitting there with the engine idling. What do you want to do?"

"Nothing yet," said Kate, putting the binder down on the workbench and turning toward the front door. "The cabin's secured, so we'll let her make the first move. What's the guard doing?"

"Waving at her to come over."

"You and Peter focus on her. Let me know if she starts toward the cabin. I've got the guard."

She peeked out the window. He stood, hands on hips with the rifle slung over his shoulder. The Jeep still sat at the far end of the clearing. Why wasn't she coming closer? Kate glanced back at the workbench. "Nick, get out the back!" she shouted and threw open the front door.

The startled guard frantically grabbed for his weapon, but Kate was faster. She got off three shots while running for the safety of the trees. The first missed, but the next two struck the guard in the leg and abdomen. He went down, writhing in pain. Gunfire came from the other end of the clearing, but Kate ignored it as she sprinted hard for the tree line.

She almost made it before the cabin erupted in a ball of flame.

CHAPTER THIRTY-SIX

Kate landed face down on the ground, the breath knocked out of her and her ears ringing. She gasped for air as she rolled onto her side. The cabin was engulfed in flames. She could hear popping noises from inside as stored ammunition went off, ignited by the searing heat.

She struggled to her feet, spitting dirt out of her mouth. Her left shoulder was bruised, but otherwise she was unhurt. She flexed it as she took stock of the situation. Nick's SUV lay on its side, two of the tires on fire and producing clouds of acrid black smoke. The south wall of the cabin had fallen onto the SUV, but the pickup was still upright, and except for some scorched paint, seemed undamaged.

More gunshots came from the west end of the clearing as Emily's Jeep turned around and started back down the access road. Talia stepped out from the trees, spraying bullets at the vehicle as it disappeared down the path.

Kate clicked her mic switch. "Everyone check in."

"I'm good," came David's reply.

"Me too," added Talia.

There was no response from Peter. "Talia, go check on Peter. David, if the keys to the pickup are in it, move it away from the cabin."

She walked over to where the guard was prostrate on the ground. He'd have eventually bled out from the bullet wound to his stomach, but he hadn't had to suffer so slow a death. He'd been too close to the cabin when the bomb went off. One leg was twisted at an impossible angle and his skin had blackened from the heat. But the death blow was the slender piece of wood embedded in the side of his skull.

An engine roared to life. She looked up to see the pickup back away from the ruins of the cabin and come toward her.

She climbed in beside him as he braked to a stop. "Did Nick make it out the back?" she asked.

David shook his head.

"Damn. Talia's trying to locate Peter. They should be over there somewhere," she said, pointing to the other side of the clearing.

"Emily?"

"She got away. Talia got off some shots but couldn't stop her." Kate looked back at the burning cabin. "She wasn't leaving any loose ends behind. We should have anticipated this."

He glanced over at her. "You can't foresee every eventuality. Sometimes you have to deal with things as they happen."

"There's not much left to deal with. Nick and Josh Griswold are dead, and Emily's gone."

David parked the truck at the south edge of the clearing. Kate got out and pushed her way into the undergrowth. "Talia? Where are you?"

"Over here. Peter's been hit."

Kate found Talia kneeling beside him, using her jacket to apply pressure to a shoulder wound. "The bullet wound doesn't look too bad, but he hit his head when he fell. We need to get him to a hospital."

"Do you know what happened?"

"I think Peter figured out why she wasn't going near the cabin. He started shooting just as it blew, and she returned fire. I tried to stop her. I know I hit the Jeep. I'm not sure if I got her or not."

"That'll have to wait. David, help me get him into the bed of the pickup."

Monica could hear a car coming down the path. Maybe the whole thing was over, but the explosion from up the hill sounded a lot louder than what she imagined flashbangs would be like. Peter wasn't answering the radio, but that didn't worry her too much. They probably had their hands full up there. She looked down at the flare gun. With any luck, this would be the team coming and she wouldn't need to put her plan to the test.

The vehicle came around a sharp curve, swaying as it bounced over the rutted roadway. Monica tried to steady her nerves and peeked around the boulder. It was Emily's Jeep. Something had gone wrong.

She picked up the flare gun. Trying to wreck the Jeep seemed like a better idea than getting into a gunfight she knew she couldn't win. But either way, Emily couldn't be allowed to get away. Not after all the hell she'd created. Not after trying to kill Kate.

A loud crash and the sound of snapping wood caused Monica to take another look. Emily had smashed through the gate without stopping. Monica stood up, pointed the flare gun at the oncoming vehicle and fired. The flare struck the Jeep on the hood and exploded in a brilliant ball of orange light. It ricocheted off the windshield and bounced straight up into the air before falling and coming to rest on the rear seat. The car veered to the left and struck a tree head on. The flare continued to burn, setting fire to the upholstery. Emily gave a glance over her shoulder before scrambling out of the car. She ran fifty feet into the trees before throwing herself flat to the ground.

Monica instinctively ducked back behind her hiding place just as the car exploded. The force of the blast caused the boulder to roll onto her foot, pinning her to the ground. The pain was excruciating and no matter how hard she pulled, she couldn't get loose. Out on the road, the car was burning, but there was no way to know where Emily was.

Monica picked up the gun Peter had given her, her hands trembling. She cursed at her own foolishness. Why had she thought she could stop Emily all by herself? Praying that the team was coming down the hill in pursuit, she tucked the hand clutching the gun behind her and waited.

∼

The explosion from down at the base of the hill startled all of them. "What the hell was that?" shouted Talia.

"I don't know," Kate answered. "Where's Peter's radio?"

Talia searched through his pockets. "He must have dropped it when he got hit. Good luck finding it in all this undergrowth."

Kate swore. And she thought things couldn't get any worse. "We've got to get down there. Talia, stay in the back with Peter and keep that rifle ready. David, you're driving."

She got in on the passenger side and pounded on the dashboard. "Go, dammit. Drive!"

∼

Monica heard footsteps approaching. She tried once more to pull her foot free without success. When Emily came around the boulder, Monica could see the anger smoldering in her eyes. A trickle of blood ran down the side of her face and onto the collar of her jacket. She held a gun in her right hand.

"Who are you?" she demanded. Monica shook her head and said nothing.

Emily looked down at the base of the rock. "You're not going anywhere. Do you have a vehicle down here?"

"No. It looks like you're stuck. You might as well surrender."

Emily smiled. "Surrender to a woman who can't even stand up? Sorry."

She raised the weapon. Monica pulled hers out from behind her and saw the surprise in Emily's eyes.

They fired simultaneously.

Kate stuck her head out the window. "That was gunfire. Faster, David."

"If I go any faster, we'll end up wrapped around a tree. We're almost there."

They rounded the last curve as David braked to a stop. The gutted Jeep was burning, and the fire had spread to some of the surrounding foliage. A tree felled by the force of the blast lay across the road, eliminating any hope of getting down to the highway. Nobody was in sight.

"Talia, stay with Peter. Keep that rifle ready and watch for Emily. David, you take that side of the road. I've got this one."

Kate slipped out of the truck and into the trees, staying low and using whatever cover she could as she moved closer to the Jeep. A boulder to her right caught her attention. If she were Emily, that was where she'd hide. She circled around behind it and peeked past a large oak tree. Someone was lying on the ground. She raised her weapon, but then relaxed. That red hair could only belong to one person. She stepped out of hiding and started toward the rock. Monica's right arm came up, the gun pointing right at Kate.

"Relax, Monica. It's me."

The arm dropped back to the ground. "It's about damn time. What the hell happened?"

"I have the same question," Kate replied, looking over at the Jeep.

"I didn't know how else to stop her, so I shot it with the flare gun. Then it blew up like there was a bomb in it."

"There was. She was planning an attack somewhere in the city. Where did she go?"

Monica pointed down the path to the highway. "That way, but I doubt she made it too far. I shot her."

"She wasn't armed?"

"She had a gun, but it jammed, or maybe it was empty. She

ducked back out of sight before I could get off another shot. Now get me out from under this damn rock."

David arrived at the scene. "No sign of her."

"Talia will keep watch. Help me get this thing off her leg."

David looked around and picked up a fallen limb large enough to use as a pry bar. He wedged it under the boulder. "I'll tip it over a little. You pull her out."

Kate kneeled down and wrapped her arms around Monica. David put his shoulder into it and pushed. The rock rolled slightly to one side and Monica cried out in pain as Kate pulled her clear.

David got down on his knees and examined her leg. "It's broken right above the ankle. Another candidate for the hospital."

Kate pulled out her phone and checked the display. "I've a signal, but it's weak. Call 911. And then call ISA. I'm going after Emily."

Kate moved past the burning Jeep onto the access road. The county highway was a couple of hundred yards further down the hill. Emily might try to carjack a passing motorist, but out here in the woods it might take a while for somebody to come by. There was still time to find her.

A blood trail led across the road, but instead of continuing down the hill, it led off into the trees. Kate followed with her gun drawn.

"She didn't go down to the main road," she whispered into her comm unit. "She's somewhere in the woods. Anybody have an idea why?"

"It's an ambush," said Talia. "She wants you to follow the trail while she doubles back behind you. Don't fall for it. Find some cover and make her come to you. She doesn't have any other options."

"It looks like she's losing a lot of blood."

"Then it shouldn't take long."

Off to her left, Kate saw a rocky outcropping. At its base was something not quite a cave, but more like an alcove with vines partially shielding the opening. She pulled the vines apart and went inside. She put a fresh magazine into her gun and waited.

After five minutes went by with no sign of Emily, Kate wondered if Talia might have been wrong about Emily's intentions. She was about to emerge from her hiding place when she heard a rustling in the bushes to her left. Emily stepped out from behind a tree and started back toward the road. She was limping badly with blood stains down the front of her jeans. Her weapon dangled from her right hand.

Kate waited until she was clear of any available cover and stepped out past the vines, her gun arm extended in front of her. "Hold it right there, Emily, or whoever you really are. Drop the gun."

Emily slowly turned toward her. Her face was deathly pale, and she looked like she might collapse at any moment. Her eyes went wide with recognition. "You!"

"Yeah. Me. Now put the gun down."

"And go to prison?"

"Or bleed to death first. Personally, I don't care which. Now I'll tell you one more time. Put it down."

A ghost of a smile flickered across Emily's face. "That's not possible." She said something in Farsi and raised her weapon.

Kate fired four times, putting each round squarely in the middle of her chest. Emily fell backward onto the ground, sightless eyes staring up at the green canopy overhead.

Kate walked over to where her body lay in the dirt. An expanding pool of blood oozed from underneath her and stained the ground a dull red. She picked up the gun and checked the chamber, ejecting the live round before tossing the weapon aside.

"Kate, are you okay?" She could hear the concern in Talia's voice.

"Yeah. She's dead. Did you get hold of anyone?"

"ISA has been notified and the local emergency response is on the way."

"Good. I'll be there in a few minutes."

Kate stared at the body of the woman who had brought such chaos into her life. Images of Dan, Jason Collier, and Phil DeCosta flashed through her mind. She saw Boris with his brains splattered across a wall in Moscow. She heard Monica's screams as she was gunned down in Riyadh. More bodies than she could count were scattered in the wake of this woman.

"Bitch!"

Kate spat on the corpse and turned back toward the only people she wanted to be with right now.

CHAPTER THIRTY-SEVEN

Peter paused outside Carl's office, waiting for Ella Kinsmore's consent before entering the inner sanctum. His shoulder ached. The pain meds helped some, but he left them at home this morning. He couldn't afford to be at less than his best today, not when so much was at stake. Kate's presence had been requested as well, but Peter had no idea where she was. After her debriefing, she dropped off the map. Nobody had heard from her for two days and all attempts to call her went straight to voicemail.

"You can go on in, Mr. Schilling," said Ella, dutifully fulfilling her role as gatekeeper. "They're waiting for you."

Peter joined Carl and Warren Sinclair at the conference table and gingerly eased himself into a chair.

"How's the shoulder?" asked his boss.

Peter winced as he tried to get comfortable. "The joint needs to be replaced. They tell me it'll be as good as new, but the soft tissue has to heal before they can go ahead with the surgery."

"Glad to hear it. The good as new part, I mean. I wouldn't have dragged you in here when you're still recovering, but Warren asked for a briefing on the outcome."

"I was coming in today, anyway. Paperwork doesn't take medical leave. What would you like to know, Senator?"

Sinclair leaned forward with his hands clasped in front of him. "All of it. If this ever ends up in front of the committee, I'll need to know the facts."

"I doubt it will come to that. We've buried it pretty deep."

"I'm sure you have, but I used to be a Boy Scout."

Peter grinned. "Be Prepared," he said, reciting the Boy Scout motto. "Okay, the bottom line is that Iran was behind it. The Russians had an agenda of their own, but the spy operation was all Iran. They replaced an American citizen, Emily Nassar, with a sleeper agent who embedded herself at the CIA. She was using Nick Mueller as a source and Susan Reardon's chief of staff, Josh Griswold, as a conduit. Mueller claimed he was being blackmailed and supposedly Griswold was as well. But since they're both dead, we may never know for sure. Iran passed some of the intel on to the Russians when it suited their purposes. They also tried to stop Kate by hiring a Russian OPG organization to track her down and kill her."

"Thank God they failed."

"God had little to do with it. Kate figured it out. She prevented the delivery of the missiles and stopped Russia from going ahead with their plans, at least for now. I'm sure they'd still like to regain the level of control and influence they used to have in eastern Europe. We can't consider this the final solution to the problem, and we need to remain vigilant. But for now, we're back in calmer waters."

"Quite an accomplishment for a novice."

"She had a face-to-face with Vasily Kosygin," said Carl. "It wasn't something I would have approved."

"If she hadn't, we'd be looking at another war in Europe right now," said Peter.

"I realize that. But …"

Sinclair held up his hand. "She got the job done, and that's what matters. What about Susan Reardon?"

"Susan was being used," said Peter. "They gave her just enough information to draw our attention toward her and away from the real spy. Her ambitions led her to see it as an opportunity instead of the ploy it actually was. Is the president going to let her take the reins at the CIA again?"

"He won't get the chance. I met with her yesterday. She overstepped and I told her so. I also told her if she tried to return to her job, the committee would have some questions she might find uncomfortable to answer. With her record and reputation, she'll have plenty of opportunities in the private sector. What about Mueller? His father could be a problem."

"He was told his son died in an accidental explosion of stored propane tanks while he and a friend were using the cabin to do some hunting. There was nothing in the autopsy to refute that."

"And the spy?"

"DNA analysis proved she was not the real Emily Nassar and that she was of Iranian descent. That's as much as we'll ever know."

"So, what happens now?"

"None of it will be made public," said Carl. "The official story is that Emily resigned her job at CIA and went to Egypt where she has family. We made sure there's a paper trail to support that. The body was cremated."

"Sounds like you cleaned things up satisfactorily. What's the situation in Russia?"

"Malkin resigned the presidency and while they're saying it was for health reasons, it seems more likely it was a bloodless coup. Vice President Grinkov assumed the office, but Kosygin and others are taking advantage of the situation to assume more power. He's been named Director of State Security, a position that didn't exist until now. It will bear watching, but things seem stable for the moment."

"And Artisimov?"

"Dimitri Artisimov and Alexander Kruzov were instrumental in resolving this. Both have been offered asylum, but neither has accepted. They want to return to Russia."

Sinclair frowned. "Is that wise? They committed acts of treason."

"Yes, but they didn't do it for money or to advance the interests of Russia's enemies. They acted to stop a foolish adventure by a misguided leader. The current government recognizes that fact and has disavowed the actions of the Malkin regime. I don't know what awaits them back home and neither do they, but they're both loyal to their country and wish to return. All we can do is give them our thanks and wish them well."

Sinclair settled back in his chair. "So, it's like nothing happened. A war that would have stretched across the Middle East and Europe and might have gone nuclear was narrowly avoided and nobody will ever know."

Peter smiled. "That's what they pay us for."

"What about Kate Malone?"

"She's taking some time away."

"I'd like to meet her."

"That might be a problem, Senator. I'm not sure she works for us anymore."

∽

Kate sat at the back of the church. Dan's casket had been placed at the foot of the altar flanked by a colorful array of flowers and wreaths. The pews toward the front were filled with family and friends dressed in the somber colors appropriate to the occasion and listening as the pastor read from the Bible. The passages comprised the usual funeral liturgy meant to comfort those left behind and give meaning to a life choked off in the blink of an eye.

Her eyes surveyed the mourners. The circumstances of Dan's death fell under the veil of national security, and these people would never know the truth. With the cooperation of the FBI, ISA constructed a plausible story for public consumption and the evidence to back it up had been produced or manufactured. Officially, the explosion at her apartment was the result of a gas leak. A report supposedly filed by the State Police stated that Dan's body had been found inside the burned wreckage of a car at the bottom of a gorge in Virginia. The death had been ruled an accident. His family would never know what really happened to him and maybe that was a blessing, but the memory of that day could never be purged from her conscience.

As the service ended, she slipped out of the sanctuary, hoping no one had noticed her. She stood outside taking deep breaths, trying without success to bury her guilt beneath a veneer of normalcy. Coming here had offered a small hope of finding some solace, but all she felt was pain.

"Excuse me, but are you a friend of Dan's?"

Kate turned to face a young woman wearing a black dress and making a weak attempt at a smile. Her makeup had fallen victim to the tears, but her eyes still radiated an inner strength. "We were co-workers. He was a good guy, and I thought I'd come for the service. I hope I'm not intruding."

"Not at all. I'm Diane. Dan was my brother."

Kate tried not to avert her eyes. "You have my condolences."

Diane nodded. "I'm sorry, but I have to ask. Your name's not Kate, is it? He told me he was seeing someone from work by that name. He seemed, I don't know, like maybe he was in love."

The words hit her like a punch in the gut. "No. I'm ... I'm Maria. Look, I should go. I'm taking you away from your family."

"We're having people back to the house. You're welcome to come."

"Thanks, but I can't. I need to get back to work."

"Sure. Well, we appreciate your being here."

Kate walked back to her car and sat in the parking lot, watching the people trickle out of the church. Maybe some of them had gained comfort from the service, or at least some closure, but she came away with neither. Her only closure had come with the death of Emily Nassar, and it had provided little in the way of comfort.

Her phone rang, displaying Monica's picture. She almost let the call go to voicemail but touched the answer icon instead. "Hey, Monica. Now's not a good time."

"It'll have to be. Talia and David are leaving tonight. They want to talk to you. Where are you, anyway?"

"I went to Dan's funeral."

"Oh." A long and awkward pause ensued. "Was it ... I mean ... hell, I don't know what to say. Are you okay?"

"Yeah, I guess. As okay as I can be given it was my fault. You don't just walk away from that, you know?"

"You've been avoiding everyone."

"I haven't felt much like company."

"Beating yourself up isn't going to make it easier."

"Pretending it didn't happen won't either."

"We're meeting at Del's at 2:00. You'll come?"

Kate wasn't in the mood for socializing, but she couldn't let Talia and David leave without saying goodbye. Not after all they'd been through together. "I'll be there."

She hung up and looked back at the church. Another chapter of her life had closed forever. "I'm sorry, Dan," she whispered. "I'm so sorry." She wiped tears from her eyes and started the engine.

∽

Del's Tavern was a neighborhood establishment located only a block from Monica's apartment in Georgetown. Before Riyadh, this had been their usual Friday night spot for drinks and dinner after work. Kate paused inside the door and took in the familiar sights, sounds and aromas that brought back memories of easier days. She spotted Monica waving at her from a booth near the back.

"You look like hell," said her friend. She moved her crutches out of the way as Kate slid in beside her.

"I haven't been sleeping much lately." She looked across at Talia and David. "Hi, guys. Monica says you're heading home tonight."

Talia nodded. "We wanted to see you first. I'd ask if you're okay, but I'm guessing not."

"I'm sorry I've been MIA for the last couple of days. I needed ... I guess I don't know what I needed."

A waitress placed four beers and a plate of nachos on the table. Kate ignored both. "How do you do it?" Her voice was almost pleading. "How do you come away from all the crap we went through and just keep going? Doesn't it ever get to be too much? Don't you ever want to say screw it and walk away?"

"Every time," David replied. "How do we do it? Like this. With people who understand. When you're in the middle of a mission, there's no time to think about those things. There's a job to do, and it's worthwhile and needs to be done. Afterward, when there's time to stop and breathe, the doubts and the guilt and the regrets are turned loose to prey on your mind. But the basic truth is still the same. The job needed to be done. It can be dirty and maybe you do things that gnaw at your conscience later, but that's not the bottom line. Are you sorry we stopped what could have turned into a nuclear confrontation?"

Kate shook her head. "That part I'm okay with. It involved hard things, but if we hadn't kept going, even more people would have died. It's the collateral damage that keeps eating at me. Boris in Moscow, the innocent woman who got sprayed with nerve gas in London." She looked away. "And Dan. How am I supposed to live with that?"

"It isn't easy," said Talia. "And it's why the first rule exists."

"Yeah."

Talia patted her on the arm. "It takes time and there're people you can talk to."

"That helps?"

She shrugged. "It's not magic. There's no way to make it all disappear. But yes, it helps. Don't push people away, Kate. It's the worst mistake you could make."

"On another subject," said David, "we were asked to pass along an invitation. Director Niminsky recommended you be presented with a Medal of Honor and the president agreed. It's the highest commendation the government can award a civilian. And you're not even Israeli."

"I'm not sure I want to be commended for what I did. People died. Accepting an award would feel wrong somehow."

"You're going to refuse?"

"I'll think about it. Tell the director I'm honored by the invitation, but there are things I need to deal with first."

Talia nodded. "We'll tell her, and she'll understand. She spent years in the field herself. But what about you? What are you going to do now?"

"After my debriefing, Peter offered me a job. He thinks I belong in the field."

"What do you think?" asked David.

It was the question she'd been asking herself for days. "Do I want to put myself through that again? Could I? Even if I wanted to? The job offer in New York might still be open. It would mean a lot more money and nobody's going to be shooting at me. My old job in analysis is still there as well. I was pretty good at it." She took a drink from her beer. "Or I could say to hell with the whole thing and go back home. Dad could use some help with the farm."

"Can I give you a piece of advice?" asked David. "Give yourself some time. Personally, I think you're meant to be in the field fighting the battles that need to be fought, but I won't try to minimize the heavy load that goes along with that."

"I agree," added Talia. "Whatever choices you make, we'll always have your back. If you don't want the commendation, fine. But get your ass to Israel anyway. You have friends there."

Kate reached over and took each of them by the hand. "Thanks. You guys were my sanity through all of it, and I'll never forget it."

David waved the waitress over and asked for the check. "We need to get back to the hotel and pack. Let us know what you decide. And if you just want somebody to talk to, pick up a phone. That's what we're here for."

Kate gave them each a hug as they started toward the door. Talia stopped halfway and retraced her steps. "One more thing. Whatever you decide to do will make no difference to us, but you're a badass. I would take you as a partner in a heartbeat with no questions asked. I mean that."

Kate smiled for the first time in days. "Coming from the top badass of all time, that means a lot. Thanks."

Talia nodded and followed David out the door.

"So, what now?" asked Monica.

"Right now, I have a lot of thinking to do. I'll call you soon."

Whenever she needed some space or just time to think, Kate usually headed for the west end of the National Mall and the Vietnam Memorial. She stopped at a kiosk and purchased a small wreath before walking along the black granite wall engraved with the names of the soldiers, airmen, marines, and sailors who lost their lives in the war. She stopped at the midway point and placed the wreath at the base of the wall. Reaching out, she touched the name of Lt. Col. Richard Malone, U.S. Army.

"Hi, Gramps. It's me again. I'm all mixed up and I could use some advice."

Kate took a seat on the bench and let her eyes wander along the seemingly endless sea of names. Her grandfather had died long before she was born, but she still felt a connection to him. She'd read the letters he sent home to his family and listened to her dad's stories about his father.

One of the first things she did upon her arrival in Washington was come to the memorial to find his name. She was a stranger in a new city and nervous and uncertain about her future. Just sitting here had given gave her a sense of belonging. He was only a name engraved on a wall, but sometimes it was like he was here with her, a calming presence when she was most troubled.

Back in grade school, she had a teacher who, once a week, would inspect the storage compartment of everyone's desk. If she found it too messy for her liking, she dumped the contents onto the classroom floor and made you put everything back arranged in a more acceptable way. Kate felt like someone had done the same thing to her life.

Throughout the crisis, she'd relied on her instincts. It was like when she played soccer back in college. With the game on the line and the ball suddenly at your feet, you didn't have time to consider your options. You followed your instincts and training and took your best shot. If you couldn't do that, then you didn't belong out on the field.

She looked back at the wall once more. These men and women had died in the line of duty. They may have lost the struggle, but despite whatever doubts they carried with them, they faced the challenge head on. Kate understood that completely because she'd never flinched from a challenge in her life.

Her father sat her down the night before she left for a new life in Washington. "You're an adult now and the world's out there waiting for you. You'll always be my daughter, but now I need to step back and let you go. You'll screw up sometimes and make decisions you may come to regret, but every time you fall down, make damn sure you get right back up. Face life head on and don't back down from anything. You've always made me proud, Kate. And you always will."

Her thoughts turned back to her grandfather. He certainly hadn't backed down. "Okay, Gramps. Here goes."

Kate reached into her pocket and pulled out her phone. "Peter, it's me. If I take you up on your offer, the first step is training, right?"

"Of course. You never should have been out there without it."

"And if I change my mind, I can back out anytime? Assuming I even pass the course?"

"I doubt that will be a problem, but yes. I don't want anyone working for me who doesn't believe they should be there."

She took a deep breath. "Then I'm in."

"The last time we spoke, I got the impression you'd had enough."

"Yeah. It's what happens when you ignore the first rule."

"The first rule?"

"Never mind. I had a talk with someone who set me straight. The analysis section will have to get by without me. But first I need a little time off. I have to find a place to live."

"Take what you need. Just out of curiosity, who did you speak with?"

She looked over at the granite wall. "You wouldn't understand. I'll be in touch, Peter."

Standing up, she placed her hand on her grandfather's name once more. "I did it, Gramps. Wish me luck and I'll let you know how it turns out."

Heaving a sigh, she headed for Constitution Ave. to hail a cab.

∽

**The Story Will Continue In
Kate Malone Book 2**

THANK YOU FOR READING TOO SOON A SPY

We hope you enjoyed it as much as we enjoyed bringing it to you. We just wanted to take a moment to encourage you to review the book. Follow this link: Too Soon A Spy to be directed to the book's Amazon product page to leave your review.

Every review helps further the author's reach and, ultimately, helps them continue writing fantastic books for us all to enjoy.

∾

Also in series:
Too Soon A Spy

∾

Calling all thriller fans: be the first to discover groundbreaking new releases, access incredible deals, and participate in thrilling giveaways by subscribing to our exclusive Thriller Newsletter. https://aethonbooks.com/thriller-newsletter/

Want to discuss our books with other readers and even the authors?

JOIN THE AETHON DISCORD!

Don't forget to follow us on socials to never miss a new release!

Facebook | Instagram | Twitter | Website

∽

Looking for more great thrillers?

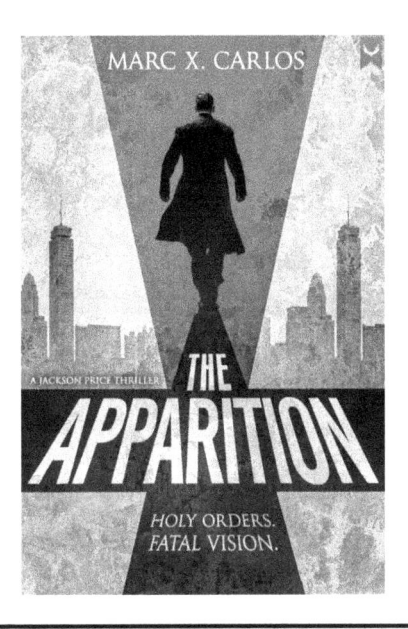

The truth shall set you free. But for one young lawyer, it might just cost him his life... A popular priest is accused of a horrific assault and tied to the murders of two other women. Jackson Price and his mentor race to uncover the motives of his accuser. At the same time, detectives uncover a checkered past of inappropriate behavior with women and mental health issues. The case may hinge on the truth of an apparition and the impact it has on everyone involved. As the case races through the criminal justice system, Jackson finds himself caught between reality and the delusions of a killer. One could end his short career; the other could end his life. Strap in and follow the investigation to the thrilling end! **The Apparition is a gripping psychological legal thriller with high stakes suspense and vivid courtroom drama. From debut author Marc X. Carlos, it's inspired by one of his real cases as a career criminal defense attorney with extensive experience in high profile crimes, courtroom technique and crime scene investigation.**

Get The Apparition Now!

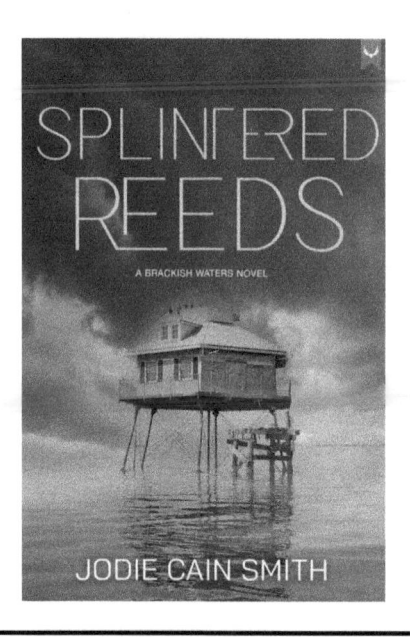

When no one is left to save you, save yourself or die trying. The one constant in Jules' life is family —the plentiful Martin clan. Domestic terrorism brought the Martins together under one roof to endure food scarcity, punishing Gulf Coast heat, no electricity, and no indoor plumbing. One outhouse for twelve people is no way to live, but at least they are safe. For now. With every setback and stolen dignity, Jules questions whether she wants to survive at all. She keeps the family fed, hunting and fishing along the shores of Mobile Bay while avoiding both US Army patrols and The Knights, a homegrown militia group determined to convert all of Bellefontaine to their radical ideology and rid the seaside community of anyone who stands in their way. When two members of The Knights set their sights on Jules, violence lands on the Martins' doorstep, threatening everyone connected to the family. The one bright spot Jules finds is in a chance meeting with an 11-year-old looter who gives her a new sense of purpose and a reason to survive. She sees herself in the rebel-boy— independent, foolishly fearless, and capable of making costly mistakes. Will she be able to protect the boy from rising violence? Or will they both become victims? **Deliciously Southern and with a break-neck pace, Splintered Reeds is a timely domestic terrorism thriller that explores the fallout of a divided nation, the strength of family, and the journey through the complexities of grief, and the fight for autonomy in a world turned upside down.**

Get Splintered Reeds Now!

∽

A shocking, twist-filled mystery thriller perfect for fans of Michael Connelly, Harlan Coben, and D.D. Black. Fame. Money. Murder. Charismatic ex-soldier Evan Drake works for Los Angeles's rich and famous as a "fixer" of their problems. But when a beautiful young woman hires him to find a missing man, Evan steps into a dark conspiracy that may not be fixable. He tries to piece together the clues - a Hollywood home break-in, posts on the dark web, a secretive tech company with a revolutionary new product - but the more he learns, the more elusive the truth becomes. Soon, he's not only fighting for answers, but fighting to keep himself and other innocent people alive. **Don't miss the start of this mystery thriller series from #1 Amazon bestselling author Ted Galdi about an ex-soldier who works unofficially as a "fixer." Grab your copy today!**

Get The Cassandra Trap Now!

For all our Thriller books, visit our website.